I0638266

A
Hero's
Nature

Books by Sandra Ardoin

Contemporary

Hidden Veil Hometown
A Musician's Heart
A Horseman's Mission
A Hero's Nature
A Father's Promise
(Next in Series)

Love at Christmas Inn
Love in Second Bloom
Leaving the Past Behind
Lost in Winter's Wonderland
Longing for Second Chances
Box Set

Stand Alone Books
A Love Most Worthy
Renee

Historical

House of Fire - Coming
A Lady Divided

Widow's Might
Unwrapping Hope
Enduring Dreams
Rekindling Trust

Barnes Brothers
The Yuletide Angel
A Reluctant Melody

Short Stories
Daphne's Day Out

A
HERO'S
NATURE

HIDDEN VEIL HOMETOWN
BOOK THREE

SANDRA ARDOIN

Corner Room Books

©2025 *A Hero's Nature* by Sandra Ardoin
Corner Room Books, Salisbury, North Carolina, USA

For more information on this book and the author visit:
www.sandraardoin.com.

All rights reserved. This book or any portion thereof may not be reproduced in any form, stored in a retrieval system, or transmitted in any form by any means—electronic, photocopy, recording, or otherwise—without prior written permission of the author, except for the use of brief quotations in a book review. For further permissions, please contact the author through her website: www.sandraardoin.com/contact.

A Hero's Nature is a work of fiction. Names, characters, and incidents are products of the author's imagination or are used for fictional purposes. Any resemblance to actual persons, living or dead, is entirely coincidental. Any mentioned brand names, places, and trademarks remain the property of their respective owners, bear no association with the author or the publisher, and are used for fictional purposes only.

All Scripture quotations, unless otherwise indicated, are taken from the Holy Bible, New International Version®, NIV®. Copyright ©1973, 1978, 1984, 2011 by Biblica, Inc.™ Used by permission of Zondervan. All rights reserved worldwide. www.zondervan.com The "NIV" and "New International Version" are trademarks registered in the United States Patent and Trademark Office by Biblica, Inc.™

But he said to me, "My grace is sufficient for you, for my power is made perfect in weakness." Therefore I will boast all the more gladly about my weaknesses, so that Christ's power may rest on me.
2 Corinthians 12:9 NIV

One

"Reagan!"

Shaina shouted her name as soon as she walked through the back door. Not a good way to start the day.

Reagan Hartwell entered the Abbott Veterinary Clinic's reception area. "What's wrong?"

"This." Shaina pointed to the computer screen.

Reagan stared at the day's appointment schedule until the name on the three o'clock appointment stared back in what seemed to be letters three times their normal size. "Please don't tell me I did that."

Shaina winced. "I'm afraid so."

Reagan pressed her palms to her temples. How had she scheduled an appointment for her boss at the Brantwell farm on a clinic day?

But she knew. Oh, how well she knew.

Every year. These types of mistakes happened every year around the anniversary of Matt Becker's death. She turned into a distracted, incompetent pea-brain. To many people, it would seem an insignificant error, easily rectified. No big deal. To Reagan, it was a symptom of her short-term ineptitude. "Trey is particular about not mixing the appointment days. He will kill me."

Laughter spurted from Shaina. "Like that would ever happen. You are his golden child, the Elizabeth to his Darcy. Jane to his Mr. Rochester." She practically sighed when referencing the literary characters.

"Oh, please."

Yes, Reagan and Trey were friends and worked well together, but if she kept messing up, he would fire her—golden child or not—and she wouldn't blame him. Thankfully, the workweek had one more day after today. She vowed to concentrate on nothing but her job. Meanwhile, she would pray her absentmindedness didn't ruin Trey's business.

"Stop reading those romance novels and watching Hallmark movies, Shaina. They're warping your definition of what real-life love is all about." It was both beautiful and painful.

Her friend jerked back in her chair as though trying to dodge the sharp words thrown at her.

Reagan's stupidity and short temper weren't her friend's fault. "Sorry. I just . . ."

"It's okay, but I'm getting concerned." Shaina's chair swiveled to face her, and Reagan jumped back to avoid being hit by the woman's legs. "I'll never meet my Mr. Rochester in a small town like Hidden Veil. Look at Harmoni. She's been here five years and hasn't met a soul, of the ever-after kind, I mean."

Reagan bit her tongue on the opinion that Shaina's aunt, while sweet during those infrequent times when she socialized with others, was a bit too timid to attract a man's attention.

Shaina grabbed the coffee cup sitting on the warmer at the

corner of her desk. "I don't want to turn thirty like Harmoni and still be single."

Says the twenty-five-year-old to the already thirty-year-old woman. "You have time. You'll find someone."

Since when had Reagan become an expert on romantic love? Several people had called her fickle because she dated and dropped guys after a month or two. They didn't understand the favor she was doing those men.

I've had enough of your selfishness, Matt. We're done.

The memory of writing those words pierced her. One day, the anniversary of her fiancé's death would come and go with only a twinge of remembrance from her. Maybe. Until then, she would live with the knowledge that her own selfishness cost him his life.

"I do love it in Hidden Veil." Shaina gazed out the large front window of the waiting room with a dreamy look, as if she saw her prince riding into the parking lot on a white steed. Reagan saw only empty blacktop.

"Trey reminds me of Darcy. You know, the handsome, strong, and silent type."

Handsome? Yes. In a boy-next-door way.

Silent? Not like Harmoni Basinger, but he wasn't one to waste time on unnecessary words.

Strong? Although slim in build, he was no slouch in the muscle department, not when he treated large animals—horses and cattle. Yet, his gentleness with small animals had drawn pet parents to use and recommend the clinic.

Strong of faith and character? There, Trey excelled.

Which made him too good for her.

An unexpected discomfort settled in Reagan's chest. Was her friend and co-worker saying she had romantic feelings toward

Trey? It wasn't the first time over the past few months that Reagan had felt this poke in her heart when speaking of him. It couldn't be jealousy, but whatever it was, it was inconvenient and unwelcome.

Shaina's fair cheeks darkened. "Don't get me wrong. I'm not crushing on Trey. I prefer the Mr. Rochester type. You know, a little broody and mysterious. But I can see how someone else would consider him a romantic hero." She eyed Reagan as though making a point.

The poke in her chest eased, and Reagan nodded to the computer, ready to drop the talk of romance. "I'll give the Brantwells a call and reschedule." She pulled a sticky note from a pad on the desk to make herself a note so she wouldn't forget.

As the clinic's business grew, so did Reagan's duties as both vet tech and office manager, the latter a role she'd stepped into when Trey hired her as his first employee three years ago. A role that, with their increased patient load, had grown overwhelming. Not that a heavy workload was an excuse for her mistakes at this time of year.

"I've already left word," said Shaina. "If I don't hear from one of the Brantwells in the next hour, I'll call again."

Reagan breathed an internal sigh of relief. "Hiring you was one of the best decisions I've made."

Shaina turned back to the computer. "I'm glad to help where I can."

For weeks now, Reagan had considered suggesting Shaina take over the office management so she could concentrate on her tech duties. It may be time to approach Trey about it. "You are a lifesaver."

Shaina winked. "I know."

Reagan walked around the reception counter and unlocked

the front door for soon-to-be-arriving patients. She straightened a print hanging on a side wall over a row of five chrome and midnight blue plastic chairs. All the whimsical photos in the room displayed colorful images of cats and dogs—some wearing sunglasses and others wearing hats. This photo was her favorite. An Australian Shepherd with clear blue eyes sported a straw cowboy hat, a red and white paisley bandana tied around its neck, and a piece of straw dangling from its mouth. It spoke to the country girl in her.

A few minutes later, Reagan double checked the clinic's readiness for the day's first appointment. A loud voice coming from the reception area caught her attention and sparked the barks of dogs recuperating in cages in a nearby room. Their barks competed with a man's verbal abuse.

As she hurried down the cool hallway toward the front, Trey stepped out of his office, slipping his lab coat on over blue scrubs, his standard clinic attire. On days when he treated large animals, he wore hiking pants and heavy boots.

He pulled the tortoiseshell glasses propped on top of his head down to rest on his nose. "What's going on?"

Reagan strode alongside him. "I was on my way to find out."

In the waiting room, a hulking, middle-aged man stood at the front counter. He held a shivering black Labrador Retriever in his arms and berated Shaina for asking him to wait.

Trey stopped at the man's side. "Is there a problem, sir?"

Reagan had to hand it to him. In a case like this, his mild-mannered personality beat her shoot-words-now, apologize-later brand of discussion.

"This dog needs treatment. I see no one else here, yet this woman wants to work her in." With his head, the man gestured toward the empty waiting area. "The animal is a valuable asset, and we can't afford to lose her while you finish your morning coffee."

Reagan observed the dog, about seven or eight months old. The poor thing shook like most animals brought to the clinic, sensing it was a place to fear, rather than a place of healing. But those glassy eyes reflected more than fear. Her focus slid back to the face of the man whose bombastic noise only added to the animal's distress. She searched her memory for his identity but came up blank.

Trey placed his hands on the dog's ears and gazed into brown velvet eyes. "How long has she had a fever?"

"I only arrived this morning. Dad said she's been sluggish for the past day and won't eat." He lowered the dog to the floor, and Reagan spotted swelling on the inside of a front leg. Trey knelt to look at it. The pup's shaking eased somewhat under his tender touch, and she licked his hand.

Reagan flashed a polite smile. "Sir—"

"The name is Marshall Burnside."

Only one Burnside lived in Hidden Veil. This man was not him. "What is your dog's name?"

"I don't know."

Her eyebrows arched. "You don't know her name?"

"I didn't check her papers before bringing her here. My father called her Bud. He calls all of them Bud. I'm only here because Dad asked me to bring her."

Now it made sense. "Your father is Oren Burnside?" When Trey glanced at her, she said, "The elder Mr. Burnside owns a kennel on Steel Gate Road." It was less actual road than potholes and rough pavement.

"I remember the place." By his flat tone, Trey must know the kennel was in much the same shape as the road used to reach it.

"We'll need some information before I can treat your dog."

Shaina pulled out the required paperwork and handed it to Burnside's son, who grunted but walked to a chair to fill it out.

Reagan accompanied Trey down the hall. He stopped outside his office. "Come get me when he's finished." He paused. "We both know you can take care of this yourself, Reagan, but I'm afraid if I don't handle his 'valuable asset' personally, it will set Burnside off again."

"I agree. The man is insufferable." She stepped closer. "Burnside Kennel wasn't always a rundown wreck. When I was growing up, it was a respected business. The Burnsides bred and trained prize-winning Labrador Retrievers, and Mrs. Burnside showed dogs in New York at the Westminster Kennel Club Dog Show. The kennel slid downhill after she passed away a few years ago. I've heard her husband slid downhill with it."

"Loss is hard on many people."

Was he speaking of her now? If he only knew the truth. "I'll get everything ready and see if he's finished filling out the form."

When Shaina handed her the paperwork, Reagan scanned the information, what little Burnside had filled out. At least he'd signed the important line on the back side—consent for treatment. She picked up the puppy. "We'll take care of her. It won't be long."

An English Springer Spaniel mix howled from his spot in the far corner. "I see you, Chauncey. I'll be back for him soon, Mrs. Ferguson."

"Take your time."

What a difference in attitude from the man whose voice thundered through the room a short time ago.

Back in the treatment room, she gave the paper to Trey and placed the pup on a mat covering a stainless-steel exam table.

Trey read the information on the New Client form as she took the dog's temperature.

"He doesn't know much about the pup's history."

Trey laid the paper on the counter. "If he isn't part of the everyday operation of the kennel, I can understand. I guess this little girl should count herself fortunate he consented to treatment." Trey slipped on a pair of latex gloves while whispering soothing words to ease the dog's fear. He examined the infected gash on the leg. "It's long but not too deep."

After Reagan injected an anesthesia near the wound, they worked together to clean the injury. Afterward, Reagan fetched Mr. Burnside and led him to the consultation room. The man consumed the air in the small space, so she waited at the open doorway.

"How is the dog?"

"She'll be fine. No stitches, but Dr. Abbott gave her an antibiotic injection." She recited various wound care instructions. "Before you leave, we'll get her an Elizabethan collar."

"You mean one of those silly-looking cone of shame things? No, thanks."

Trey joined Marshall with the pup. "It's for the dog's good, Mr. Burnside."

"And a neon sign to potential buyers that my father doesn't take care of his dogs. You've treated her, Dr. Abbott. She'll be fine."

"The pup shouldn't lick the wound." Trey crossed his arms. "I'm sure you don't want more infection to set in and cause greater problems for her and more expense for you. If you won't use the collar at your father's kennel, I can keep her here for a few days."

Reagan looked away and sucked in her lips to keep from

smiling at her boss's quiet coercion.

Mr. Burnside huffed. "Don't be ridiculous. My father has years of experience dealing with dogs and an entire building to house them."

Trey removed his gloves and tossed them in the can by the door. "Then, I'm sure he'll understand. As Ms. Hartwell said, you can get the collar—no charge—from the receptionist."

No charge? Oh, now that raised Reagan's hackles. Why should they bend over backwards for the pompous cheapskate? One glance at that sweet puppy lessened her ire . . . some. Their duty was to the Lab's welfare, even if it meant kowtowing to Burnside.

Trey smiled as though the man was a good friend. "Keep her separated from the other dogs, watch her, and follow the instructions Reagan gave you. I'm sure your dog will be fine, but call me if necessary."

Burnside gathered the poor pup into his arms again. "How much will this visit set my father back?"

Reagan's boss was a man who rarely lost his temper, but Trey's tight jaw muscles and widening nostrils said Burnside tempted him. "Reagan, tell Shaina to prepare a bill for sixty-five dollars."

She stared at him. "Sixty-five?" That was much less than the normal charge for the services he'd performed. First the free collar, then a discount on today's treatment. Couldn't he bestow his charity on someone more deserving?

Figuratively putting on her office manager hat, she graced Trey with a pointed look that said, "We need to talk."

As she walked down the hall to grab a collar, Mrs. Ferguson leaned over the reception desk. "Briar Park, the company that owns the string of nursing and rehabilitation facilities, called my

Uncle Ted looking for land around Hidden Veil. He would like to sell them the Burnside property."

Reagan stopped outside the supply room behind Shaina. Ted Main of Main Realty? She hadn't heard that Oren Burnside wanted to sell the kennel. What would happen to the dogs?

Shaina listened but said nothing that would encourage the gossip.

"He says Mr. Burnside is behind in paying his property taxes, and the county wouldn't feel bad about taking the land. I feel sorry for him, but when my dad broke his hip, Mom had to drive over twenty miles one way to visit him while he went through rehab. We need that kind of place around here, and my uncle says Briar Park has an excellent reputation. Even Mr. Burnside's son wants him to sell."

Reagan could imagine that, if it involved money, Marshall would sell his father out.

"Uncle Ted says Mr. Burnside refuses. Someone needs to convince him it's time to retire."

Even though the place might not be up to her standards, Reagan had no desire to see the man lose his property because of delinquent taxes. But Mrs. Ferguson was right. If he couldn't care for the dogs, he should retire.

Hidden Veil could use a nursing facility in the area. Matt used to complain each time the family, especially his mother, faced a long drive to visit his grandfather in a nursing home. He regretted being unable to see the man more often and wished there had been a place for him closer to Hidden Veil. Matt would rejoice at this chance to help others.

She had her own list of people who could have benefited

from having such a place nearby.

What would it take to convince Mr. Burnside to sell? Could Reagan be that someone Mrs. Ferguson spoke of, and if so, would helping to see Matt's wish come true relieve some of the guilt inside her?

Two

Before leaving the consultation room, Trey had conducted a quick argument with himself over providing the services of his clinic at such a deep discount. Given Burnside's less-than-mannerly behavior toward Shaina and Reagan, why had he felt a need to reward the overbearing attitude? Obviously, Reagan didn't approve. But he hadn't done it for the man's sake. He'd looked into the troubled eyes of the injured puppy and the words tumbled out.

He'd walked out the door as Reagan returned with the e-collar. "Sixty-five."

"Yes, Dr. Abbott." She'd hit the right tone with her answer, but the scowl on her face told him it took everything in her not to argue.

That bold, opinionated streak drew him to her. She knew when to let it fly free and when to rein it in. Most of the time, anyway. No one walked away from her confused about where she stood. For Trey, that was both appealing and the bane of his existence.

Trey poured himself a cup of coffee and took it to his office to finish the paperwork he'd started at seven o'clock this morning. A relaxing coffee break. Ha! He couldn't remember the last time he'd had that luxury.

He sank into the chair in his cramped office and turned on the radio in time to catch the news. He tuned most of it out until the broadcaster mentioned a wildfire out west—ten thousand acres and only fifteen percent contained.

Kaine.

Trey's younger brother, a smokejumper in Idaho, was likely in the thick of the action. Like their dad, Kaine thrived on firefighting and went into the Forest Service straight out of college. He'd made Dad proud by following in the footsteps of three generations of Abbott men, jumping into the profession with eager feet. Unlike Trey, who followed in the career footsteps of a family friend. His choice made him the black sheep in a family of soot-covered white sheep.

At the knock on his office door, thoughts of his brother vanished, and he prepared himself for the impending blast. "Come in, Reagan."

Trey's office door pushed open. She stood in the hall—five feet, five inches of adorable dynamite. As usual, his heart betrayed his brain, racing at the sight of those green eyes smoldering with the need to express her opinion, and knowing he was destined to keep his emotions in check. How long could this continue?

He waited as Reagan stepped into his office.

"Good guess, knowing it was me at the door."

"It wasn't hard. I only have two employees—"

"Two full-time employees and two who work part time." She plopped into the chair by his desk, her brunette ponytail bouncing from side to side. "Speaking of employees, I'd like to suggest a change."

He had expected a different subject from this visit. A suggested change was okay, as long as she didn't say she was leaving. That might solve the problem of keeping his feelings for her secret day after day, but missing her would create a different problem. "What did you have in mind?"

"I'd like to hand the clinic management tasks to Shaina. She's good at her job and has grown well past the duties of receptionist and sometime-assistant."

He couldn't disagree. "That means a substantial raise." Combined with his own plan—

"I'm aware of that. I'm also aware I'd take a cut in pay."

She should know better than to think he'd cut her salary. He didn't pay her all she was worth to begin with. "Am I overworking you?"

"I'm fine, but the practice is growing, Trey. Something has to give soon. Besides, I don't want to lose Shaina."

"I agree. Let me see what I can do." He leaned forward with his arms crossed on the desktop. "Since you bring up the subject of change, I have one of my own."

Wariness dipped her eyebrows. "Oh?"

"I'm bringing in another vet."

She sat straight in the chair. "Wow. Okay, it's understandable. When?"

He enjoyed catching her off guard occasionally. "Soon."

"Want me to put out feelers? I can contact the College of Veterinary Medicine at NC State. Or were you wanting someone more experienced?"

"I've already talked to a friend, the vet who encouraged me to go into practice. He recommended someone. If things go well, she can start in a couple of months."

"I didn't know you were looking for someone." Did he hear hurt in her voice?

"I only learned of the opportunity a few days ago. Like you said, the practice is growing, and you've known of my long-term plan for expansion." If it worked out, they would also need one more vet tech, maybe two—more money in salaries. Success came with challenges. "She'll be here next week to look around and meet everyone."

"Okay."

Reagan had drawn out the word like it wasn't really okay. What was . . .?

Aw, man. How had he forgotten the anniversary next week? He'd call and reschedule. After all, he wanted his prospective co-worker to see his practice in its best light, and that wouldn't happen with Reagan in a fog.

"So, you didn't say how you guessed it was me at the door and not Shaina."

Her statement brought him back to the moment she stood at the door. "I expected to see you as soon as Burnside left. You're as subtle as a disco ball in a dance club."

"Being coy is a waste of time and energy." She laughed. "A disco ball?"

"I fell asleep watching *Saturday Night Fever* the other night."

They both liked older movies, so she'd get the reference. "I haven't met Marshall Burnside's father yet, but there are rumors. It was those rumors that prompted me to cut my bill. Besides, this incident gives me an excuse to visit the kennel and see the condition for myself. If they give me a hard time, I'll remind them of my generosity."

"Charles Abbott the Third,"—her eyebrows bounced—"Master Spy."

Trey grinned and shook his head. "Just a friendly visit."

"From what I've been told, the elder Mr. Burnside is almost a recluse, and heaven only knows the condition of the other dogs."

"Other than the cut, the nameless puppy we saw this morning seemed well taken care of."

Reagan frowned. "Still, during your friendly visit, you can talk him into a going-out-of-business sale."

"One accident doesn't mean the place needs to be closed, Reagan."

"Even if the dogs are better off? And maybe it's been more than one accident, just the first you've treated. I wonder why Marshall Burnside came here. I thought his father used Dr. Michaels."

"Michaels retired recently."

"I hadn't heard. I guess that means you'll get the kennel's business . . . for as long as it lasts."

Regular visits by Marshall Burnside? Trey restrained a groan.

She rubbed the arms of her chair—back and forth, back and forth—a rare sign of nervousness. "Since you're so understanding about accidents, I have to tell you I *accidentally* made a mistake."

He stiffened. Not another one. "What happened?"

"It's worked out." She stopped rubbing and sighed. "I scheduled an appointment at the Brantwells today. Shaina caught it, though."

Another employer might breathe fire at her. However, Trey had learned to live with the issues that tormented her this time each year. It didn't mean he had to like the reason for those issues.

"I'm sorry, Trey."

"Just try to be more careful."

"I promise." She stood and checked her watch. "Next appointment is in three minutes."

His gaze followed Reagan out the door. He needed to keep a better eye on her. Earlier in the week, she'd forgotten to give Mrs. Hensley's new kitten its second feline panleukopenia vaccination, overcharged one client, and undercharged another. Now, it was a scheduling error.

All but two weeks out of the year, she was an ideal employee—capable, smart, conscientious—the best vet tech he'd known. Those other two weeks? She turned into a distracted klutz.

Next Thursday was the eleven-year anniversary of her fiancé's death in Afghanistan. Trey expected her to be even more unreliable as the actual day drew closer.

Eleven years! Each one hard on her. Each one hard on him and not simply as her employer. How many times had he prayed she would move on from her grief and see him as more than a friend and the man who paid her salary? How many times had he prayed to be a hero she immortalized . . . like Matt Becker?

Man up, Trey. You're an Abbott. Abbotts aren't afraid of the smell of smoke!

After over a decade, his father's angry words still festered inside him, like the infection in the Lab puppy's cut. It wasn't smoke that scared him. It was the reason for the smoke.

Admitting to a fear of fire wasn't his worst failing, not when compared to the time his inaction almost cost a life. He thanked God it hadn't. But that day's humiliation would remain his secret. He respected his father but could imagine the man's disappointment if he knew of that failure.

No, he stood little chance of competing with the memory of a fallen soldier who had once saved his team from certain death. Certainly not as the weakling his father believed him to be.

Not as the weakling he knew himself to be.

Home safe and sound and still employed.

What a busy Friday! Under normal circumstances, Reagan would fix a quick supper, flop onto the recliner in her living room, and turn on the TV, losing herself in some mindless movie.

Day-by-day, she was becoming more of an old woman. And she hadn't even hit thirty-one!

Reagan opened the side door that gave entrance into her breakfast area and adjacent kitchen. She tossed her purse on the table, fighting the fatigue that came at the end of a trying week. Yet satisfaction sizzled through her, providing her with something she hadn't felt yesterday or all week, really—success.

The success of a day this week without a screw-up. That was worthy of celebration.

She dug her phone from her purse and sent a text to her sister, Brianna.

Movie and popcorn at my place tonight?

Reagan added ice to a glass, then poured herself some tea while she waited for Bri's answer. Winter was over, spring was in full bloom. It was time to brew the sweet tea. Time to enjoy the mild weather before the temperatures rose, along with the humidity.

Her phone dinged, and she read her sister's response.

Sorry. Can't. Studying.

With a sigh, Reagan whipped off a text, assuring Brianna it was fine and they would get together another night.

She texted Macie Newman and received another rejection. Her son Alex had a soccer game. Reagan's thumbs slid over the keys.

Hope he kicks a dozen goals.

Jo Callahan had already mentioned a trip to Raleigh, where her husband Kyle would perform a special church concert this weekend. The newlyweds were taking the opportunity for a little getaway alone time.

Alone time. Reagan had plenty of that. Even when she went

out on a date, she often felt alone. It was her own fault. Had she never sent Matt that letter years ago . . .

She shook the thought from her mind.

Hands on her hips, her shoulders surged up and down with a hefty and audible exhale in the quiet of her home. What now? She could call any of a dozen guys she knew. More than one would offer to take her out tonight. Not an arrogant thought. Simply experience.

The idea appealed to her as much as the chicken and rice casserole she'd made two days ago. She should have gotten Chef Macie Newman's recipe . . . so much better.

She shoved a plate of the leftovers in the microwave, pressed a couple of buttons, and walked into her living room to grab the TV remote. Halfway through heating her meal, the newscaster began a report about a spreading wildfire in Idaho. Her immediate thought went to Kaine Abbott, Trey's brother. Was he involved in fighting the fire?

She grabbed her phone, called Trey, and heard heavy breathing when he answered. "Dr. Abbott."

"You sound out of breath, Dr. Abbott."

He chuckled. "It's Lulu."

"She was on the run again?"

"Yeah. I can understand what her previous owners went through. Not that I condone what they did."

Of course he wouldn't. It was why he'd taken in the Tennessee Fainting Goat when Lulu's owners moved away a few months ago, leaving her to fend for herself. The new homeowners called Trey after they frightened her and she froze, then fell over. They handed Lulu off to him, hoping he'd find her a new home.

So far, he hadn't looked very hard. He denied it, but Reagan knew he'd grown attached to the goat.

"What's up?"

The microwave dinged, but she remained in front of the TV. "I just saw a news report about a wildfire in Idaho. Are you aware of it?"

"I heard yesterday."

"Have you talked to your brother?"

"Not yet. I tried calling but didn't get an answer. I'm sure he's fine." The cautious note in Trey's voice told her his confidence in what he'd said ran only word deep.

"I'm sure he is."

Maybe he needed someone to help him take his mind off of the worry. "How about a movie and popcorn tonight?" Why was she stuck on watching a movie and eating popcorn?

After a slight pause, he said, "I can't. I told Kyle I'd dog-sit Davey. Unless there's an emergency, I don't want to leave him alone on his first night here."

"Oh. Okay." Had he paused to decide whether to leave Kyle's bullmastiff for a while, or had he looked for an excuse to turn her invitation down?

Reagan waited for him to invite her over to his house. It wasn't like they never shared time together in their off hours. But he didn't. She couldn't decide if she was okay with that or disappointed. "Well, I'll let you get back to your dog-sitting duties. I'll see you at church."

"Sure thing."

Not long after she'd ended the call to Trey, a familiar tune drowned out the news. She picked up the phone and eyed the name on the screen. Scott Hendrix. She tried to put a face to the name. When it came, she groaned.

He was the good-looking tech she'd met at a conference she'd attended last month. "Hello?"

"Reagan Hartwell?"

"Yes."

"We met—"

"Yes. I remember." *You were the hotshot who ogled every woman in the place.*

She supposed he expected his response—a low, sexy chuckle—would give her the vapors. Vapors? Ugh! Shaina's references to nineteenth-century literature were rubbing off on her. "What can I do for you?"

"I've been thinking about you. I know it's late notice, but how about dinner tonight?"

A date with Hotty Scotty? She guessed, because it took him almost four weeks to contact her, she must be at least number three or four on his list of prospects. She could be farther down the line, since he'd given her little notice.

Hendrix was a loser, but wasn't dating a loser better than dating someone she really liked? Better than hurting that person through her eventual self-centeredness? Better than sitting at home by herself?

Reagan eyed the plate with the casserole. "What time will you pick me up?"

Three

Saturday night, Reagan followed Bri into Ricardo's, the restaurant only a couple of blocks from her home. When her sister suggested dinner here, Reagan surrendered without an argument.

"Would you have come with me if I'd suggested anywhere else?" Her sister, Brianna, a petite brunette with a perky face and attitude, was a college junior on her way to a business degree that didn't trap her into a particular industry. She could afford to be perky.

"Sure I would have. I just wouldn't have enjoyed it as much."

Few people denied Brianna what she wanted. First, she was the baby of the family and used to getting her way. Second, if she didn't get it immediately, she had perfected the ability to finagle others into seeing her side.

Frankly, right or wrong, all three Hartwell sisters possessed stubborn opinions and headstrong actions. But Reagan's older sister, Paige, had a mother's heart, and Brianna made it a point to see the bright side of just about everything. And Reagan? Daddy called her Miss No-nonsense. He was right. She didn't suffer fools gladly, not even herself.

Reagan Anne Hartwell was the biggest fool of all. On the cusp of the day of the year that punctuated that fact with a big, black exclamation point, she was happy for tonight's distraction.

The smells of dishes like fajitas, burritos, and enchiladas set off a growl in her stomach. She'd had little appetite lately, but if any food could tempt her, it came from the kitchen at the back of this building owned by Rick Burns.

Rick also owned the place across the road, the Red Dog Diner. Most Hidden Veil residents were aware of his ownership of both places, but the food was so good here, they didn't mind that a Scots-Irishman owned a restaurant that specialized in Mexican food.

Reagan leaned close to her sister to be heard over the sounds of mariachi music coming from overhead speakers. "Let's ask for something in a corner."

"How about there?" Brianna pointed to an empty booth across the room.

"Perfect."

Within minutes, they had given the waitress their order. While they waited for their food, they munched on tortilla chips and salsa and washed it down with sweet tea. Brianna wiped her hands on a paper napkin. "Mrs. Mendelsohn saw you out with a guy last night. Who was he?"

How quickly they'd come to the reason for the invitation. "No one I want to see again."

Bri stared at her as the waitress placed their meals on the

table. After the woman walked away, she said, "You seriously need to stop, Reagan."

Brianna Hartwell: perky, opinionated, and bossy.

"Stop what?" As if Reagan couldn't recite the coming lecture word-for-word.

"Dating losers. You don't like the guys you go out with, but you're afraid to find someone you can like."

Perky, opinionated, bossy, and blunt.

And telling Reagan nothing she didn't already know about herself. "I thought you were taking business courses at that college, not psychology."

"Don't get mad. I only said what we've all wanted to say to you for a long time."

"I didn't ask for your judgment on my love life."

"Well, maybe you should ask for someone's judgment, because you're getting nowhere on your own." Brianna played with the tines of the fork peeking out from a rolled napkin next to her arm. "I didn't mean to start an argument. I'm worried about you. If you *had* asked me, I would have said there was no need for you to look any further than . . ." She glanced around and lowered her voice. "Trey Abbott."

"You and Shaina are plotting! He's my boss and a friend. Nothing more. Besides, I can't date him without risking my job."

"Poppycock."

"Poppycock?"

Bri wrinkled her nose. "You have me watching old movies now. Anyway, you two are always together in social settings. You even share meals together."

"So Trey and I eat a meal together once in a while. Those are not dates."

"You don't have non-dates alone with our other guy friends. Why him?"

"Easy. Kyle is married. Lane is engaged, and Sutton is . . . Sutton." While they were all good men, Trey was the only one she would spend time with in a private setting. He was kind, thoughtful, had a calming presence, and never came on to her. Her stomach clenched at that last reason. Why not?

"In my opinion—"

"Oh, yes, please tell me your opinion." Reagan rolled her eyes.

The sarcasm failed to daunt Brianna. "You're afraid."

Reagan set her jaw. "This is no longer a topic of discussion. You're not my mother."

"Oh, like you were *my* mother when you ordered me not to volunteer at Healing Springs?"

Until last summer, Reagan had still been angry with Lane Becker for what she perceived was his role in his brother's enlistment in the Army. She never realized Lane blamed himself. Since then, she'd forgiven him and wished him well in his attempt to use equine therapy to help veterans and others with PTSD. She'd even become close friends with his fiancée, Macie.

"You're right. I overstepped with that decree, and I apologized for it."

"I'm just saying you ought to give Trey a chance. Everyone knows he looks at you like you hung the moon."

Everyone? How, when he never hinted to Reagan about it? Even if they admitted to shared feelings, it would go nowhere. It couldn't, for reasons he would never be privy to.

"Besides, he's sweet"—Bri's eyebrows jumped—"and hot."

The iced tea slid down the wrong pipe, choking Reagan. Her sister thought Trey was hot? Good looking behind those glasses and shy smile, yes.

Okay, he was no strain on the eyes.

But if others realized how little she deserved a man like Trey, they would stop trying to push the two of them together.

Reagan pulled a tee-shirt over her head and snugged it down around her hips. She leaned over the bathroom sink and stared into the ancient mirror at the shadows under her eyes. "You will be extra vigilant this week."

The thought of work carried her back to Trey's announcement about bringing on a new vet. It surprised her but made sense considering the growth in their workload. She liked the smallness of their clinic, the camaraderie and familiarity of working with one doctor. How much would reporting to a stranger change the dynamics?

Reagan added a bit of blush to her pale cheeks. What if she didn't get along with the woman? Her hand dropped, her fingers opened, and the brush fell into the sink. Trey had the only vet clinic in Hidden Veil. Leaving it meant also moving away from her hometown, her family and friends, and starting over. A new job would take her away from Trey.

On the positive side, it would give her some breathing room.

Over the last several months, something had changed in their relationship. Something elusive. Like entering a room and catching the slightest whiff of perfume, a fragrance subtle enough to be imagined.

Reagan could pinpoint the exact time and place when she first noticed it. Last November, Jo Ella Ledbetter—as of January this year, Jo Ella Callahan—had invited their friends to her coffee shop, Jo E's Java, for a Friendsgiving. Trey had spoken fewer words than normal that day. Then she'd watched him drive away from Jo E's early with some lame excuse about work.

She never questioned him about it because . . . well, probably because she sensed it was something better left a mystery. Something she didn't want to know. Still, it planted a seed that felt like hope inside her. A seed she would never allow to sprout.

Reagan plucked a dark brown hair from the green shirt and dropped it into the trash can by the bathroom sink, then tied her long hair back with an elastic band. When was the last time she'd had her hair cut? Three months ago? Soon it would be as long as it had been when Matt was alive.

This was getting ridiculous. She should be over his death by now. She should get on with her life. So why couldn't she? A simple answer, really. If she had displayed one ounce of maturity and compassion, he would still be alive.

I've loved you for years, but it was your idea to enlist. Reagan hadn't seen the letter since mailing it, but somehow, she had it memorized—at least, the truly cutting parts.

She sponged a layer of foundation under her eyes to hide the darkness. If only she could use it on her conscience to cover the darkness of her regret.

Grabbing her purse from atop her bed, she stuffed her phone inside, then snatched up her keys and headed for the side door off the kitchen, slamming it behind her. She backed her Honda out from under the carport and stopped at the end of the driveway, studying her small, almost eighty-year-old frame home.

She cherished the old house she had inherited from her grandmother—the one her grandparents had lived in for almost sixty years. The idea of selling it and moving left her close to hyperventilating. And how ironic in light of her suggestion that Oren Burnside sell his place.

Reagan had given the exterior of the house a cheery face, painting it a light gray with white trim and black shutters. In the summer, she used the front porch as an outdoor haven, planting whimsical flower pots and sitting on a brightly cushioned rocker.

The interior was another story. Little by little, she had painted and repaired and brought it into the twenty-first century. It still needed a lot of work, but Reagan had done her best on a meager budget. Her next major project was to remove the fiberboard ceiling tiles in the kitchen and install more modern light fixtures and new countertops. All in due time. For now, she had to concentrate on her job, or there would be no money to do renovations.

Once she reached the highway on her way to the clinic, she switched the radio on. The station played Eric Church's "Love Your Love the Most," one of Matt's favorite songs from before he enlisted. He'd always crank up the volume, saying it spoke so much of what he felt for her.

Her vision swam. Why had she ever sent that letter?

As she approached Steel Gate Road, she brushed away the tears from under her eyes, no doubt smearing her makeup, then she reached over and punched the button, turning off the radio. She couldn't take hearing that song this week.

As she returned her attention to the road, something small and light-colored moved into her peripheral vision. It loped across the highway and darted in front of her car. She swerved to miss it and slammed her foot on the brake. The Honda left the road and bounced through the tall grass, launching the car toward a mature pine tree.

The vague thought flashed through Reagan's mind that she might face her late fiancé sooner than she'd ever expected.

But another face streaked across her vision like a comet, an image with kind dark eyes behind adorable tortoiseshell glasses. In its wake, the sight left a trail of longing. Why hadn't she been a better person, one worthy of someone like him?

Four

Trey glanced at the time on the dash of his Ford F-150. Forty minutes until his first appointment. Oversleeping, then driving into town to fill his gas tank had eaten into his usual minutes of easing in to the morning routine and made him late.

He rubbed his tired eyes. Middle-of-the-night emergencies were not uncommon for him. He loved his job, no matter what his family thought of it, but he risked burnout if he didn't bring another veterinarian into the practice.

Over the weekend, he ran the numbers, including Shaina's promotion and adding a second tech to take some of the load off Reagan. It would be tight, but another vet would allow for more business.

He read the time on the dash clock and grimaced. He should arrive at the clinic with a few minutes to spare, enough time to get in a half cup of coffee and go over his schedule for the day.

The thought of coffee brought back Marshall Burnside's accusation on Friday. He chuckled. Burnside sure got Reagan's goat.

Trey crested a slight hill and leaned over the steering wheel, staring out the windshield. A car sat angled in the calf-high grass up ahead. At this distance, he couldn't tell if someone had parked or broken down. He slowed the truck, ready to pull over and offer help.

The closer he got, the clearer the picture. The front of the familiar car rested against the trunk of a pine tree, crushed and concave like a fortune cookie. His heart jumped into his throat. It couldn't be. But deep inside he knew.

He steered the truck into the grass as panic stole his breath. The magnet on the trunk of the Honda—Noah's ark with a line of animals marching up a ramp—confirmed his fear.

Trey bolted from the truck, phone to his ear and a 911 operator on the other end. After jogging to the car, he cupped his hand to the driver's side window, and peered inside. Reagan slumped in the seat with her forehead resting against the steering wheel. Her dark hair covered her face, and blood dripped onto the white nylon fabric of the deflated airbag.

"Reagan! Lord, please let her be all right." Thankfully, the fire and EMS station wasn't far.

He tried both front and back doors. Locked. Ran around to the passenger side. Same thing. He slapped the window, but she didn't move. Although he often teased her about pushing the envelope on the speed limit, he'd always thought it would result in a ticket, not speeding head-on into a tree. Why didn't she listen?

Trey looked for other signs of trauma as the faint whine of sirens reached his ears. The blessed sound grew closer with the emergency vehicles. He ran to the edge of the road and waved down a sheriff's SUV. Deputy Higgins, owner of a sweet orange tabby named Daffy, climbed out. "You okay, Dr. Abbott?"

"I'm fine. I wasn't involved, but the woman inside the car hit a tree. The doors are locked." He ran a hand through his hair, frustration gaining a solid foothold on his emotions. "I can't get her out."

"Calm down. Fire and EMT are right behind me."

The deputy had no sooner spoken than a fire truck topped the hill, followed by the rescue squad. As the EMTs exited their vehicle, Trey took a step back toward Reagan's car. The sheriff's deputy held out a hand. "You'll have to move away."

Trey pointed to the car. "That's my employee." *She's my . . .* She was his friend. Nothing more. Maybe he should have chanced telling her how he felt long ago.

"Reagan Hartwell?"

Familiarity—the beauty and burden of living in a small town. "Yes."

"I understand your concern, but I still want you to stay back."

Trey waited as instructed but remained close enough to watch every move. And pray. Within seconds, the sheriff's deputy had opened the car's door. Reagan stirred, and a relieved breath whooshed from Trey's lungs.

As the first EMT reached the car, he said, "Aw, Reagan. What have you done to yourself?"

Trey's gaze darted to the emergency worker. "You know her?"

"We grew up together . . . dated a time or two."

Of course they had. And as usual, it hadn't lasted. "How is she?"

"They'll check her out at the hospital."

While the EMT—Trey didn't even want to know his name—examined the semi-conscious Reagan, a second person rolled a stretcher through the grass toward the car. A short time later, Trey moved back to remain out of their way as they eased their patient onto a gurney.

"I'm here, Reagan. You'll be okay." His words had no effect on her, but he felt better after hearing himself say them.

Lying on the stretcher, Reagan looked at him, glassy-eyed and bewildered. A red-stained gauze bandage covered a portion of her forehead over her right eye. He suspected, in her confused state, she struggled to place him, which drove another spike of pain through his chest, a non-verbal assault on his feelings for her.

The first emergency worker nodded to Trey. "We'll head to the hospital now. You can follow if you'd like."

"Thanks." Trey reached for Reagan's hand and wrapped his fingers around hers, trying to warm the chilled skin. She didn't respond except to stare at him with a shining gaze of helplessness that tied his stomach in knots.

He leaned closer, prepared to press a kiss to her forehead, then jerked upright. She wouldn't thank him for even an innocent gesture made while she wasn't in her right mind and others watched. "I'm praying and will see you soon."

Within minutes, they had loaded Reagan into the ambulance and departed. It was about a twenty-minute drive to the small regional hospital. At least, it didn't appear to be a life-or-death trip.

Thank you for that blessing, God.

Trey turned toward his truck to follow the ambulance, thankful she had awakened and moved on her own. Deputy Higgins flagged him down. "Hold up, Dr. Abbott. Before you go, I'll need some information from you."

Trey glanced down the road, tempted to tell the deputy he'd contact him later, but he understood the need for a proper report. Already, the sound of the siren had faded into the distance.

He made quick work of answering questions regarding the accident and opened his truck door as the deputy drove off. The rustle of nearby brush and a tiny yellow head poking around a small tree stopped him from climbing into the cab. Round brown eyes stared at him with both fright and pleading. No time to waste, but he wouldn't leave the pup alongside the road to be hit by a car.

Trey crouched. He forced his voice to soften. "Come on over and say hello." The wary dog whined. "I won't hurt you."

It took soft words and a couple of patient, nerve-racking minutes to coax the Labrador Retriever puppy from behind the tree. It crept to Trey, head low and belly dragging the ground. He scooped up the dog, cradled him in his arms, and soothed the animal's shaking with soft strokes over his head and along his back. A somatic mutation—a gene mutation commonly known as the black spot phenomenon—blackened a portion of the puppy's right ear. Odd, but harmless.

Trey looked around. "Where'd you come from, huh?" He could guess, since the Burnside Kennel was close by, and the only breed raised there was Labrador Retriever.

He checked his watch. The ambulance probably neared the

small hospital's emergency room by now. He'd drop the puppy at the clinic and ask Shaina to call Reagan's sister, then have her cancel his morning appointments. He would return the puppy to the kennel later.

Had the accident have happened to any other employee or friend, Trey would make the hospital visit. Of course, he couldn't fool himself into thinking the same motivation would rush him there.

Had she ever experienced such a throbbing head? And her chest ached with every breath.

Lying prone on an examination room bed, Reagan reached up and touched her forehead. Her fingers brushed a bandage, and her mind rustled up the image of a doctor leaning over her to close a cut with stitches.

"They'll come out in about ten days." A smiling, middle-aged nurse entered the cubicle, her voice too loud for Reagan's comfort. She pulled the curtain across the track, enclosing them in privacy. "Do you remember anything about what happened to you, sweetheart?"

Reagan started to shake her head and thought better of it. She closed her eyes and tried to think past the headache. She breathed in the cool, clean air inside the room and struggled to recall whatever caused her to end up here. Fog mired her memories.

The drive to work. Had she lost control while speeding? Had

her annual screw-ups reached a new high?

Wait. Something streaked in front of her car, right? She swerved. Had she hit it? "The last thing I remember is seeing something small and yellow crossing the road." An animal, surely.

"Ah. Sounds like that's why you ran into the tree."

"I ran into a tree?" With the way her head and body ached, she had no trouble believing it.

The nurse eyed the cardiac monitor by the bed. "Don't work yourself into a tizzy. You suffered a slight concussion, but you were one fortunate young woman. Not many people play chicken with a tree and come away from the experience with nothing broken. Otherwise, the worst is the gash on your head. You'll be sore for a while, girlie."

With slow and cautious movements, Reagan touched the area below her neck where her chest ached.

"Seat belt bruise." The nurse studied the machine. "The doctor will be in shortly to talk to you. If he's satisfied you have someone to watch over you for a couple of days, you can leave."

Someone to wake her every few hours and make sure she was still alive? With Reagan's parents out of town, she could stay at their place with Brianna but really didn't want to leave her house. She could ask Brianna to stay with her. Would her sister want to leave the privacy she'd been enjoying? "I'm sure I'll be okay."

"You might ask the woman in the waiting room."

"What woman?"

"She said she's your sister and the man with her is your employer."

43

Trey was here? How had he learned of her accident? A cloudy impression emerged of him smiling down at her. Although he'd said something, he may as well have mimed the words. A memory or a dream?

"Are you ready to see them?"

"Yes, please." She pulled the warming blanket they'd given her up to her shoulders, covering the thin and ugly gown she wore. "Where are my clothes?"

"In the bag, along with your purse." The nurse pointed to a chair in the corner. "But stay in that fashionable gown until after the doctor sees you and says you can leave us."

Once the nurse walked away to fetch Brianna and Trey, Reagan did her best to straighten her hair, wishing she had a brush and a mirror to see the results. She paused while running her fingers through her hair. It wasn't the first time Brianna saw her disheveled.

Reagan let her arm fall on the mattress. Since when had she cared what Trey thought of her appearance?

Five

Brianna rushed into the exam room. Fortunately, she stopped short of hugging Reagan and adding to her physical misery. "You've had us so worried. How do you feel?"

"Sore, but the nurse says I'll be fine. They'll release me soon."

"Are you sure? That was quite a hit you took." Trey stepped forward, squeezed her fingers, then drew back before she could recover from the shock of the unexpected warmth running through her.

Weird. It wasn't as if they had never touched. They often worked together in close quarters, but that sudden sense of . . . of . . . She had no name for it. She only knew the feeling had never happened before. It must have been a stress reaction.

Reagan studied Trey. Some idea, some recollection, tried to wiggle into her thoughts, but it never fully formed. At least, he seemed oblivious to her reaction a moment ago. That settled it. She'd simply felt the result of a traumatic experience, like an earthquake's aftershock.

"I'm ready to go home." She grimaced in apology. "You

probably won't see me at the clinic for a couple of days, Trey."

"Take the rest of the week. Give yourself plenty of time to recuperate. I don't want you to return until you're one hundred percent better."

His soft voice and the concern in his eyes reassured her. Then she realized he probably worried she would continue to mess up at work. She couldn't blame him when it was a matter of preserving the integrity of his business.

"I won't need a week."

Brianna scowled. "Do as he says, Reagan."

She didn't have the energy or focus to argue with either of them. Still, what would she do for a week? Tackle some of the million little things to be done around the house? They required a sound body—something she couldn't lay claim to at the moment. Reason enough to stay home.

She ignored Bri and asked Trey, "Were you at the accident site?"

"I was on my way back from town when I saw your car." He winced. "You scared years off my life. Don't do that to me again."

"It wasn't on my agenda." She studied his tired eyes and the mussed hair that looked as though he'd pulled the ends through his fingers. She couldn't say which of them looked worse, but she suspected her accident hadn't put those shadows under his eyes. "Late night last night?"

"Cow caught in barbed wire." At her grimace, he said, "It looked worse than it was. She'll be all right."

"You should have called me."

"No need to ruin your sleep."

"Things from this morning are fuzzy. I have visions of seeing a yellow dog in the road." The type of animal was more than she'd recalled a few minutes ago. Maybe her memory was coming back.

"I found a yellow Lab puppy hiding nearby. I've taken him to the clinic for now."

"A yellow Lab?" Her temper rose, the blood pounding inside her head and adding to her headache. "It happened near Burnside Kennel, didn't it?"

Trey nodded. "I found him hiding in the bushes alongside the road. Don't worry, I'll handle the situation."

He'd known the argument she'd planned to make. He had a way of deciphering what she would say next, even when she wasn't sure herself. Still, she needed to get it off her chest. "I'm telling you, that place is a menace to the dogs there. Burnside should close it down and sell out." She considered telling him what she'd heard last Thursday about Oren's back taxes but hesitated spreading what amounted to a rumor.

Trey shrugged, not agreeing or disagreeing, so she changed the subject. "You saw my car? What condition is it in?"

"Not good. The front end is crushed. I called Harley to tow it to his shop."

Everyone in the county trusted Harley Whitman to repair a vehicle right the first time. The man had more work than dealer shops. She would have chosen him, too. "Thanks."

"Do you need a ride home?"

"Actually . . ." Reagan turned her attention to her sister. "The nurse says someone should stay with me for a day or two. Want to keep me company?"

"Sure." Brianna laid a hand on Reagan's shoulder. "I'm just thankful your injuries weren't worse. When they spring you from this place, we'll stop by Momma and Daddy's to pick up my things."

"I appreciate it."

"I haven't called them yet. I wanted to wait to see you."

"Smart thinking. I'll call them later."

"Well, I'm glad you're okay and have a ride home. I'd better head back to the clinic." Trey pointed to her. "Don't let me see you before next Monday."

She had no intention of going anywhere but home—after a stop at her parents' house. But a whole week around the house?

Trey backed toward the curtain. He watched her as if he wanted to memorize her features out of concern she'd disappear. She caught herself seeming to do the same thing. Oddly, Sunday morning at church could have been the last time she'd seen him. The thought left her sad and confused.

Brianna's gaze shifted between the two of them, even though she had no way of feeling this strange current that passed between Reagan and Trey, one Reagan wasn't sure she wanted to interpret.

"Let me know if you need anything."

"I will. Thank you, Trey."

He nodded and disappeared, pulling the curtain closed behind him.

Reagan pressed a hand to her aching forehead and gave it a slow count of ten to ensure Trey had left the area. Then she turned to her sister. "Okay, out with it. I know whatever you want to say is boiling inside you, ready to spill over."

A satisfied smirk popped out on Bri's face. "He is so gone over you."

"Don't be ridiculous." But what if it was true? How had she missed seeing his interest during their three years of working together? Or were these recent feelings on his part?

But something had passed between them—something that

belittled her attempt to brush it off earlier. How was she to deal with this unexpected response? Did she want to explore it further? And, if so, would it end the way most of her romances ended?

No. It wouldn't end that way, because she had no intention of starting something between them. Trey didn't deserve to be hurt by someone like her.

Even though he told himself to turn around, that he had work to do, Trey pulled into Harley Whitman's station on the north side of Hidden Veil. He parked near the garage, left his truck, and scanned the car-filled lot, looking for Reagan's Honda. He spotted it at the side of a large aluminum-framed building.

Horror overshadowed his mood once more at seeing the broken windshield and the hood crunched into a V shape. He'd known loss—family members like his maternal grandparents, a couple of classmates. This was different, though. This was Reagan.

And thank God he hadn't lost her.

His heart sank. No thanks to him, though, when he'd done nothing to save her. She'd needed him, and he couldn't even open the car door. Some hero.

This morning gave Trey a tiny taste of what Reagan must have gone through when she first learned of her fiancé's death. The fear. The nausea. How had she survived? He had barely held himself together when he saw her in the hospital.

Then there was that touch. It brought to life the meaning of a good kind of hurt. Squeezing her hand had sent an odd shock wave of pleasure through him, something he'd never experienced in the past.

"She's a mess, ain't she?"

Trey blinked at the voice. Harley meant the car, right? "Yeah."

Standing at Trey's side, he wiped his greasy hands on an old rag while chewing the ever-present tobacco. He smelled like motor oil and sweat and the "chaw" he would spit out soon. With his long, bushy beard and shoulder-length hair, he looked like a 19th-century mountain man in a mechanic's jumpsuit. Contrary to his rough exterior, Harley was one of the most faith-filled Christian men Trey had met in Hidden Veil.

"Can it be repaired?"

The man grunted.

"I assume that's a no."

"Ain't nothin' gonna fix that. For one thing, the frame's bent. All that car's good for now is a few parts and recycled metal." The man spit brown liquid onto the ground. Funny how he could aim a yard away and hit the target. "God was lookin' out for that little lady. How is she?"

"Banged up, but going home."

Harley nodded. "Tell her I'll keep the car here. Once the adjuster gets a look, she can let me know what to do with it."

Trey pointed to the back of the trunk lid. "Mind if I take that magnet? I think she'll want it."

"Help yourself, then come on inside. I took some other personal things from the car, like her phone. Found it under the passenger seat. Must've fallen to the floor when she hit the tree."

"I'll get everything to her."

Once Trey pulled onto the highway a few minutes later, he drove through town, turning toward the clinic, the route he'd taken this morning. Had it been only a few hours ago? He approached the road leading to the Burnside Kennel and slowed the truck. Should he stop and let the Burnsides know about the accident and the escaped puppy waiting at the clinic?

After glancing at the clock on the truck's dash, he hit the accelerator. This morning's agenda had gone by the wayside, but Shaina had sent him the afternoon schedule, which was packed with appointments. He'd pay Burnside a visit later.

He walked through the back door to the reception desk. Shaina asked about Reagan, her tone chastising him for not calling her with an update. He apologized and explained they'd be on their own for the rest of the week. He hoped so, anyway, but knowing Reagan, he'd give her two days before she returned.

"How's the puppy I brought in?"

Shaina's cheeks reddened on each side of a wide smile. She disappeared under the desk and reappeared, holding the squiggling Lab in her arms. The pup's tongue darted in and out with the attempt to lick Shaina's face.

"He should be in a crate."

"I couldn't help it. He's so sweet." To prove her words, the dog bounced up, his tongue aiming for her mouth. She turned her head, and he found her cheek.

"You realize you can't keep him?"

"I wish." Shaina sighed. "I don't think Harmoni's creepy lizard would make a good playmate." She shivered.

For the first time in hours, Trey laughed. Harmoni Basinger kept a menagerie of creatures most people found repulsive. Her preference in pets unnerved them.

He held out his hands for the puppy. "After I examine him, he's going into a crate in the back until I can return him to his owner."

"You know where he belongs?"

"I have a strong suspicion."

Shaina's expression turned fierce. "So do I."

Ignoring the comment, Trey ruffled the fluffy coat of the puppy and dodged the tongue that slid across the corner of his glasses, blurring a lens and his vision. He removed the glasses and stuck them in the pocket of his lab coat to clean later. He only needed them for seeing long distance, anyway. "When is my next appointment?"

She checked the computer screen. "One-fifteen."

"That gives me time to grab a little lunch." And get his head back into the veterinary game.

The puppy whined. Trey smoothed a hand over the dog's head. "It's okay."

He should be angry that the animal almost got Reagan killed, but one look into those happy brown eyes and all was forgiven.

Six

Tuesday evening, Trey followed Shaina into the clinic's parking lot. He sat the pet carrier on the passenger side floorboard of his truck. "It's been a long day."

"I'll be glad to have Reagan back." Shaina poked her index finger through a hole in the plastic. The puppy that caused Reagan's accident licked her finger like it was a beef-flavored treat. "Are you sure he can't stay with us?"

"He isn't a stray. He belongs to Burnside." Most likely.

Though Trey had planned to return the dog to the kennel yesterday, his schedule prevented it. "You did a great job today, Shaina."

"Thanks. I'll see you tomorrow." She climbed into her car, a sporty, two-door Mustang convertible, and slung rocks as she leadfooted it out of the parking lot.

Trey shook his head. He couldn't remember being that free-spirited in his mid-twenties.

A few minutes later, he bounced down the road to Burnside

Kennel, pulled up the drive, and stopped alongside a cement block building behind a rundown farmhouse.

Exiting his truck, he stood with his hands on his hips. Dogs barked in the background as he scanned the area. It was a beautiful property, located at the top of a hill covered by hardwoods and pines. The out-buildings looked shabby, neglected, but he sensed they had good bones.

No other vehicles in sight meant the son probably wasn't here. Good. He couldn't deal with the guy today. But where was Oren Burnside?

The screen door at the house slapped shut. Bent over a cane, an older man Trey assumed was the one he sought shuffled forward with an unsteady gait.

Trey met him halfway. "Hi. Are you Mr. Burnside?"

"Oren." His gravelly voice rose barely above the cacophony of barking that hadn't stopped since Trey's arrival. "What can I do for you?"

After seeing the rundown condition of the kennel, Trey hoped he hadn't made a mistake in bringing the wandering puppy back home. "I'm Dr. Abbott from Abbott Veterinary Clinic down the road."

"You tended my little girl's cut."

"Yes, sir."

"Appreciate it."

"I believe I have something belonging to you." He pulled out the carrier from the truck and removed the squiggling puppy.

"I recognize this boy." Mr. Burnside chuckled. "He's a naughty one. Dug a hole under the fence out back and slipped away. Thanks for returning him."

"You should know he caused an accident yesterday by running across the road."

The old man's gray eyebrows shot up. "Accident? Anyone hurt?"

"My friend went to the emergency room, but she'll be fine."

"I'm sorry. Glad she's all right." He glanced around. "I don't have much."

Was he worried about a lawsuit? Trey couldn't speak for Reagan, but she wasn't the type to sue. "How long have you owned this place, Mr. Burnside?"

"Twenty-odd years."

Reagan wanted the kennel shut down. Based on Burnside's age and physical fragility, Trey couldn't argue with the practicality of closing it. But it embodied a man's life, livelihood, and memories—things not easily shut down.

Oren pointed to the puppy and shuffled to the block building. "Let's get him back where he belongs."

Trey held the door and stuck to the man's side in case he lost his balance. The interior, cleaner than he'd imagined, had a well-thought-out set up. The right management or a new focus could turn it into an amazing place again. Maybe a boarding kennel with daycare facilities?

Trey had seen the toll it took on an older man forced into retirement. After the sale of his farm, his own grandfather had lost his zeal for life. Trey hated to see that happen to Oren Burnside.

After a few more minutes of conversation while he checked on the puppy he'd treated last week, Trey left to deliver the box of items Harley had taken from Reagan's car and, yes, to satisfy his concern over her healing.

Brianna answered his knock. "Hi," she whispered. "She's sleeping."

Reagan lumbered toward the door. "I was resting my eyes."

Even with tired eyes and tousled hair, no other woman ratcheted Trey's heartbeat like she did. "I brought you your things from the car."

Brianna took the box from him, reached inside for Reagan's cell phone, and handed it to her.

"Thanks." Reagan stuffed the phone in a back pocket of shorts that showed off well-sculpted legs. "How are things at the clinic?"

"Shaina's doing a terrific job helping me with patients."

"I told you she was good."

With that lackluster statement, Trey read her mind as though subtitles flashed above her head. Why would she think they didn't need her? "True, but she's not a tech, and the work overwhelms her at times. She mentioned she can't wait for you to return to take some of the load off her shoulders."

"I'm sure I'll be well enough to return Thurs—" Her face lost a little of its color. "On second thought, I'll be in on Friday."

Thursday was the anniversary of Matt Becker's death. Would the date ever hold only good memories for her?

For Trey, it was an annual reminder of his inability to measure up to a dead man.

By Wednesday morning, Reagan had gotten her fill of cramped

spaces, sappy romance novels, and by-gone-era movies. She walked out of her bedroom dressed in a knit top and jeans after she'd pulled her hair into a ponytail and slipped into a pair of mule sneakers.

Brianna looked up from where she sat at the breakfast table in the kitchen. She jammed her spoon into the small carton of peach yogurt. "You only wear shoes outside. Where do you think you're going?"

"Can I borrow your car?"

"Why?"

Reagan gave her little sister that big sister I-don't-answer-to-you stare.

Unperturbed, Brianna said, "Not unless I know where you're going."

"To the clinic." Okay, maybe she answered to her sister occasionally, especially when she wanted a favor.

"In that case, no, you can't borrow my car."

"Why not?"

"Trey told you to take the week off, something he reiterated when he dropped your phone off yesterday."

"Trey isn't trapped in this small house." A thousand square feet of claustrophobia.

"You're healing from a concussion."

True, she still suffered from a slight headache, but her other aches and pains had dissipated. Somewhat.

She grabbed Brianna's keys off the kitchen counter. "It was a mild one."

"Reagan—"

"I won't be gone long. I want to make sure everything is

running smoothly. Shaina has a lot on her plate." Not that she had complained when Reagan phoned to be certain Trey was out on a call.

"Then I'll drive you."

"You don't need to do that. What about studying?"

"Yes, I do. Studying can wait. I'm responsible for you. Momma and Daddy will never speak to me again if I let you take my car and crash it into another tree." Her sister's lower lip protruded just enough to make her look pathetic.

Who did Brianna think she was kidding? Their parents would never speak to her again? She was their baby.

Fine. What did it matter who drove? Reagan tossed her the keys. "Let's go." Not waiting for her sister to argue, Reagan walked out the door.

They approached the spot where she had run off the road, and she gripped the seatbelt to control the tremble running through her whole body. She could have suggested Brianna go a different direction, even if it meant driving back roads and coming to the clinic from the south, but then her sister would realize how much seeing where she could have died affected her.

"Are you okay?"

There was that question again. "Great." Reagan placed both hands on the tops of her legs, pressing down to keep them still.

As they passed the tree bearing the gouges her car had left, she remained alert to anything crossing their path. Her father told her swerving to miss the animal had been a reckless move on her part. If she hadn't, where would the poor thing be now?

In Trey's clinic, or . . . She didn't want to imagine the alternative. While she was grateful she hadn't hit the puppy, the fact it escaped the kennel made her want to throttle someone with her words. Marshall Burnside. Her eyes narrowed. Yes, she'd love to place the blame squarely on him.

Reagan pointed to the road leading to the kennel. "Turn there." She'd delay her visit to the clinic in favor of giving Mr. Burnside—whichever one she ran into first—a piece of her mind.

"Why?"

"Turn."

Brianna hit the brakes and turned right. The car bounced down the rough state road. "You're going to owe me for new shocks."

At the faded wooden sign near the driveway, its peeling letters mere shadows of their former selves, Reagan told her sister to turn again and proceed up the incline. They passed what used to be a nice two-story farmhouse. Now, it looked on the verge of abandonment—white paint faded to a yellow pall, rusted gutters, a lopsided shutter, and overgrown bushes that hid the front windows. Her sister followed the rutted stone drive to a large, cement-block building in the back.

"Stop."

Brianna parked beside a familiar sedan. Reagan recognized the silver Lexus Marshall Burnside had driven last week. The building's door opened, and he walked outside, followed by an elderly gentleman with a multitude of wrinkles that ran like rivulets over his thin face. He appeared to be in his mid-to-late seventies and toddled with a cane. One look at the feeble Oren Burnside and Reagan rethought her purpose. What if she said the wrong thing and he suffered a heart attack or something?

Yet their appearance left her no choice. She had to speak.

"Good morning, Mr. Burnside."

The elder man nodded. "Ma'am."

Marshall stepped between Reagan and his father. "What can we do for you, Ms. Hartwell?"

"Dr. Abbott said he found the puppy I almost hit Monday." Her voice dipped. "I hope he wasn't too frightened by what happened."

After giving him the impression she blamed herself for the accident, Marshall's shoulders relaxed a bit.

She focused on the elder Burnside. "May I see him . . . or her?"

"Why would you—"

"Follow me, ladies." Oren Burnside turned his back on his son's interference.

Reagan and Brianna followed him down a concrete aisle inside the large block building. The walls echoed with multiple barks. On the outside, this place stood witness to everything she'd heard about it, every reason it shouldn't exist. The inside surprised her.

As the thin man shuffled along, hunched over a cane, guilt hung over her like a cloud for making him walk to a compartment near the back.

Bri leaned close to whisper, "Go easy on the old man."

Besides the good of having a nursing facility in Hidden Veil, the safety of Oren Burnside's dogs was a prime reason for him to sell out. Someone, somehow, must convince him of it. "I'll be on my best behavior." At her sister's expression of doubt, she crossed her heart. "I promise."

But she'd feel a lot better with Trey on her flank instead of

Marshall.

The air held the smell of canines. Overall, though, the place was cleaner than she'd expected, practically spotless. In passing the half-walled compartments, a dog—sometimes more than one—stood at each chain-link gate. Some stared with hopeful or welcoming eyes, waiting to receive attention. Many barked, others whined. Only a few ignored them. To his credit, Oren Burnside greeted the animals in each compartment as though they were close friends, stopping to place a palm on the gate to receive a sniff or have his hand licked. As Marshall said, he called them Bud. She would put it down to an act, but judging by the lolling tongues and wagging tails, the dogs liked him.

Then again, the man was a canine hoarder.

Reagan turned her condemnation for the condition of the property on the son. Though probably in his mid-forties, he was able to care for his father and the dogs. As far as she could tell, though, he did little but gripe.

He banged on the chain link of a compartment. "Shut up!"

She traded a glance with Brianna, whose frown matched her own. Why hadn't Marshall hired help for his father? Because he was a cheapskate. That was obvious from his visit to the clinic last week.

"Dad, why are you doing this? Ms. Hartwell and her boss have no business butting their noses into the way you take care of your property."

Property. The dogs? They meant nothing more to him?

Oren's steps slackened—if it were even possible for them to move more slowly. He looked at his son, his brow furrowed with more than the wrinkles of age. "Well, I reckon I . . ."

When he paused, appearing as docile as the chocolate Lab in a nearby compartment, Reagan empathized with his situation. "If you'd like us to leave, Mr. Burnside, we'll go." Her heart stepped up its pace as she waited for his answer.

Like a turtle, Oren Burnside faced forward and started moving down the kennel aisle. "I don't reckon it will hurt to show these women my babies."

The growl behind Reagan didn't come from a dog.

My babies. If she was the type to let sentiment distract her from a mission, she'd wail.

Seven

Oren Burnside paused in front of a compartment holding five yellow puppies Reagan judged to be around four months old. They bounced up and down, whined, and thumped the concrete floor with their tails. One had the oddity of a black spot on its ear. Oren singled out that puppy by pointing a crooked, bony finger. "There he is."

So that little rascal caused her accident.

Brianna gasped. "Oh, he's so cute. They all are."

Reagan had to admit he was cute. She gestured toward the gate. "May I?"

"I don't think that's necessary, Ms. Hartwell." Marshall stepped near the fencing, stopping just shy of blocking her way.

What was his problem? Oh. He was probably counting the dollars he suspected she'd seek in a lawsuit.

"She can't hurt anything, son."

Reagan took that as permission. She muscled past Marshall and opened the gate wide enough to enter the cell, then shut it behind her and crouched. Immediately, three happy puppies surrounded her, jumping up and down and clawing at her pants. She laughed, but it was the oddball that interested her most. He sat on the concrete behind the others, almost as though he recognized her as the person he ran off the road. His big brown "I'm sorry" eyes pinched her heart.

She tapped her knee and called to him. With slow, stuttering steps, he approached, sniffed her hand, and placed a paw on her palm. She swept him up in her arms and cuddled him while he snuffled her hair and tried to lick her ear. His little body was jam-packed with good-natured charm.

Brianna clapped her hands. "Oh, Reagan. He's a sweetheart."

"Unfortunately, that mismark means he'll never bring the money of a show dog." Marshall stood over his father. "He's nothing but trouble. I told you we should have gotten rid of him long before now."

Reagan wouldn't put it past him to have let the puppy out, hoping he'd run away and rid his father of one troublesome mouth to feed. Surely, he wasn't that cruel.

Then again . . .

The elder Burnside's lips tightened, and a look of defiance sharpened his brown eyes. "How would you like to take him home, young lady?"

Reagan blinked several times as though the action would help her understand the question. She turned to her sister. Surely, Oren hadn't just offered to sell her a puppy. But the glow in Brianna's eyes and her encouraging grin told her it was true.

She hadn't come here to leave with a dog, especially one that cost her a trip to the hospital. What would she do with an energetic puppy—soon a large dog—in her small house? She worked all day and spent as little time at home on the weekends as possible. And who said she even wanted a pet?

But could she leave him here to crave more love and attention than Oren Burnside could provide? "How much do you want for him?"

Marshall straightened. "Naturally, my father couldn't let him go for less than eight hundred dollars. I'm sure you know he could easily ask three or four times that for one of Burnside Kennel's pups."

He wanted her pay eight hundred dollars for a dog with a "mismark," one who was nothing but trouble to them? Ridiculous. True, the puppy was a purebred, black mark or not, but who did Marshall think she was? A Kardashian?

Reagan placed the puppy on the floor, her bruised muscles groaning with the effort to bend over. Eight hundred dollars! That was miles away from her ability to pay for a dog. And what if he had medical issues? Could she afford to have him treated? Of course, Trey would provide her with a discount, like he did too often in her office manager opinion. She didn't want to grouse about others, then expect his benevolence for herself.

She'd need to purchase a bed, food, bowls, a collar and leash, a crate for nighttime, on and on. Those expenses couldn't wait. Neither could the expense of replacing her car. She had no extra money to spend on purchasing an animal, not even a sweetheart like this one.

She avoided those hopeful puppy eyes staring up at her. "I'm sure he's worth every penny, but I'm afraid that purchase isn't possible for me."

"I'll handle this, Marshall." The father glared at the son,

assuming the reins and looking stronger than he had since she'd arrived. "He's a gift to you, ma'am, an apology for the trouble he caused you the other day."

"Are you crazy, Dad?"

A gift? How much did Oren Burnside owe in back taxes? And how could she, with a clear conscience, take precious money away from him? "I can't, Mr. Burnside, but I appreciate the offer."

"My wife loved these dogs, Ms. Hartwell. She was more concerned about them going to people who would care for them than making money."

"Which is why this place is dilapidated. Mom put more emphasis on the dogs than what it took to run the business." Despite his irritation with his father, Marshall's voice softened when speaking of his mother. Maybe he wasn't a totally puffed-up peacock.

Reagan glanced around the building, listened to the whines and yips from the animals, then carried the puppy out of the block-walled cell, and shut the gate behind her before she could change her mind. "I accept, Mr. Burnside, and I'll give him a good home."

"I wouldn't have offered if I didn't think you would."

Marshall waved an arm through the air in disgust. "I've wasted too much time here this morning. I have work to do. I'll see you later, Dad." He spun on his heel, stalked down the aisle, and slammed the door on his way out.

"I apologize for my son's behavior, ladies. He doesn't approve of my holding on to this property. He'll get it eventually, and he can do as he pleases then." Oren sighed, his gaze sweeping the building. "I've let the place go. Truthfully, it's become more than I can handle. He's probably right, and I should close it down."

Words she had longed to hear. "I think it might be for the—"

"Don't you have help . . . some high schoolers to come after school?"

Reagan scowled at her sister for interrupting her attempt to get Mr. Burnside to see reason.

"No extra money to pay them."

"You have a kennel full of fine dogs, Mr. Burnside." There must be at least thirty, minus one now. "Why not sell them and the land and retire?"

"To a nursing home? That's where Marshall wants me to go. He calls it assisted living."

Reagan heard an acidic note reminiscent of his son, but how ironic that he might remain on this property if Briar Park purchased it. "I only meant that you said you can no longer keep it up. Why continue to worry over something beyond your control?"

He looked around, and his lower lip quivered. "My wife and I loved running this place."

So he kept the business out of sentimentality.

"You see that boy over there?" He raised that bony finger again to point to a black Lab lying on the cool floor in a corner, uncaged. With his gray muzzle and stiff movements as slow as his master's, he looked as though he'd occupied that same spot from the day the kennel opened. The old dog's thick tail thumped the concrete, knowing he was being talked about. "He won many a ribbon in his day and was her favorite. I could never sell him."

"That's understandable, Mr. Burnside." Brianna reached out and squeezed the man's arm, leaving Reagan to feel like a hardhearted jerk for wanting him to sell to Briar Park.

"What about the other dogs?"

"Technically, I still operate my business. I sell a few here and there, but I've lost the drive for marketing, and my wife was the trainer, so I no longer show them."

The puppy in Reagan's arms drew in a deep breath and closed his eyes, resting his chin on her shoulder. Even if she didn't keep the puppy, if she re-homed him, he'd be out of this place.

Given the chance, she'd remove all the dogs from here—all but the ancient black Lab. That was why she'd come this morning, wasn't it? To talk Oren Burnside into parting with his dogs and land? She wouldn't press the issue today, but she would be back.

Reagan—someone who never gave her heart without endlessly agonizing over it and listing the pros and cons in triplicate—was already in love with this warm, troublesome bundle of fur in her arms. Before she let reason talk her into changing her mind, she tightened her grip on her new *baby*.

One dog re-homed. Too many more to go.

The bleats coming from the pen at the rear of Trey's property told him Lulu had seen him. Good. Too often, Trey had made an unintended noise that frightened the Myotonic goat. True to her breed, she did what any of her kind—nicknamed Tennessee Fainting goats—would do. She stiffened and sometimes tipped over like a felled statue.

"Are you hungry?" When the goat answered with a pitiful bleat, he threw a section of hay into the pen, then rubbed the top of her bony head as she ate.

He really should keep her at the clinic in a compartment in the back building, but Lulu's former owners had abandoned her. It didn't sit well with him to let her feel discarded again. Besides, watching her antics, like climbing on top of the little house the previous owners of his property had used for their dog, entertained him.

Mocha wrapped her lithe cat body around his legs, begging for her share of attention. He picked her up and ran a hand along the smooth brown coat. Both animals had experienced neglect. Both found a new home with him.

For as long as he could remember, Trey had considered animals a blessing from God with their amazing abilities, intelligence, and service to people. People like the legally blind man who lived near his family when Trey was a kid. He'd lived by himself but walked the neighborhood every day, depending on Max, a Golden Retriever guide dog for his safety. Trey often asked to walk with him just to watch the dog do his job.

He halted, his body as stiff as Lulu's at the remembrance of a call three months ago. His friend, Zeke Grosse, mentioned looking for land for the organization he worked for, Forever Faithful. They trained and provided service dogs for those in need. As much as he'd wanted to, Trey couldn't help him then. Now?

He had prayed for a way to help Oren Burnside put his

property to good use. Was this it? And would it help to square him with Zeke?

Less than five minutes from the clinic on Thursday, Trey's phone trilled through the Bluetooth. He tapped the button on the steering wheel, hoping it wasn't an emergency. "Dr. Abbott."

"Well, if it isn't the infamous Dr. Charles Abbott the Third. How are you, Trey?"

Infamous? When it came to his family, probably. Still, hearing his brother's voice elevated his trying morning. "Hey, Kaine. I'm good, but how are you, man? I heard a news report on Friday about a wildfire."

The silence lasted several seconds, and Trey wondered if they'd been cut off. Then Kaine said, "Yeah. They're always intense."

Trey prayed every day for his brother and father, men who fought on the front lines of fires that wiped out forests, homes, memories—sometimes, lives. He admired them, respected them, cheered for them, but he'd vowed years ago to never be one of them. If he could, he would trade names with Kaine, making his younger brother Charles Franklin Abbott III. After all, he'd earned it. Trey was a biological Abbott only. He ran a hand down his face as if the action could wipe away the memory of the way his fear and rejection of fighting fires disgusted his family—his dad, anyway.

"How bad is it?" After pulling into the clinic lot, Trey drove the truck around back and parked. He waited for an answer from Kaine that didn't come. "Hello?"

"Actually, I'm not on the line for this one. Mind a visit?"

Kaine voluntarily leaving the site of a wildfire raised an alert. "You're not needed on the fire line?"

"They can handle it without me."

"Is something wrong, Kaine?"

"Nah. Why would you ask?"

The defensiveness in your voice, for one thing. "You've never visited me in Hidden Veil."

"My vacation weeks piled up. The boss told me to use them, so I thought I'd see your clinic and that little town you keep talking about. If it isn't a good time for you, tell me."

"No. Anytime is good." Well, maybe not *right* now. Reagan's accident had made things extra busy. But he couldn't turn his brother away. He left the truck and headed for the back door. "I guess this means I should clean and do laundry."

Kaine laughed. "Hey, I spend most of my time bunking with two guys, and we all smell of smoke. I can handle a few dirty socks and a little dust."

"Just let me know your plans."

"Will do."

After hanging up, Trey jerked the back door open and entered the clinic, his thoughts shifting from Kaine to Reagan. Today was the day. Was the normally strong and independent Reagan Hartwell hiding at home as usual, feeling sorry for herself?

Why would this year be any different?

Eight

The sun warmed Reagan's eyelids, alerting her to a new day. *The Day.*

She turned on the mattress, curled into a ball, and yanked the sheet over her head. Later, she would go to the kitchen, grab the bag of Oreos she'd purchased for the occasion, and eat them in bed. She'd stay here for as long as it suited her, for as long as she felt sorry for herself.

She did that, didn't she? On this date each year, Reagan Hartwell conducted her own little pity party and invited no one else. It was just for her. Just for the one day.

She opened the drawer on the nightstand next to her bed and pulled out a small stack of envelopes tied together with a simple yellow ribbon. She'd never summoned the courage to throw the letters away, but kept them as a reminder of her culpability.

Her index finger skimmed over the name—her name— written on the top envelope. Every year on this date, she dragged the letters out of the drawer. Matt's letters to her. During most of his deployment, they had communicated through video calls, but they both enjoyed having something tangible to keep and sometimes wrote to one another using snail mail. Knowing Matt, he kept each of her letters, too.

Reagan untied the ribbon and opened the top envelope to the rhythm of her shallow breaths. She pulled out the paper inside and unfolded it. The contents mesmerized her, as they did every year. Mesmerized, convicted, and broke her heart.

Reading Matt's last letter had become an annual ritual, maybe even a form of punishment.

> *Reagan,*
> *I only have a few minutes to get this in the outgoing mail, so I'll be quick. I tried to call you, but you must have been busy. It's been busy here, too.*

Her throat swelled. "No, Matt. I saw your call and ignored it."

> *I have good news. My time in the service these last two years, especially this deployment to Afghanistan, has been hard on you and on our relationship. I understand that. But, babe, I'm coming back to the States. I'll be stationed at Fort Sill in Oklahoma. Let's get married and you can come with me. Say yes.*

Even if she'd agree, she had no chance to say yes. His letter arrived a week and a half after he'd been killed. Almost four weeks after she wrote her own letter, the one that obviously sparked his request for them to marry sooner than anticipated.

What happened to her last letter to him? Had the Army shipped it back to Matt's parents with his things? Had they read it? If so, they never mentioned it to her. But wouldn't they wonder? She sent the letter, and within two weeks, he died.

I won't wait for you, Matt. We're done. Those words would forever haunt her.

Reagan folded the paper without reading the rest. She stuffed it in the envelope, tied the ribbon, and tossed the bundle back in the drawer. Only a coward would have ignored his call. Only a coward would have broken up with him through a spiteful letter. And only a self-centered idiot would believe her words didn't contribute to his lack of vigilance . . . to his death.

Maybe she should talk to the shrink working with the veterans at Lane's equine therapy center. After all, her issue involved the military—indirectly.

A sharp bark sounded from the other side of her bedroom wall. She rolled over and covered her face with a pillow. Quill. How could she forget about the puppy she'd brought home yesterday? The mark on his ear reminded her of a splotch of ink made by the nib of a quill pen. It seemed a perfect name.

He barked again, several times. "Okay, I'm coming," she mumbled. A short walk, a little breakfast for the dog, and she'd return to the privacy of her room.

Reagan threw off the sheet and climbed out of the warm bed. Catching a glance at her reflection in the dresser mirror reminded her that her older neighbors wouldn't want to see her walking her dog in her pajamas. She should also do something with her hair. By the time she'd prepared herself for a walk along public streets, she was wide awake and smelling coffee.

Brianna.

Maybe the concussion still affected her more than she'd realized, since she'd also forgotten her sister stayed with her.

She opened the bedroom door. Bri sprawled on the floor in front of the couch, tussling with Quill. The puppy bounced and growled. Brianna laughed, then spotted Reagan. "Good, you're up." Her eyes widened. "And dressed."

Quill ran to Reagan and jumped up on her legs. She reached down and lifted him, cradling him in her arms. "It's time this little guy went out."

"I've already walked him, but he hasn't eaten yet." Brianna stood and headed for the kitchen. "I need to get to class."

Relief ran through Reagan. She hadn't been sure how to get rid of her sister. "Thanks for walking him."

"Will you be all right while I'm gone?"

"Sure." Reagan stroked the dog's soft fur, knowing her sister hadn't referred to the injury. "There's really no reason for you to stay any longer, Bri."

"You're throwing me out?" The question held a teasing note.

"I'm saying I no longer need a baby sister to sit with me."

Bri studied her. "You're sure?"

"I am."

"Well, it will give me a little more alone-time in the house until Momma and Daddy get home." Her sister glanced around. "When I graduate, I'll be glad to find a job and move into my own place."

Reagan understood Brianna's desire to be on her own. At twenty-two, it was time for her to experience more independence.

"I appreciate the way you took care of me."

Brianna wrapped an arm around Reagan in a side hug. "What are sisters for?"

Both of Reagan's sisters had big hearts that led them to care for others. How had her parents ended up with someone as emotionally closed off as their middle daughter? She hardly remembered a time when she felt as optimistic as Brianna or as motherly as Paige. Maybe during her years of dating Matt, but the memories of their happiness grew foggier with each passing year.

After Bri packed and left, Reagan fed Quill, poured herself a cup of coffee, and grabbed the bag of cookies from the cabinet above the stove. The packaging crinkled in her grip as she carried the Oreos and her coffee toward the bedroom. A knock on her front door stopped her in the living room.

Reagan grimaced. Her friends knew better than to bother her on this day. She crossed the room and peeked through the peephole. All but this one.

After freeing a hand and hoping to keep from sloshing hot coffee, Reagan opened the door. "Macie."

A year ago, she would have ignored a knock from Macie Newman, because the woman worked for Lane Becker. Back then, Lane's name sat at the top of Reagan's "Evil People" list . . . right under her own. Once she accepted that he wasn't to blame for Matt's decision to join the Army, she'd erased his name. Now, only hers remained—along with a few guys she'd dated over the years.

"I'm sorry I couldn't come earlier, but Alex and I were visiting my parents." Macie shifted the casserole dish and bowl she carried.

Shoot. Now she had to let her inside.

Quill bounded across the room and jumped on Macie's leg. "Oh, he's so cute. When did you get a puppy?" Her eyebrows drew down. "Wait. He isn't the one—"

"The one and only." Reagan shooed the pup away. "Let Macie come in."

Once Quill backed away, Macie walked inside. "From what I've heard, God watched over you in a big way."

Reagan's spirit cringed when she realized she hadn't even stopped to thank Him. Why did she always forget, then feel like one of those nine newly healed ingrates who walked away from Jesus without a word of appreciation?

Thank you, Father. I guess it's better late than never, huh?

She pointed to the dishes in Macie's hands. "What is all that?"

"I brought comfort food."

Once a chef in a top restaurant, Macie now cooked mouthwatering meals as part of her job working for Lane and his Uncle Monte. She frowned at seeing the cookies. "Breakfast?"

Reagan held up the bag. "I already have my comfort food." *So, you can go now.*

Macie bypassed her, walked into the kitchen, and placed the dishes in the refrigerator. "The Beckers ate lasagna last night. I made extra to bring over today. I also brought an apple-pecan salad with a raspberry vinaigrette."

"I love lasagna." Reagan would probably love anything her friend made.

Rather than shoo Macie out the door to continue her one-woman sad fest, Reagan poured her friend a cup of coffee. Evidently, the will for privacy had faded with the smell of lasagna.

The two sat at the kitchen table with Quill lying on the floor at Reagan's feet. "You left to finalize the wedding plans with your mother?"

"Yes. I can't wait."

Jo had agreed to be matron of honor and Reagan a bridesmaid at Macie's wedding to Lane. Reagan's dress hung in her closet, a green swooshy, tea length style that looked like it came straight from a fifties Audrey Hepburn movie. After the wedding, she would look for a reason to wear it again.

Lane had asked Sutton to be his best man and Trey a groomsman. Reagan's heart quickened as she imagined Trey in a tux.

"What is that smile for?"

Reagan jerked upright, and the image vanished. "I hope Lane recognizes his good fortune."

"I remind him every chance I get." Macie grinned, then bit her lip. "How are you feeling about today?"

Evidently, this wasn't just a culinary wellness call. Since she and Macie had only met around this time last year, Lane must have spilled the beans about Reagan's habit. "I'll make it through. I always do."

Macie gripped the sides of her coffee cup in both hands. "I try to not butt into someone else's issues—"

"But you're about to."

"Because it hurts to see you hang on to the past as I did. After Derek died and Alex suffered his first panic attack, I refused to let the anger go. It wasn't healthy."

Reagan used the mention of Macie's son to divert the topic. "How is Alex?"

"Ron has done amazing work. Alex has come a long way in learning to deal with his fears, and I'm seeing God's provision first-hand."

Everything Reagan had heard about Ron, the psychologist helping the vets at Healing Springs Equine Therapy Center, led her to believe he might help her . . . if she sought it.

Macie sent her a pointed look. "I'm not falling for the change of subject. Reagan, you can't bring Matt back by locking yourself away one day a year. Feeling sorry for yourself is not the way to live."

Everyone assumed they knew why this day upset Reagan. They were so wrong.

"Would you like to talk about what keeps you from moving on?"

Reagan was tempted. She reined in the temptation and laughed. "That sounds like something you learned from Alex's doctor."

"Got me." Macie flashed a wry grin. "Just give what I said some thought?"

Reagan couldn't move on when she feared bringing future heartache on others. She couldn't—wouldn't—risk causing harm to someone else. Someone like Trey. It was easy to blame her reaction to his touch in the hospital on the concussion and comments by Shaina and Brianna, far harder to encourage whatever that reaction meant.

"Okay, I'll take your silence as a hint that I've interfered enough for today. I'd better get back to the ranch or Uncle Monte will be grumbling." Macie placed her hand on Reagan's arm. "Someone out there will make you happy. I hope you'll open your eyes to see him."

After Macie left, Reagan grabbed the bag of cookies and walked through the living room, Quill on her heels. She stopped at the door to her bedroom and stared at the unmade bed. It waited for her to climb in and use it as a place of regret, a place to turn away anything but self-condemnation.

Take it from me, feeling sorry for yourself is not the way to live.

Reagan chuffed a breath. What was she doing? With this day? With her life? She glanced down at the bag in her hand. With these cookies?

"God, I am one colossal mess." It was as close to a prayer of confession and petition as she could manage.

Macie's life as a grieving widow and anxious mother. Oren Burnside's inability to accept his wife's death. Both hit too close to home for Reagan. Though in different ways, in different stages, and for different reasons, all three of them had let the death of a loved one stall their future happiness.

She had grown sick of this day of remembrance. Sick of knowing people felt sorry for her. Sick of the inability to move on. Sick of letting people believe it stemmed from mourning. Sick of guilt tarnishing what she'd had with Matt.

Fortunately for Macie, she'd found Lane, and he'd accomplished wonders in helping her and her son deal with the past. She was happy again. According to Shaina and Brianna, if Reagan gave Trey a little encouragement, he would do the same for her. He would help her move on.

But they didn't know the truth or how deep her self-indulgence went, spreading deadly poison that had already taken one life. She pictured the letters in the nightstand drawer and recalled the poison pen of destruction she'd used.

Reagan returned the unopened cookie bag to the kitchen cabinet and carried Quill outside. As they played in the backyard, she mimicked his energy and carefree spirit.

By the time they returned to the house, she'd decided Macie was right. She could no longer remain in this claustrophobic space, dwelling on the past all day. Not this year. This year, she'd break out of her self-imposed prison and do something worthwhile, something to give meaning to the day. Something to make Matt proud.

And she knew just what to do.

Nine

Inside Oren Burnside's office at the front end of the kennel building, the older man sat behind a neat but scuffed desk. The wrinkles in his face deepened. "Let me get this straight, Trey. You want to lease my property for a boarding kennel and a training facility?"

"I'll lease this building, the barn, and a small part of the land for my purposes. People ask me to board their pets when they leave for vacation or business. I'm not set up for that. The whole of your property is too large for that purpose alone, though."

He really needed to expand the clinic and bring on new employees. Even though a kennel involved additional expenses, it was also another income source. It was another way to prove to his family he could make a difference and a living without using a fire hose.

"For the rest, a friend reached out to me a few months ago, seeking my thoughts about property around here for training service dogs. I didn't know of anything available then." And, to his shame, he hadn't made inquiries around the county on their behalf. "Your surrounding property could provide the space for an organization to train animals for people with special needs."

"You won't do the training yourself?"

"No, sir. I'm not involved with Faithful Friends beyond offering my veterinary services. You'll sign a separate lease with them. I do hope to donate a portion of my net receipts from the boarding kennel to help them with the rent."

Oren leaned back in his chair, his mouth drawn in a tight line. "I'll still have my house?"

"Yes, sir. That won't be part of any rental agreement."

The place was perfect for the plan he'd laid out, like God had worked in the background in the months since he'd received the phone call from Zeke.

"This is all preliminary, Oren. Before making a final decision, I'll be in touch with my friend again. We'll come up with a detailed plan. I won't do that until I know you'll lease us your property."

"Dr. Abbott, this may be a blessing. Still, let me sleep on it."

Trey shifted in the shabby, but surprisingly comfortable armchair. "Take your time, but since nothing is firm with Forever Faithful, and things may not work out, they would appreciate their involvement be kept between us."

"Fair enough. I've no desire to advertise it."

The dogs barked. Oren pushed up and hobbled out of the office. Trey followed.

Reagan stood near the outer door, looking far from feeling sorry for herself. Why wasn't she locked in her house today, as usual?

She spotted him standing next to Mr. Burnside, so he slipped around Oren and met her by the door. "I'm surprised to see you here."

"I'm returning this to Mr. Burnside." She held up a collar and leash. "I decided moping at home this year wasn't worth the calories."

His chest lightened with the possibility that she may have turned a corner on her grief.

Last year, he'd stopped by her place with a takeout order from Ricardo's, hoping to cheer her up. She'd confessed to remaining in the bed all day, saying it was typical for her each year. That day, it sank in. He could never wrest her love from the memory of the late and great Matt Becker.

Yet he'd experienced that surprising connection in the hospital. Nothing physical, but soul deep. Something he'd never felt before.

Except for the bandage clinging to her forehead, she looked her normal self. "Feeling better?"

"Can't wait for the stitches to be removed. But the headache is gone, and the bruises from the seatbelt are healing."

"Good."

Burnside scuffled up to them, his cane tapping the concrete floor. "How is the puppy, Miss Hartwell?"

She smiled at Oren. "His name is Quill, Mr. Burnside. He's happy."

"Glad to hear it."

They spoke as though they knew one another, and Trey realized he'd missed something important. "You bought a puppy?"

"I took home *the* puppy yesterday. A gift from Mr. Burnside."

She handed the man the leash. "Thanks for the loan."

She was full of surprises today.

Oren turned. "Let's go back to the office. I've been giving thought to my son's harping on me to retire and find homes for my babies. Maybe you'll have some suggestions, Ms. Hartwell."

"I'll be happy to give you my thoughts."

Reagan followed them down the aisle to the office, her voice and steps upbeat. What a change. Her cooperative attitude would please Trey if it didn't warn him that something was up.

He led her into the small space, crowded by a metal desk, file cabinets, a worn love seat in an orange and brown tweed, and a computer that could give the kennel owner a run for his money in age. Her nose wrinkled. He couldn't tell if the décor disgusted her, or she suppressed a sneeze from the layers of dust that covered the office.

Oren sat with a groan and propped his cane against the desk. "Miss Hartwell—"

"Reagan, please."

He grinned. "Reagan, the past few days have led me to accept that things can't keep going as they have."

"I agree, Mr. Burnside." She sat on the love seat, raising a small cloud of dust and dirt. "In fact, that's why I came today. It would be in your best interest to—"

Oren's hand shot up quicker than Trey would have imagined him moving. "I know what you're going to say, and I'm not ready to sell. However, Doc Abbott wants to rent my property."

Trey held his breath. They had agreed to keep things with Forever Faithful private for now. Could he trust in Oren's silence?

Reagan turned to him, and her eyes narrowed. "You want this property? Why?"

He shrugged. "We've left too much money on the table because we haven't had the space to board animals. It makes economic sense."

She shifted back to Oren. "Mr. Burnside, how many acres do you own?"

"Almost ten."

"Surely you don't need all that acreage for your purposes, Trey."

He knew where she headed. "There's a fenced play area at the rear of this building. Behind that is a decent barn and corral for large animals needing special care. As it stands now, I recommend those cases to other vets and lose business."

Although the place demanded time, money, and hard work to make it useful, Trey believed it would pay off in the long run. As for Reagan? She might need more convincing to see his plan as a positive.

A boarding kennel? Reagan stared at Trey. What was he thinking?

Yes, they routinely turned down people who asked to board their animals at the clinic. But could they fill this spacious building with enough customers to pay the bills? And what if the county took the property after Trey spent hard-earned money to renovate?

Reagan's pulse rate rose. She'd come here to persuade Mr.

Burnside to sell to Briar Park, a more valuable use of the land than a boarding kennel. How many employees would Trey add to the payroll? Three? Four? The rumored facility could help countless people through job opportunities and easing travel for families of those needing physical help.

First things first, though. "What about the dogs?" She pointed toward the main room. "What will happen to them?"

Mr. Burnside frowned. "I'll sell them. As I told Trey, I owe some taxes to the county."

Reagan leaned back, relieved that he'd told Trey about the delinquent taxes. She caught herself and sat straight. Getting her seat dirty on the dusty material was as filthy as she wanted to get. "I can help you find them homes."

"I hoped you'd say that, young lady."

Trey nodded. "Thanks, Reagan."

"I'll contact some of my friends on the dog show circuit. Some may be interested in adding to their breeding programs." A wistful looked entered Oren's eyes. Did he miss the show circuit?

"Good idea. I'll check into other reputable breeders." No puppy mills. Just thinking about those places gave Reagan hives.

"We haven't worked out the details to a lease yet. I've asked for time to think about it, and Dr. Abbott has agreed."

Then there was still hope, because she believed the people around Hidden Veil could benefit from the property more than the Abbott Veterinary Clinic.

Oren's gaze sharpened on her. "If and until we work out the details, please say nothing to others, especially to my son. There's no need to bother him with my plans."

Because he would object?

Oren's eyes gleamed with growing moisture. "I've done the dogs my wife and I loved a disservice. It's driven a wedge between me and my son."

That wasn't the reason a wedge existed between Oren and Marshall. Unlike Reagan, whose plans for the property stemmed from a more noble purpose, she suspected the son saw only dollar signs.

"My foolishness almost ended in tragedy for you and your puppy, Reagan. Guess I'm trying to say I'll take all the help I can get and be grateful for it."

A lump formed in the pit of Reagan's stomach. She had vowed to do something worthwhile today, something to set Matt's wish in motion. She owed it to him.

Trey hadn't signed a lease yet. She had time to talk him out of it.

Kaine shifted in the passenger seat of Trey's truck and winced.

"Are you okay?" Trey had noted a similar expression when his brother walked out of the airport with a slight limp and when he'd tossed his bag onto the truck's back seat.

"Just a sprained ankle."

Kaine flashed an all's-cool-in-my-world smile, but the shadows under his eyes called it a lie. Then again, he had caught a red-eye flight. It could be nothing more than fatigue.

"Thanks for picking me up. I probably should have gotten a

rental at the airport. Where can I find one in Hidden Veil?"

"Don't worry. I use this vehicle most of the time, so my SUV is available." Trey chuckled. "Besides, Hidden Veil has no car rental agencies."

Kaine's shoulders relaxed. His brother might look a little haggard today, but Trey's average physique and his quieter personality contrasted with Kaine's normal athletic build and bad boy good looks. Dark hair almost touched his shoulders. A scruffy beard accentuated high cheek bones. And the large tattoo on his upper arm—silhouettes of firefighters in front of a burning forest—was a nod to his job.

Tattoos had never appealed to Trey, but Reagan had dated her share of guys with them. He tried to imagine what he might get to represent his life in ink. A sad-eyed puppy? A cute little kitten? Sounded about right for him—something helpless and non-threatening. He huffed.

"Something wrong with *you*?"

Trey shifted in his seat, grasping the steering wheel in a tighter hold. "No."

They spent much of the drive from the airport talking about inconsequential things. Kaine asked about Trey's practice, the weather, and the pros and cons of small-town living, even though the town Kaine lived in wasn't much larger than Hidden Veil.

Trey turned the tables with a few questions of his own, ending with, "What did Mom and Dad say when you told them about your trip here?"

"I didn't tell them."

"You do plan to visit to Raleigh before going back to Idaho, right?"

Kaine stared out the passenger side window.

Why was he acting so weird? "When did you talk to them last?"

His brother's muscled shoulders grew rigid under the black T-shirt. "About a month ago."

A month? Kaine was Dad's favorite, the one who'd followed in the footsteps of past generations of Abbotts. The two of them spoke once a week, whereas Trey spoke more with their mother. With Dad, the conversation usually devolved into insinuations of disappointment. *I'm so proud of Kaine. He's a born firefighter.* It took little imagination for Trey to hear the rest of what wasn't said, *What happened to you, Trey?*

Kaine's fingers beat a rhythm on his knees. "So, you dating anyone?"

A swift change of subject. Interesting. Trey understood his brother well enough to know something was wrong. Pushing him to explain would only cause him to clam up. There'd be time during his visit to learn the truth.

"Not at the moment." When was the last time he'd taken a woman out more than once since moving here? He usually excused his lack of romance as having no time while setting up his practice, but he knew better. And this was something *he* didn't want to discuss. "You?"

Another long pause. "Not at the moment."

Thankfully, that ended the conversation about women.

Trey checked the rearview mirror. With no one following, he slowed the truck and pointed to the right. "That's the clinic. I live in the house next door."

"Convenient setup."

"Saves on gas." Trey grinned at his brother, then drove past the properties. "I'll take you into town, what there is of it." Why was he downplaying the place he'd chosen to make his hometown?

"How's Reagan doing after the accident?"

"She's good." He pointed to the scarred tree as they passed it. "It happened there."

Kaine grimaced. "She was lucky."

"The Lord was looking out for her."

And for that, Trey was grateful. Every time he'd passed the site this week, he'd cringed at how differently things could have turned out. He still saw that baffled and frightened green gaze as she stared at him from the stretcher bed. Over and over, he'd tried to put himself in her place, to imagine how he would react had her accident left him grieving. How long would it last for him? Ten years? Twenty? A lifetime?

Trey shook off the morbid thought and continued down the two-lane highway that ribboned through downtown Hidden Veil. He pointed out the various hot spots in town. Locke's Old-time Drug Store and Soda Fountain. Yesteryear Antiques and Collectibles—a store still run by ninety-something-year-old Garnet Clark. The wooded park with a small stage, cast iron benches, and picnic tables for community gatherings and concerts. The city had already placed a sign at the entrance advertising the upcoming community dance—the Blossom Bash.

He waved at Jo Callahan, who cleaned the tables on the sidewalk in front of her coffee shop. She waved back.

"There's a church on every corner." Kaine frowned at Hidden Veil's Baptist Church and the Lutheran church across the street.

A minute later, Trey pointed to an old building shaped like a Quonset hut. "That's my church. It was a feed store until they built a new one. On warm days, you can still smell the feed and fertilizer. It's a contemporary service with an engaging pastor. I think you'll like it."

"Yeah, probably not." His brother's hard expression left no room for discussion about his faith, or lack of it. Something else to ferret out when the time was right. "Wow. I see why you brag about the town."

Trey chuckled and turned around in the parking lot of the Red Dog Diner. The brothers had grown up in North Carolina's capital with its sights and history and traffic. "I'll admit, it's a far cry from Raleigh."

"Bro, this place isn't on the same map." Kaine turned to him. "You really like it here?"

"I do."

"Why?" Ordinarily, his brother would follow the question with a cockeyed grin. There was no grin, simply a sincere attempt to understand.

"You mean, why not a larger place with more opportunities for entertainment and dating?"

"You are kind of hidden away from a social life. No pun intended."

Kaine was right. The founders tucked the town into an area several miles from the nearest McDonald's and Walmart, not to mention a movie theater and the bars Trey didn't frequent. "I have plenty of friends, and you know I've always liked small towns."

Their grandparents on their mother's side had lived on a tobacco farm in a tiny eastern North Carolina community. Economically poor, but rich in faith and friendship.

"Yeah, well, small towns fill the state, so I'm asking, why Hidden Veil?"

Trey took a moment to think over his answer. "The first time I drove through, I stopped for lunch at the diner."

"That ancient restaurant where you turned around?"

"They serve great hamburgers."

Kaine grinned. "Then I'll let you buy me one or more while I'm here."

"Maybe I'll let you buy me one . . . or more."

"We'll see. Okay, so . . ." Kaine rolled his hand through the air, prodding Trey to continue with the answer to his previous question.

Trey recalled his feelings during that drive several years ago. "People smiled and waved as I drove by. Customers in the diner said hello and introduced themselves."

"That sounds like pure country nosiness."

Trey laughed. "Probably. Really, it felt like coming home, like God said, 'This is where I want you.' So I did some research into the area and its opportunities. When it came time to set up my practice, I chose Hidden Veil. I haven't regretted it." He glanced at his brother. "What do you like about Idaho?"

Once more, Kaine shrugged and turned his head to stare out the passenger window. Conversation over . . . for now.

Ten

Trey left the highway and drove down his gravel drive. He raised the door of the garage but parked the truck outside. Lugging his canvas bag, Kaine followed Trey into the kitchen. Again, his brother had shown discomfort when walking.

"Why don't you let me take that upstairs for you?"

"No. I've got it." Kaine inspected the large bright area with its stainless-steel appliances, including a gas range and double oven. He whistled. "Your kitchen begs for a woman who likes to cook."

Trey ignored the hint about his marital status. "This room was about the only one that didn't scream 1970s when I bought the house." One day, he should replace the yellow sink and matching counter in the downstairs half bath, then tackle the upstairs.

Kaine peered out the sliding doors leading to the sunroom. The ample windows afforded a wide view of a large backyard dotted with trees. "Nice place, Trey."

His chocolate and white cat wound her body around Kaine's legs and *meowed*. "Mocha, let him get settled first."

"Mocha, huh?" Kaine picked up the cat. "You always did like your chocolate and your cats."

"She wandered onto the bank's property downtown around six months ago and stayed for several days. When no one claimed her, a teller brought her to the clinic." Despite Kaine's earlier statement, Trey picked up the bag. "Your room is upstairs." He led his brother through the den, past his own bedroom, and up the stairs to one of the two bedrooms on the second floor. He dropped the bag on the bed. "I'll let you unpack. Soda?"

Kaine handed Trey the cat. "That'd be great."

A few minutes later, Kaine entered the kitchen. Firefighting gave him an adrenaline rush. So, with a wildfire raging in his state, something he'd normally be on the front lines fighting, Trey again wondered the reason for the sudden visit. He slid a can of Cheerwine—his brother's favorite soda—across the surface of the kitchen island.

Kaine popped the top and took a swig. "Man, I've missed this. I had a Raleigh friend send me a case a few months ago. It didn't last long."

Trey had no desire to discuss local soft drinks. He wanted some truth. "Okay, out with it."

His brother eyed the soda can as though reading every ingredient. "Out with what?"

"I've been in Hidden Veil three years, and you've never shown an interest in visiting. Why now? Why during a big fire?"

Trey tagged along as Kaine ambled into the sunroom and stood at the wall of glass overlooking the backyard. "I told you. I had vacation time to use." He pointed toward the small enclosure near the tree line. "Is that a goat?"

"Yeah. Her family abandoned her when they moved away."

"Some family. So, you took her in?"

Trey shrugged. "I'm looking for a new home for her."

"Don't tell me. The goat's name is Hershey."

Trey laughed. "It's Lulu, and no, I didn't name her."

Kaine joined him in laughter. "You really have gone country."

Trey exhaled. Why question someone who found excuses to avoid talking about himself? "You asked about local entertainment. The Blossom Bash Community Dance in the park takes place around the middle of the month."

"Blossom Bash?"

"It's a celebration of spring. Always a good turnout. Do you think you'll be here?" A not-so-subtle way to ask how long his brother intended to stay.

"Will you go?"

"I usually do." Last year, Trey went with Reagan—as a friend. It was a rare occasion when she had no date. Given the surprise of seeing her at the kennel on Thursday, could this be the year he asked her to accompany him as more than a friend, and she said yes?

Kaine crushed the empty soda can and tossed it in the trash. "Sounds like something we shouldn't miss."

And it sounded like Trey had a couple of weeks to pry more answers from Kaine. With his brother's ability to avoid the subject, it might take that long.

Reagan stood in the exam room, her focus on the computer screen. She brushed a dark lock of hair away from her forehead. The tips of the stitches near her hairline pricked her fingers. She dreaded the scar the wound would leave. What woman wanted to look like the business end of a hockey stick met her face?

Had the accident really occurred only a week ago? It seemed a month. At least, she was back to work—mentally and physically.

Reagan punched the keys to finish entering her notes regarding a schnauzer she examined a few minutes ago.

"Help."

Reagan had just entered the last notation when she heard the harsh whisper. She jumped from her seat, ready to save Shaina from an aggressive animal in the waiting room, a fight between patients, or a demanding owner. "What's wrong?"

Shaina stood at the door to the room, face flushed and mouth set in a scowl. "Trey's brother is at my desk."

That was it? No emergency? Reagan's muscles relaxed. "Kaine? Why the fuss? You're acting as though he has two heads."

"One is plenty, and I'm not fussing. I'm angry." She leaned into the room. "Come see for yourself."

"Sure. I've looked forward to meeting him." Reagan brushed past her. "Did you tell him Trey is out?"

Her friend set her jaw, eyes flashing. "You'll regret it, and I told him, but he won't leave."

Reagan stopped in the hallway. "Why would I regret meeting him?"

"Because he isn't . . ." Shaina's voice turned into a hiss. "He isn't Trey."

Reagan fought a grin. "None of us are." *No matter how much we might wish for his kind-heartedness to rub off on us.*

"This guy is barely above Marshall Burnside in manners."

"Everyone is above Burnside."

Shaina crossed her arms in front of her, a sign of stubbornness. "Yeah, well, I'm telling you, those two could arm wrestle for the title of Jerk of the Year."

"Wow. You really dislike Kaine Abbott." Reagan sighed. "Okay, what did he say to rile you?"

"For one thing, he said he never thought he'd find someone like me working for his brother."

"That's it?" More than once, when speaking of his brother, Trey had called Kaine a willing beacon, drawing the opposite sex to him. "Sounds like he was flirting with you."

"I know flirting when I hear it. I didn't hear it. He took one look at me and turned grouchy." Her voice rose on that last word. She took a breath, and her volume decreased a notch when she said, "After I told him Trey wasn't in, he growled— *growled!*—then reached over the counter and turned off the warming pad I use for my tea, simply because there was no cup sitting on it. Never mind that I'd only just removed it. Then he ordered me to turn the warmer off when I'm not using it. Can you believe his nerve?"

"He's a firefighter. I guess that's how he thinks."

"Well, if Kaine Abbott wants to be a bear, he can return to Idaho, look a grizzly in the eye, and growl at him, not me."

"A week and a half ago, you told me you like the brooding

type. Darcy and Rochester, remember? Isn't that the way all gothic heroes act? They walk around all frowny-faced and grumbling?" Reagan couldn't imagine an attraction to that type of man. Probably because she often saw those characteristics in herself.

"I said brood, not rude." Shaina's scowl implied she was about as pleased with Reagan as she was with Kaine Abbott. "Consider yourself warned."

"Done."

Once the two of them reached the front desk, Shaina raised her chin and took her seat, ignoring the man with the dark brown hair, brown eyes, and beard. Reagan understood why Trey described his brother as he did. Though not exceptionally tall, Kaine had an air of confidence—arrogance, according to Shaina—and the deep tan of a man who spent most of his hours outdoors. With the exceptions of Shaina and herself, she could understand why he drew the attention of women. "Kaine?"

He stepped closer, his gait uneven. Had he hurt himself? He caught the hand she held out in greeting and didn't let go. "You must be Reagan."

"It's nice to meet you." She slipped her hand free.

"You, too. I was told my brother's gone."

"Trey has several large animal appointments this afternoon. We don't expect him back until after hours."

"Shame. I came to see the clinic." Kaine scrutinized the waiting room as though he expected to find Trey hiding behind a chair or the tall dracaena in the corner. "I should have checked with him first."

"He stays busy. How long will you be visiting?"

"My plans are fluid, but I'll be here long enough that we'll probably run into one another again." Within the beard, Reagan spotted a dimple at the side of his mouth when he smiled. "I hope so, anyway."

Oh, he was a flirt. "I'm sure we will."

"Trey mentioned a dance later this month. I may stick around for it. Will I see you there?"

If he weren't Trey's brother, she might encourage an invitation. After all, Kaine impressed her as being no different from any of a dozen guys she'd dated—and dropped. But because he was Trey's brother, she didn't want to boost his interest. "I have patients to attend, but if you'd like a tour, Shaina can show you around."

The growl from behind the desk told Reagan that Kaine wasn't the only bear in the vicinity.

His grimace landed on Shaina. She hadn't exaggerated his antagonism toward her. Strange. "Thanks. Maybe another time."

After he said goodbye and limped out the front door, Shaina grunted. "See?"

"I saw a nice enough guy. Are you sure you didn't say something to upset him?"

"I had no chance. One look at me and he acted as though we'd met before. Like he thought he—" Shaina sank back in her chair, her eyebrows dipped in what appeared to be speculation.

"What's wrong?"

She leaned forward. "Nothing. You're right. I guess I was a little too sensitive."

That was a quick turnaround. "Okay, well, it sounds like Kaine plans to stick around for a while, so play nice."

"Will do." Shaina straightened a stack of papers on her desk, not looking at Reagan. "So, you didn't answer him. Who's taking you to the Blossom Bash?"

"I'm not sure I'll go this year."

Oddly, she couldn't summon an interest in a date with a guy she barely knew. Dare she ask Trey to go—as a friend, like they did last year—without risking misinterpretation by certain Hidden Veil matchmakers? She might convince some of her friends to go as a group. No dates. Then again, most of her friends were seeing someone, engaged, or married.

Unless Shaina wanted to go with her.

"I suppose you'll go with Chase?" Chase Taylor was Shaina's on again, off again date. He seemed like a nice enough guy, but theirs was a convenient relationship rather than one with sparks.

"I don't know."

Reagan tilted her head and rolled her eyes toward the ceiling, making a show of thinking. "I can suggest someone else." Her lips twitched.

Shaina glared at the door Kaine had used to leave the clinic. "Last . . . man . . . on . . . Earth."

Eleven

"If you wipe that glass one more time, it will shatter."

Reagan dismissed Shaina's warning and ran a rag over the front window of the waiting room. Again. "It never hurts to double check."

"Double check, fine. Obsess, no."

The office hadn't opened yet, but in a few minutes, they would meet the veterinarian Trey hoped to hire, Carolyn Nakano. Reagan wanted everyone to see the clinic in its best light, but today was special.

She glanced at the ceiling. Maybe she should have grabbed a ladder and cleaned the light fixtures.

The front door opened and a petite woman walked inside wearing black dress pants and a silky turquoise blouse.

Too late for the lights.

Long, straight black hair draped over the woman's shoulders, and her smile lit up her heart-shaped face. Reagan's eyes popped at the woman's beauty and the graceful way in which she approached the front desk. Was Trey aware of Dr. Nakano's Hollywood gorgeousness? How much had her attractiveness inspired his decision to hire her?

No, that wasn't Trey. He'd be more interested in her dedication and the quality of her work. For some reason, she wanted to tack "hopefully" to that thought.

The woman held out her hand. "Good morning. I'm Carolyn."

Reagan gathered herself. After shoving her hand forward, she realized she still held the rag. She stuffed it in a pocket of her scrub pants before clasping Carolyn's hand. "I'm Reagan Hartwell. I'm sorry for the need to reschedule last week, but Dr. Abbott insisted I be here to meet you."

"No worries." Dr. Nakano eyed the stitches in Reagan's forehead. "How are you feeling?"

She waved off the inquiry, not wanting to give this woman the impression she couldn't do her job. "Fully functional."

Shaina left her desk and scurried around the counter. "I'm Shaina Weber, office manager and receptionist."

"Carolyn." The woman smiled. "I look forward to working with both of you."

Thirty-two and with a brand new DVM certificate to hang on a wall, would Dr. Nakano—Carolyn—be a know-it-all, eager to prove herself? Or would she fit well into their small staff? Reagan struggled to prepare for all the changes about to take place at the clinic.

Carolyn glanced around. "I'm supposed to meet with Dr. Abbott."

"Right here." Trey entered the room from the hall.

She smiled and shook his hand. "It's nice to meet you in

person."

"You, too."

Reagan studied Trey's reaction. She could swear he stood a little taller. Seriously, did glue stick to Carolyn's hand, forcing him to hold it for so long?

Trey turned to her. "We'll talk in my office for a few minutes, then if you'll show her around?"

Reagan planted a beaming smile on her face. "Be happy to."

With a slight tilt of his head, Trey paused and let his curious gaze probe her as she had him. Maybe she had overdone the cheery voice? A moment later, he guided Carolyn down the hall, and Reagan's lips drooped back to normal.

"Wow." Shaina took her seat at the reception desk.

"Right? I didn't expect Miss Universe."

Shaina laughed. "Obviously. She walked in, and I thought I'd need to pick up your jaw up from the floor. Then when Trey entered the room, two sets of retractable claws shot out."

Retractable claws? "What?"

"I'm talking about the look on your face when Trey met Dr. Nakano."

"Don't even start with that romantic nonsense."

"Your eyes may already be green, but they—" The front door opened again, snagging Shaina's attention. A frown replaced the mischievous smile of a moment ago.

Reagan glanced over her shoulder as Kaine walked inside the clinic, his limp almost gone this morning. He carried a small white box with *Sweet Times Bakery* in green letters across the top.

From the corner of her eye, she noticed that, even though no cup sat on its base, Shaina pressed the "On" button to the mug warmer and mumbled under her breath, "Make my day, Smokey the Grouch."

Reagan turned a snicker into a cough as she faced Trey's brother. "You're up and about early."

"Trey brags on the bakery downtown, so I tried it out." He set the box on the counter and lifted the cardboard lid. "I brought pastries."

Cheese Danish. Bear Claws. Cinnamon buns. Reagan's mouth watered. "They look great."

He shoved the box toward her. "Have one."

She reached out to grab a Danish. Thinking better of it, she withdrew her hand. "Thanks, but we have a visitor this morning, and Trey wants me to show her around. Maybe later."

"That's right. I forgot Trey said the potential new vet was coming today. I guess he's with her now?"

"Yes."

Kaine's glance bounced off Shaina and onto the cup warmer. He frowned but didn't comment. "How about you, Shayla? You look like you could use something sweet."

Shaina stilled and studied Kaine. Reagan had never seen that shade of pale on her friend's fair-toned face. Then her skin reddened, and her expression reflected a strange mix of outrage and shock. Reagan waited for an explosion, but Shaina regained control and graced him with a syrupy smile. "The name is Shaina, and my daddy always said I was sweet enough."

His mood did a one-eighty. "Yeah, I'm sure he did." He aimed a grin at Reagan, but it lacked the pleasure of a moment earlier. "Tell Trey I'll see him later. Enjoy." Before she could respond, he slid the box of pastries across the counter and walked out the door.

Reagan tried to ignore the sweet smell in the air and rested her forearms on the counter. "What is it between you two?"

Shaina sighed and switched off the coffee warmer. "I really don't know why he doesn't like me, nor do I care."

"I hope he gets your name right next time."

"My guess is, over the years, he's breathed in too much smoke. It's fogged his memory."

Reagan had met Kaine Abbott's type over and over—carefree, no commitments, no serious emotions.

Just the type of guy she usually dated.

Trey walked into the narrow building on Main Street that housed his accountant's office. Zeke had responded to his inquiry about the property with enthusiasm and had sent detailed needs for the facility.

Even though he still hadn't heard from Oren, a cancellation at the clinic left Trey with time to check his finances, to see how much he could afford to invest to get his plans off the ground.

"If it ain't the good-looking Dr. Abbott, Miracle Healer." The woman behind the desk peered at him over her readers.

Trey laughed. Since treating her cat's intestinal inflammation last spring, Frieda Armstrong frequently sang his praises. "You're good for my ego, Frieda."

"I don't say what I don't mean." She removed the glasses.

Time to get down to business. "Now, what brings you in here?"

"I don't have an appointment, but does Jack have a minute?"

She rose from the chair. "Let me check."

Trey made a decent living as a veterinarian in the small, rural area. He even had a nest egg, thanks to an inheritance from his grandparents, but that didn't mean this was a financially sound idea. Jack would tell him how much he could risk.

While waiting for Frieda to return, Trey's gaze skimmed the room in the old building, from its brick walls to the tin ceiling to the Victorian bookcases and small tables—all the furniture had price tags dangling from them. As the son of Garnet Clark, owner of Yesteryear Antiques and Collectibles, he used his office as an advertisement and extension of his mother's business.

Frieda reappeared. "He has thirty minutes before an online meeting, so go on back, Dr. Abbott."

Contrary to the front portion of the financial adviser's office, Jack's personal space was as twenty-first century and technologically up-to-date as anything found in a large IT firm. It made sense, since the sixty-something man dabbled in technology as a hobby.

"Thanks for seeing me on short notice."

"Glad to see you any time." Jack shook his hand and gestured to the gray barrel chair in front of a minimalist desk with a gray metal frame and light wood top. "What's on your mind?"

Trey told him of his plans for the kennel. "If things go as planned, I'll need some capital for the work and materials to get it ready."

Jack leaned back in his chair. "I think you have a worthwhile idea, Trey." From the depth of his frown, he clearly wanted to say more.

"But?"

"But Ted Main expects to sell that property to a company ready to build a nursing and rehabilitation facility. The mayor and county commissioners know the condition of Oren's operation and wouldn't mind seeing it go away. I spend a lot of time talking to people. I don't know the truth of it, but I've heard, if he doesn't sell out soon, they're ready to take the property for back taxes. I'd hate to see you spend money for nothing."

"Oren told me about the taxes. He's willing to close his business and sell his dogs to pay what he owes. He isn't ready to sell his house and land. I'm sure our political leaders don't want to push a senior citizen out of his house."

"I'm sure Mayor Hildenberg would push her own mother out of her house if it meant seeing the town grow and the people happy. She has visions of Hidden Veil becoming a destination town like Blowing Rock in the mountains or one of the coastal islands. That requires taxes such as would come from a company as large as Briar Park—more than Burnside would ever owe." He chuckled. "I've lived in this town all my life. It's nice, but why does she think tourists will come here for a vacation? It isn't like we have the mountains, the beach, or historical sites as a draw."

"We have a lake."

Jack scoffed at that. "Wouldn't put it past her to advertise it as the beach."

Trey laughed, unable to argue the point. "Why that property? Surely, something else is available."

"Not according to Ted. Most properties in the area are too

large or too small. He also said it's centrally located in the county, scenic, close to town, and there is no competition. Briar Park has eyed this area for a long time, and they can wield a lot of clout. Don't discount the hostility you may face. People would welcome one of their centers, because it's a good distance to visit loved ones in other facilities."

Did Oren realize how close he was to losing his property? Weren't the powers that be willing to take his desires into consideration? "I understand, but Oren's property is ideal for what I have in mind, too."

"You know people when they have their minds set on something. Just realize, if you go through with this, Trey, you'll buck the system. Not to mention you'll butt heads with Burnside's son, Marshall. He's pushing as hard as anyone to sell to Briar Park."

The mayor and council. Marshall Burnside. His neighbors. Was his plan worth antagonizing everyone, some of whom use his services? He couldn't afford to lose business with the added salaries and other expenses.

"Where do you stand, Jack?"

"As you know, my mother is in her nineties. She's in good health for her age, but we don't know about tomorrow. For me, Briar Park has the edge."

"Fair enough."

The accountant turned to his computer. "Let's see what you can do."

Trey had a healthy retirement account, so for the next few minutes, they talked of ways he could access the money he needed without risking his funds. Once they finished examining his account, Jack advised how much he could afford to spend. He stood. "Thanks. Things are still in a planning stage, so until they're worked out, I'd appreciate you not mentioning my purpose for the land."

"What I told you isn't a secret, so I didn't betray anyone's trust. You can depend on me to keep quiet."

Trey left the office. The physical welfare and convenience of neighbors versus the safety and happiness of adults and children who were strangers. Did one outweigh the other?

The rescheduling of the last appointment before lunch allowed Reagan to sneak in a much-needed haircut. She walked out of Locke's Drug Store, where she'd picked up a sandwich and drink from the soda fountain section, planning to eat her lunch while waiting for her turn at Naomi's salon.

As she approached her rental car, she glanced up. Trey stood on the sidewalk across the street. She opened her mouth to call his name, then shut it after realizing he stood outside his accountant's office. Had he seen Jack about his personal account or that of the business? And, if it was business related, did it pertain to his proposal regarding Burnside's property? She stopped herself from running across the street to ask.

She studied Trey, that downcast look, as though he'd received bad news. Had he discovered he wasn't in a financial position to lease Oren's property? Would the idea die a sad economic death? While she hoped so for the sake of her Hidden

Veil neighbors, his plan had excited him. Seeing him disappointed would be like experiencing that disappointment herself.

Yet his persistence in taking over the Burnside property would force her to decide if she could get behind it. She climbed into her car, tossing the bag with the sandwich on the passenger seat. Why was life so complicated?

A quick trip around the block, and Reagan parked in the gravel lot behind Shear Delight. Walking in the back door of the converted 1930s frame house, Reagan set her lunch on the kitchen counter and called out, "I'm here, Naomi. Let me know when you're ready."

"Give me a few minutes, hon." Naomi Griffith was no more than a decade older than Reagan and called everyone "Hon," no matter their age or gender.

Reagan had devoured half her turkey sandwich when Naomi called her into the room she'd set up as a salon. When she bought the house, the hairdresser hired Sutton to tear out the wall between the living room and dining room and exchange the old sink in the nearby bathroom for the type used in a hair salon. Naomi lived upstairs.

After being seated in the only swivel chair and swathed in a cutting cape, Reagan relaxed as Naomi took the scissors to her hair. They discussed everything from her accident to Kyle Callahan's new Christian music album to the upcoming dance. As always, Reagan learned a few things she hadn't known.

The back door opened and closed. Through the reflection in the mirror, Reagan watched as Sally Ann Cooper walked toward the front of the room and dropped into a chair placed under a picture window.

"Be with you in a moment, hon."

"Take your time, Naomi. How are you feeling, Reagan? I heard you had an accident."

Reagan didn't dare move her head to speak face-to-face with Mrs. Cooper for fear Naomi would give the ends of her hair more than a trim. "I'm good. My car . . . not so much."

"They totaled it?"

"I'm afraid so. I'll look at new ones over the weekend." If the insurance check arrived in time.

"That Oren Burnside. When's he gonna think of others besides himself? He can't keep up that property no more. If he had a lick of sense, he'd sell out. I guess y'all heard there's a company wanting that land for a nursing home."

Under her breath, Naomi said, "Bless her heart."

"I heard something about it." Reagan didn't blame Mrs. Cooper for her opinion. Her husband had suffered a stroke and never fully recovered. A local rehabilitation center would make Sally Ann's visitation easier. It would have made the Beckers' lives easier.

How many others in Hidden Veil saw things the same way the Coopers did? How many enemies would Trey make if he thwarted the plans of Briar Park?

She cared too much for Trey to stand by and let him ruin his reputation in the community. She'd failed to make him see reason last week. Who else would have more success?

Even though Oren said he wanted to keep the potential lease from Marshall, more than likely, he'd already told his son. If so, discouraging Trey may be unnecessary. If not, dare she approach

Marshall Burnside about it?

The idea disgusted her. In working against Trey's plan for the kennel, she would betray their friendship, right? Maybe not a Judas-sized betrayal, but it felt like one. And if he found out, size may not matter.

Twelve

Trey's truck rolled up the gravel driveway to the Vance farm. He passed the 1920s two-story frame house on his way to the barn. He'd heard that a decade ago the farmhouse barely stood under peeling paint and rotting wood. Junk cluttered the yard and the fields grew wild. The place had served as little more than a structure supporting a rust-stained metal roof that provided dubious cover for a large family. Today, a multitude of replaced wood siding boards gleamed with white paint, and the new green metal roof shimmered under the sun.

The inside of the house and the outbuildings were works in progress. Small evergreen hedges and azaleas peppered the foundation, and clumps of daylilies formed a border along a new concrete and flagstone walkway leading to the front door. The yard provided a colorful show in spring and early summer. Gone were the junkyard vehicles and weedy fields. Today, this property was a working farm surrounded by a spring corn crop planted in neat dirt rows.

Sutton saw him parked near the barn and set down the hammer he'd used to nail a new board to the side of the chicken coop. A flock of at least twenty chickens parted to make a path for him as he joined Trey at the bed of the truck. Sutton pulled off his work gloves and stuffed them into the waist of his jeans. "You're late."

Trey checked his watch. "Two minutes."

"Forgiven. This time. Rocket's in the barn. I'll get him." The big man ambled away.

After unlocking and lifting the lid to a compartment in his truck box, Trey pulled out his instruments, ready to examine Sutton's roping horse. Rocket was a fine chestnut Quarter Horse and his friend's splurge in life.

When Sutton returned, leading the gelding, Trey studied his gait for soundness. Though he'd only ridden horses a handful of times, Trey admired the animal's stocky and muscular form. "Any problems?"

"He's good."

While Sutton held to Rocket's lead, Trey ran his hands over the horse's body, checking for anything out of the ordinary. He administered shots, then picked up the float to file the sharp edges of the horse's teeth.

Rocket jerked his head up, objecting to having his teeth floated. Sutton gripped the side of the halter. He ran a hand over the horse's back, speaking softly to settle him.

When Trey finished, he patted Rocket's neck and packed up. "I see no problems. Call me if something comes up. Otherwise, I'll check him again in another six months."

"Good." Sutton leaned his hip against the truck. "I heard

Reagan tried to kill a tree."

Even though social settings threw Sutton and the Hartwell sisters together, the animosity Sutton held toward them was no secret. He might have a beef with the family, especially the oldest daughter, Paige, but for Trey, mocking Reagan and her accident went too far. "I'm sure she would appreciate your concern." Trey regretted his sharp response.

On second thought, he didn't, because his friend's grin said it went right over his head. "Don't get your stethoscope in a wad, Vet Boy."

Or Sutton baited Trey, who swallowed it as easily as the fish swallowed Jonah. The big farmer's demeanor sobered. "What happened?"

Could the passing of years be softening his bitterness? "She swerved to miss hitting a dog, hit a tree instead, and wound up in the emergency room." The image of her slumped over the steering wheel still haunted him. "Thankfully, the injuries were minor."

"Wouldn't want to be that dog if she ever finds it."

"I found him. An escaped Lab puppy from Burnside Kennels."

"Figures." Sutton issued the one word as a complete explanation. Maybe it was.

"Oren gifted him to Reagan. She'll give him a good home and be a great dog mom."

Sutton laughed. "You're hopeless."

"What do you mean?"

"I mean, you walk around with your heart on your sleeve like you hope Reagan will snatch it to have and to hold. Tell her she's the love of your life and get it over with."

Trey leaned his backside against the truck as though unaffected by the statements. His feelings for Reagan were so apparent? Who else knew? Did she? "I'm that obvious?"

"Yep. For a long time." Sutton grew serious. "Tell her, Trey."

"You don't like the Hartwells. Why are you so interested in me telling Reagan how I feel?"

Sutton laid a hand on his shoulder. "Because no matter my opinion about the family, you're a friend, and friends don't let friends remain miserable in love."

"Friends don't let friends make fools of themselves, either. After all this time, she's never gotten over Matt Becker. He was her hero, someone who gave his life for his country." Trey pushed his glasses up to rest on the bridge of his nose. "I'm an ordinary guy—not brave, not exciting, not someone who sees to others' safety and freedom."

"You're a solid guy. A good guy. Plus, you save people's pets and livestock every day. To her, that must count for a lot." Sutton's brown gaze pierced him. "You also have what Matt can't give her."

"What's that?"

"A shoulder to cry on. An ear to listen. A warm hand to hold."

Trey fought to keep his eyes from popping behind his glasses. He'd never heard sappy romanticism from the oft-cynical Sutton Vance. But his friend had a point. Trey was alive and Matt wasn't.

But a live body wasn't enough to make Reagan forget her soldier. If it was, she'd have found someone to take Becker's place by now. Oh, yes, he'd paid attention to her dating habits. How could he avoid it when she and Shaina yapped about their love lives in the clinic? The walls weren't so thick their voices didn't carry.

Plenty of guys had tried to win Reagan's heart, only to last until they got too close or too demanding. She never bragged, never snickered or blamed them for the breakup. In most of the conversations he'd overheard, she expressed regret at ending the relationship. But it was her choice. Always her choice.

And he couldn't stomach being one of the rejected.

Sutton turned to lead his horse back to the barn. He called out, "Seems to me a hero is just someone who puts someone else's safety before his own. Isn't that what your Bible says?"

Greater love has no one than this, than to lay down one's life for his friends.

Trey pulled away from the truck at the spiritual wisdom from the unbelieving Sutton. When had the guy read the book of James?

He saw before him the image of a soldier, a man clad in full combat gear, saving his team from an IED. Another image overshadowed it, one of a scared college student facing a man with a gun. Unlike Matt Becker, Trey had never attempted to lay down his life for anyone.

His father was right about him.

"Done." Reagan placed the last box of gauze sponges on the shelf. With a supply order this large, she and Shaina had worked between patients since yesterday to inventory and organize it.

"Finally." Shaina marked the number of boxes on the inventory list. "Not that I'm complaining—I'm truly grateful— but shouldn't my promotion to office manager mean I could have assigned this job to one of our high schoolers?"

"Shared responsibility is the hallmark of a small clinic."

Shaina huffed. "You made that up."

"Not at all. It came in a fortune cookie."

Shaina laughed. "I'll have to remember that the next time Harmoni protests cleaning the bathroom. She'll hear that shared responsibility is the hallmark of a small household."

Reagan's phone buzzed, and she hauled it from the pocket of her lab coat. "Hello?"

"Hey, babe."

She hung her head, mentally kicking herself for not checking the number before answering. First, boring inventory. Now, a call from Hotty Scotty Hendrix. Could this day get any more annoying? "Hi, Scott."

"I'm in the area, so I thought I'd pick you up and take you to supper."

He'd called a couple of times since their first and last supper date, but she ignored his calls. Some people couldn't take a hint. She mouthed to Shaina that she would be outside, then walked out the back door. "Sorry. I can't go. I'm working."

His decade-old Camaro rounded the building. "And here I am." Without taking his eyes off her, his smile disarming, he left the car and joined her near the door. Good-looking, tall, blond, and already tanned. She imagined him on a California beach, a surfboard under his arm as he jogged to the water to ride a wave. "I can wait until you hang up your stethoscope."

The man must have cotton stuffed in his ears. "No, Scott. I told you after our one and only date that we weren't compatible."

He placed his hands on her hips. "It was a hectic day, and I was a little off my game. Let's try again."

"I'm in no mood for games."

Lulu's faint bleat came from the direction of Trey's house, reminding Reagan he would return from his appointment at Sutton's place soon.

She grabbed Scott's wrists, intending to shove his hands off her body. The sound of tires on gravel announced a vehicle's arrival. Trey's pickup rounded the building and rolled through the parking lot. She backstepped, trying to put distance between her and Scott, but the jerk hung on. It was an instinctive move, not one she consciously made, but one that still smacked of guilt.

"There's my boss. Now let go of me."

Still wearing that smirk, he removed his hands from her hips. "Okay, we'll forget tonight. But as I drove through town, I saw the sign for an upcoming dance. How about we go together?"

She couldn't help but chuckle at his audacity. He was outrageous. "Scott, I—"

"Great. Put it on your calendar."

Before she could lay into him for his overconfident nerve, Scott hustled to the Camaro and set it in reverse.

"Coward." Reagan couldn't decide if the comment referred to him or her.

During the drive back to the clinic from the Vance farm, Sutton's definition of a hero ran through Trey's mind. Because of it, he'd almost blown through a four-way stop along the highway. Thankfully, no cars had entered the intersection.

His friend had given him a simplistic, yet biblical, characterization of what it took to be a hero in someone else's eyes. If his plans regarding Burnside's kennel worked out, would Reagan see him as someone who, in a minor way, brought hope and safety to others?

Nothing about it put Trey in danger. Not like Matt. Not like his father and Kaine. In fact, the opposition would claim his idea would provide him with personal gain, and he couldn't argue against it. Not with any conviction.

He drove into the clinic parking lot and around to the back. Near the door, a smiling stranger faced Reagan. His hands spanned her hips. With the sound of his truck wheels on gravel, they both looked up. She retreated a step, chin tilted down.

His back teeth clenched with the recognition of that predatory look directed at Reagan. He'd seen it on his brother's face more times than he could remember. With Kaine, the beard added to the image of a wolf on the hunt. His brother enjoyed his conquests, and it appeared this guy did, too.

Trey parked in his normal space and sat behind the wheel a moment, his gaze on the brick wall of the building. Would she turn the tables on this guy as she did on others she'd dated?

He could confront them or let it drop. Backing up and driving away wasn't an option. He climbed out of the truck.

You walk around with your heart on your sleeve like you hope Reagan will snatch it to have and to hold. Tell her she's the love of your life and get it over with.

Reagan laughed and said something to the guy. He grinned like he'd won the lottery and said something back at her. Within seconds, he was gone.

The upcoming Blossom Bash gave Trey the perfect opportunity to do that hard thing and ask her to go with him. Not as a friend, but as his date. Because Sutton was right. If he did nothing—said nothing—one day she would find a man she couldn't walk away from, and he would lose her without a fight.

Trey eyed Reagan as she watched the car disappear around the corner of the building. Had she found him already?

Thirteen

With Quill sprawled across her lap, Reagan sat in her kitchen, pen poised over the notepad on the table. After turning down Scott's supper invitation, she had nowhere to go this evening. That didn't mean she would sit around idle, watching TV.

Oren Burnside had given her a list of his dogs—ages, registered names, pedigrees. Using her laptop, she scrolled through websites of breeders of Labrador Retrievers interested in obtaining new dogs. She had whittled the list down through the sales of two dogs to families in her church, and another dog to a couple who had seen her flyer on the bulletin board at Jo E's Java. But the others?

"I don't know, Quill. Is this a waste of time?"

The little rogue stared at her and whined, then slashed her chin with his wet tongue. She wiped away the dampness. "Okay. I'll keep going."

Reagan placed the puppy on the floor. "I'm seeing my future dominated by a spoiled, utterly adorable bundle of fur with the quickest tongue in the Southeast."

Why hadn't she gotten a canine companion before now? She'd lived alone for years, her social engagements a series of emotionless dates. Like the one with Scott. She gritted her teeth at the thought of today's fiasco. She should have run after him and set him straight about the dance. At the least, she could call him now. Why didn't she?

Trey. His tight-lipped reaction when he saw her with Scott had frozen her to the gravel. Not anger. Not jealousy. More like alarm. Maybe that was too strong a word. But his expression had sure struck a chord of alarm in her. A flashing red light that warned of the accuracy of her sister's opinion regarding Trey's feelings for her. It scared her to think she would allow him to sneak under her radar and zero in on her heart.

Reagan picked up her phone to call more people about the dogs. No, it hadn't hurt for Trey to see her with Scott.

For the next thirty minutes, she spoke with three dog breeders, surprised by the esteem they held for Burnside Kennels. One business showed an interest in seeing which dogs were available. She immediately emailed them the list Oren had given her. The other two passed but wished her well in finding suitable homes.

Once all the dogs were gone?

She hadn't heard whether Oren agreed to Trey's proposition. If he hadn't, she could talk to Trey, try to persuade him to abandon his plan to lease the property.

Reagan stood and stretched, then wandered to the refrigerator and peered inside. Not eager to cook, she looked for leftovers for her supper, but the shelves held nothing of interest. As she pondered her meal, the front doorbell rang. Quill barked and ran to the door. Trey stood on the porch, holding up a bulging paper bag and a cardboard tray with two drinks in his hands.

She invited him inside. The aroma of Italian food trailed behind him as he stepped into her living room, no longer looking as though he cared about what he'd seen a couple of hours ago.

"I hope you brought supper for two." She followed him into the kitchen.

His brow creased as he glanced at the bag. "Oh, did you want something?"

"Don't tease me, or I might mug you for whatever you brought."

He chuckled. The bag crinkled when he set it on the counter.

She read the restaurant name printed on the bag. "Subs?"

Sometimes, one or the other of them picked up his favorite hamburger from the Red Dog Diner and her enchiladas from Rick's, then they would eat while watching a movie together. If weather permitted, they often took the food to the park and watched the kids play on the playground. They were good, platonic times spent with someone she—

Reagan cleared her mind of the previous thought and pointed to the food. "My refrigerator is empty, so you are my hero."

His mouth twisted in an unexpected pained expression before it flattened out. "I thought I'd switch things up this time and brings subs."

Sounded good to her. "What kind?"

"Meatball for me. Ham and Swiss for you." He pulled out the wrapped sandwiches and two bags of chips, then passed the meatball sub under her nose, giving her a whiff of the Italian spices. "Or we can go half-and-half."

"Yes, to the second suggestion."

"I thought you'd say that." He removed his glasses and set them on the kitchen table, providing a clearer glimpse of those deep brown eyes, as velvety as Quill's.

Reagan washed her hands at the sink. For the first time, she experienced a twinge of nervousness over Trey's visit. Normally, she enjoyed a meal with him without thinking twice about what the evening might bring. Tonight's odd edginess had her wondering just how profoundly the change in their relationship ran, especially since the hospital visit. At odd times over the past couple of weeks, she had imagined them together like this more often—sharing meals, sharing laughter. Sharing emotions that went deeper than friendship.

She silently grumbled at Brianna and Shaina for influencing this nonsense in her head.

After pulling plates from the cabinets, she carried them to the table while Trey pulled the sandwiches from the bag. Noticing his glance at the laptop and notepad, she said, "I made some calls about Oren's dogs."

"Any interest?"

"Only one. They all mentioned their respect for Burnside Kennel, though."

"I'd hate for them to see the place now and damage that respect."

She pulled a knife from a drawer, cut both sandwiches in half, and laid them on a plate. "Has Oren signed the lease?"

"He's still thinking it over."

Then there was still time. "I can't imagine the cost involved in renovating the building."

"I think it's doable."

"What made you decide to lease the kennel?"

He paused in the middle of cutting the deli sub in two. "We can use the business."

"But we don't need the entire property. Why not encourage him to sell the rest of the acreage?"

"To the company wanting to build a nursing home?"

He knew? Why not? She'd heard it from two people.

Reagan pulled out a chair across from Trey and flopped into it. "I know you want to help Mr. Burnside, but you could help so many more people by convincing him to sell the property to Briar Park."

"Reagan." He cut the meatball sub in half. "In time, you'll understand."

"What is there to understand? It's to the advantage of the dogs and Oren, not to mention the community."

"I'm sure other places around the county fit the company's requirements."

Her back stiffened. It was up to her to change Oren Burnside's mind about his property, because Trey was no help. He refused to consider anything other than his plan. It meant he'd leave his suffering neighbors out in the cold.

His plan. She'd never known him to be mercenary . . . never known him to be like her. Until now.

Reagan couldn't let it go. Worthy as it was, she couldn't see beyond her own stubborn goal for Oren's property. She couldn't see Trey as also having something worthy in mind.

Yes, a nursing home/rehabilitation center would benefit Hidden Veil residents. But properly trained service dogs benefited people all over the country.

He stared, unfocused, at the sandwiches in front of him. *Am I making a mistake by ensuring a lonely old guy can remain on his property for as long as possible, God? Am I the one who is stubborn?*

One day, he may be one of those lonely old guys. Who would look out for him? What if he needed help and people to care for him around the clock?

Reagan removed the drinks from the cardboard tray. "You're not the only one who wants to help Oren Burnside."

Trey placed half of each sub on the plates. "Let's agree to disagree and not talk about it anymore tonight."

After a quick prayer, he picked up his half of the ham and Swiss, figuring he'd ease into the question he'd come here to ask—one with the potential to change his life. "May I ask you something?"

She set down the meatball sub. "Go ahead."

Trey fumbled for a way to phrase his question without causing her more concern, then went for it. "Something changed for you this year. What happened—other than the accident?" He didn't bother to go into details. She'd know what he meant.

Reagan clenched her fists on either side of the plate. "For one thing, I met Oren Burnside and heard how his wife's death still affected him. Then he gave me that little guy over there." She tipped her head in Quill's direction. "And that morning, Macie visited me. After she left, feeling sorry for myself seemed like a waste, so I decided to do something worthwhile with the day."

"You went to the kennel."

"And met you there."

"Well, I'm glad about the change." Trey only hoped she'd turned a permanent corner on that problem, for her sake.

Her fists unfurled like the petals of a rose. "Me, too."

He wiped his mouth with a paper napkin from the restaurant. What did her change of heart mean for him? If he were ever going to ask, now was the time. "There is something else."

"Okay."

He pressed forward to do that hard thing. "The Blossom Bash is coming up. I thought we might go together this year." Her mouth twitched, a nervous tick rather than a hint of humor. Then she breathed deeply, in and out. With each breath, Trey's hope died a little. "You have a date already."

She shook her head, then nodded. "I do."

That two-word statement chilled Trey like the sight of a butcher knife in a house of mirrors. "The guy from the parking lot."

"We met at the conference last month. He asked me to go to the dance with him."

Trey finished his half of the ham and Swiss. Seeing them together this afternoon should have prepared him. But after confirming his suspicion, his stomach soured too much to eat the meatball sub.

"I'm sorry, Trey."

Sorry she already had a date, or sorry that he invited her to go with him?

While he'd taken care before now—or thought he had—to

control the depth of his feelings around her, surely, she had an inkling. According to Sutton, everyone else knew. Why not her?

"No, it's fine. You never mentioned going with anyone else this year, so I thought we could team up. You know, two friends line dancing in the park." Trey grinned but cringed inwardly at the cowardly and false attempt to save face.

Quill jumped up, whining for attention, his front paws clawing Trey's leg. Perfect timing. Now they could change the subject. "How is this guy's training coming?"

She laughed. "He's a work in progress."

For another hour, they talked of topics that went no deeper than a sliver. The whole time, he hurt from the knife that cut through layers of false bravado to expose his weakness. When the sun faded and Reagan turned on the lights, he said, "I'd better go. I want to check on the Sheridans' dog before calling it a day."

"Okay." She followed him to the front door. "See you tomorrow."

Trey started his truck, but sat starting at the little house, wondering if she cared enough to watch as he left. Right now, he felt like he'd poured inadequacy, fear, loneliness, rejection, and hopelessness into a blender, set it on high, then drank it.

Matt Becker had spotted an explosive device in the sand and saved his fellow soldiers' lives. He was a hero. And Trey? He'd spotted a blond-headed explosive in his own parking lot. Rather than it being the dud he'd hoped, it blew up in his face.

"Ms. Hartwell?"

She frowned. Another spam call? "Who is this?"

"Marshall Burnside. I'm returning your call."

Her heart skipped. Because Trey refused to back off a lease with Oren, she'd placed a hasty call to Marshall last night. With no answer, she left a voicemail. The ethics and repercussions of the call weighed on her all morning. Oren had asked her to keep the news to herself, but the decision was too important for him to make alone, right?

Had Marshall never returned her call, would she have tried again or considered it a sign to drop her idea? But he had phoned . . . if at an inconvenient time.

"Yes, sir. Give me a moment, please." Reagan glanced at Shaina and mouthed, "I'll be back."

Uncomfortable talking inside the clinic, she walked down the hall, her nerves tingling. What she was about to do was best for all concerned—Oren, the dogs, her friends. And Trey. What if the people of Hidden Veil turned against him? He didn't need to risk his financial future on a project that may not pan out. If she hadn't believed it was for everyone's good, she would never have called Marshall. Still, a doubt lingered. She tried to outrun it by bursting out the back door into the afternoon sunshine.

Once in the parking lot behind the building, she raised the phone to her ear. "I'm sorry, Mr. Burnside. I couldn't talk inside."

"I'm out of town, but saw your message. What is it, Ms. Hartwell? If this is about your accident . . ."

A garbled voice over a loudspeaker told her he called from a crowded public area. Even so, she didn't miss the acerbity in his voice.

Why did her heart beat at this frantic pace? The man didn't frighten her. "I'm calling about your father's property."

"What about it?"

"Has he told you he's considering a lease to Dr. Abbott for a boarding kennel?"

For several moments, she heard only background noise. Clearly, he hadn't hung up. Then he spit out a curse. "I'm out of the country and haven't spoken to my father in a week."

"I think you and I have a common interest."

"And that is?"

"We both want to see him sell his property to Briar Park, not lease it."

"Have they signed the lease?"

Stones crunched beneath her feet as she paced. "Not yet."

"I'm about to catch another flight and won't return to the United States until next week." His sigh broke through the airport noise. "Convince your boss he should abandon his plan to lease Dad's property."

Fat chance. Trey seemed primarily concerned about helping Oren Burnside remain lost in his memories, something that, after years, Reagan now realized was a road to hopelessness. "I've tried to talk him out of it, Marshall. I'm only letting you know, because I care about what's best for your father, Trey, and for the people of Hidden Veil."

"Do you think I don't want what's best for Dad?"

Reagan left the question alone, judging it rhetorical.

"I'll talk to my father when I return. It's a conversation I don't want to have over the phone. In the meantime, try again with your employer."

"Fine. I'll do what I can." Reagan disconnected the call, feeling as though dirt clung to her clammy skin.

She turned to go back inside the building and jerked to a stop. A few feet away, a man smiled at her. Somehow, he had crept up on her without a sound.

How long had Kaine Abbott stood there, and how much of her call had he heard? Her pulse thrummed as she tried to remember her side of the conversation and how it would have sounded to him.

"Sorry. Did I scare you?" He stepped closer, walking across the stone with hushed footsteps. No wonder she hadn't heard him approach. Without the limp, he had the peculiar quiet trait of a cat.

"Not at all." She held the phone up. "I had to take a call and ..." Why explain? Slipping the phone into her lab coat pocket, she sought something to say that would take his mind off wondering about the call. "Are you enjoying your time here with Trey?"

He nodded. "It's been a few years since we've gotten together, just the two of us."

"How do you like Hidden Veil?"

"It's a nice little town." He laughed. "A bit boring. At least I thought so."

She studied him. What did he mean?

When he stared back, she said, "There's a strong resemblance between you and your brother." Down to the way their hair waved when it became too long, as was Kaine's. However, Trey was slimmer in body and his brown eyes reflected a meekness she didn't see in this man. That bold tattoo of forest firefighters on Kaine's upper arm, right below the sleeve of his tee-shirt, fit him.

She tried to picture Trey flaunting a tattoo and failed. He wasn't the type.

Those dark eyes turned serious. "My brother is a good guy, don't you think? He deserves the best from his friends."

Warning received. "Trey is a great guy and a terrific vet. People around here respect and admire him."

"What about you?"

"What about me?"

"You've been friends for a long time?"

"Since I started working for him. Why?"

"I don't know. I got the idea you and Trey were close."

It took her a moment to realize what he implied. Reagan's jaw clenched with irritation. Why were people suddenly interested in romanticizing her relationship with Trey? "If you're asking if we've ever dated, he's my boss, Kaine, and we're friends."

"Shame. With the dance coming up, I thought the two of you—"

"I have a date."

"Ah. The guy on the other end of your phone call?"

Reagan's stomach plummeted. Since the experience with Matt, she'd made a point of taking charge of her life and future, doing what she wanted, not following the whims of others. People rarely got the better of her. But his interrogation convinced her she had met her match in Kaine Abbott . . . in this situation, anyway.

"No." She forced a smile. "I really should get back to work."

"Yeah, sure."

As she left him in the parking lot, she prayed for his silence.

Fourteen

Trey parked his SUV next to Lane's truck at the boat launch near the lake's dam. Before Thursday, he'd looked forward to kayaking with his friends today.

One at a time, Kaine and Trey lifted the two kayaks from the top of the vehicle. Trey only owned a one-seater, so he arranged with Devyn McCall at Hidden Veil Hideaway to rent one of his kayaks. Normally, Devyn and his family only rented to those who stayed in their cabins, but he'd made an exception for a friend.

They carried the kayaks to where Lane, Sutton, and Kyle waited near the boat launch.

Sutton's smirk warned of friendly taunting to come. "You're late again, Vet Boy. This is getting to be a habit."

Trey had worked extra hours on paperwork and his plans for Oren's kennel in order to have this Saturday afternoon free. Carolyn couldn't join the practice soon enough. "You weren't at the clinic in the middle of the night, Farmer Boy."

Sutton laughed. "And I never will be."

Trey introduced Kaine to his friends, then the men launched the five kayaks and paddled along a relaxing, scenic route close to the shore.

Lane glanced at Trey, concern carved in the wrinkles on his brow. "You sure you're up to this?"

Sound sleep had been a distant dream this week. Still, he must look worse than he thought. "I'm good. But don't be surprised if you look over and find me asleep." The placid water, fresh air, and bird calls could undo him.

Kaine bumped Trey's kayak with his paddle. "Don't fall in and expect me to jump in after you. My life-saving days are over."

Trey glanced at his brother. Kaine remained close-mouthed about his problem, and Trey respected his privacy. He focused on forgetting everything but the tranquility of his surroundings, including his disappointment over not being the man to take Reagan to the dance.

Sutton and Lane paddled side-by-side ahead of Kyle, Trey, and Kaine. The tree canopies hanging over the water provided shade as they hugged the shore. Once they moved out a little deeper, the spring sunshine beat down on them, giving them a taste of the coming summer temperatures.

No jet skis or high-speed boats were allowed on the lake, which enhanced the quiet of the background against the gentle swish of their paddles through the water. Every few minutes they came upon someone fishing in a small boat, moving slow but steady with the speed of their trolling motors. Greetings were little more than a nod or a whisper amplified across the lake's surface.

"Where's your shadow, Lane?" Sutton squiggled in the ancient, closed kayak. Not a good swimmer, it was a wonder he found any physical comfort in the space with his bulk wrapped in an old and thick canvas life jacket. The rest of them wore newer, less cumbersome vests.

"Alex is following Uncle Monte around today, probably drawing pictures of Monte's every move while learning how to tend the cattle." Lane grinned and dipped his paddle in the water with the smooth motion of a man with years of experience. "Next week, I'm bringing him to your place so you can teach him how to farm."

"Don't even joke about that. I have enough kids hanging on my shirttail."

"How is Alex progressing?"

"Good." Lane glanced at Kyle to answer his question. "Macie lets him do more and more these days."

"No more helicopter mom."

"Yeah." Lane paused with his paddle in the air and stared into the cloudless, perfectly blue sky. "I can't wait until next month."

Kaine slowed his kayak. "What's happening next month?"

"I'm marrying Macie."

An image of Reagan walking down the aisle as Macie's bridesmaid invaded Trey's mind. Halfway to the altar, it morphed into her wearing a wedding gown. Her long dark hair, covered by a veil, hung over her shoulders. No, no veil. She wasn't the fancy, veil-wearing type.

Oh, man. He had to stop.

"If you were smart, you'd take your time." Sutton's voice interrupted Trey's self-admonishment.

"That's envy speaking." Lane flashed a wicked grin. "Admit it. You're hankering for the good fortune Kyle and I found. You're asking yourself when it will be your turn."

Sutton flicked his paddle across the surface of the water, splashing Lane and soaking his T-shirt. They burst into the shared laughter of two lifelong friends.

Trey paddled around a limb in the water. *Envy.* Lane would never realize how close he'd come to describing Trey's emotions when thinking of the wedding.

Kyle shook his head, a smile on his face as he paddled past them. "I hate to one-up you, Lane, but I have news of my own."

The horseman slowed his paddle. "New songs?"

"A couple, but not what I meant."

Trey admired Kyle for his conversion from writing and performing mainstream country music in a Nashville band to writing and performing Christian country songs. It hadn't been easy for him, but doors opened after a well-known artist included one of his songs on his first Christian album.

Sutton snorted. "Do you plan to tell us, or will you continue to sit in that kayak wearing that smug grin?"

"Davey gets a sibling later this year."

Trey hadn't gotten to be thirty-four without having friends go through the first child experience. "Congratulations."

"Yeah. Congratulations." Lane maneuvered his kayak alongside Kyle's and fist bumped the guy. "Jo must be over the moon."

"Already?" asked Sutton. "Didn't you two just get married in January?"

"We agreed before the wedding that we didn't want to wait and would leave the timing up to God. Even so, it caught us by surprise."

"I hope you know what you're doing, but congrats, man." Everyone but Kaine knew Sutton's sullen well wishes stemmed from his personal viewpoint on fatherhood.

"Thanks, guys. We're excited, but honestly, I think Vera is floating higher than both of us over the prospect of a great-grandchild."

A teen boy about fourteen rowed past them in a canoe. In the bow, a girl a little older held a calico cat in her arms. The animal appeared content on the water, but Trey noticed that neither teen wore a life vest.

They paddled several minutes through calm water in a companionable silence, until Sutton asked, "Are any of you going to the dance?" He cast a glance Trey's way.

Trey rammed his paddle deep in the water—so deep he almost lost it—and ignored his friend.

Lane and Kyle acknowledged their planned attendance.

Sutton eased his paddle through the water. "If you need a date, Kaine, Nadine Schutz asked me if there'd be any good-looking, single guys for her to dance with."

"Pass." The word shot out of Kaine's mouth like a cannon ball, blowing a hostile hole through Sutton's teasing.

Lane slowed his kayak and glanced at Kaine. "Sutton is pulling your chain, man. Ms. Schutz is at least seventy-five and Hidden Veil's head librarian. Besides, my Uncle Monte has first dibs on a dance with her."

Kaine's smile never reached his melancholy eyes. "I'll let you do the foxtrot with a senior, Sutton, and I can't wait to see it."

Lane turned to Trey. "We haven't talked about it, but who

are you taking?"

Trey's arm muscles hardened until he could barely paddle the kayak. *I'm sorry, Trey.* He should have known Reagan had found a date. When hadn't she? He broke out in a sweat having nothing to do with the sun, and his heart raced until he expected it to burst into tiny pieces. "I don't plan to go this year."

Sutton's gaze shot to Trey, but for once, the farmer kept his remarks to himself.

Trey had tried his best to forget the other night. One moment, he had settled in to enjoy relaxation on the lake. The next, he was picking up his shredded heart.

The others stopped to discuss the dance, but Trey paddled on. Maybe trying to outrace the memory of hearing Reagan say she already had a date for the night. He laid the fault on himself for being slow with his invitation—spineless as a jellyfish. He looked back and found he'd put more than fifty yards between himself and his friends, who still hadn't moved. They sat in their kayaks yapping like old men.

"Watch out!"

A splash and a yell yanked Trey from his defeatist attitude. Up ahead, the girl with the cat floundered in the water, her arms batting the surface. The drenched cat clawed her shoulder on its way to the top of her head. The boy stood in the rocking canoe, shouting that she couldn't swim.

After removing his life vest and slipping his arm through an armhole, he slung it over his shoulder. Trey kicked off his flip-flops, tossed his glasses near his feet, and dove into the water.

Reagan spread the colorful 1950s cotton tablecloth with its large and bright red flowers—another Nana Hartwell inheritance—on the ground. She placed her small cooler on the edge to prevent the gentle breeze coming off the lake from ruffling the fabric. She covered her mouth to hide a yawn.

Jo handed her a Jo E's cup—the lid marked with a big, black R. "You look like you need the caffeine."

Reagan gladly accepted the iced mocha with a smile and settled on the spread.

"You didn't have to come, you know." Jo sat across from her. "We would have missed you but understood if you'd said you were tired."

"What are you talking about? I've looked forward to today." Reagan raised the cold cup. "But this will help. Thanks."

"Is something wrong?"

Yes. "Why would you think that?"

"I don't know. Maybe the fact that Quill keeps whining for your attention, but you haven't noticed. You seem distracted."

Reagan glanced down at the puppy and ran her hand over his pale-yellow head. She would have left him at home, but her friends insisted she bring him today. "Sorry, little guy."

A frown wrinkled Jo's brow. "You haven't answered my question."

Was something wrong? Was she distracted? Sure. She had been since Trey asked her to the dance on Thursday night. He'd framed the invitation as one of friend to friend, but his face said it was more. His face said he expected a date. So she'd squashed that idea—and his feelings?—by using Scott's invitation as an excuse.

Though pleasant at the clinic yesterday, Trey had been uncharacteristically quiet, even for him. Shaina asked if they had argued. Argued? No. Trey rarely argued.

Added to her problems was the pressure to find homes for Oren Burnside's dogs. So far, she'd gotten commitments for four more of the dogs—the younger ones. That left twenty-two. At this rate, she'd never reach zero.

On top of everything, a sense of foreboding shrouded her. When would Trey discover she had called Marshall, going behind his and Oren's backs? Surely Kaine would tell his brother what he'd overheard, even if he didn't understand it. But she had done it for Trey's sake, his and the people of Hidden Veil.

Yes, she'd almost cancelled her attendance at today's picnic. Almost. "Don't worry about me. I'm good."

Macie joined them, holding down another corner of the tablecloth. Sliding out of her flip flops, she crossed her legs and patted the ground, urging Quill over. "He's such a happy little thing."

Reagan snorted and tossed Macie the end of the leash to keep the happy little thing from pulling her arm out of its socket. "He's spoiled."

Jo reached over and ran a hand over Quill's back. "Bring him by the coffee shop. You know I keep dog treats."

"So you can spoil him even more?"

Her friend laughed. "What are friends for?"

Quill jumped up, getting in Macie's face and making it difficult for her to sip her sweet tea while trying to keep the curious puppy at bay.

"Quill, let her finish her drink." Reagan picked him up and

placed him on the grass, tossed him a small squeaky toy to occupy him, and apologized to her friend.

"He's fine." Macie gazed at the lake. "Alex is fond of Gypsy, but she's Lane's dog. He'd love to have a puppy of his own."

Reagan recognized an opportunity when she saw one. "How about a little Lab puppy?"

Macie's brow furrowed. "I thought you were keeping Quill."

Reagan laughed. "You can't have *him*. Oren Burnside has too many dogs in his kennel that need homes—some of them puppies."

"Oh, I don't know, Reagan. They're purebreds and expensive, I'm sure. I was thinking about a rescue dog."

Reagan recalled the price Marshall Burnside quoted for Quill. Honestly, it was a generous price when his father might have gotten more. However, Oren's greatest concern was that the dogs go to good homes. If she couldn't find those homes, the animals might need a rescue. "These dogs aren't much different. I think he'd be open to an offer."

"Gran knows Mr. Burnside," said Jo. "She says the poor man can barely get around. The responsibility of keeping up the kennel must weigh on him."

Reagan dipped her chin, hiding her displeasure from her friends. "It does. In fact, I told him I'd help to find new homes for his dogs."

"I've heard there's a company that wants his land." Jo grinned. "You know how customers like to talk."

"We could have a nursing facility here." Reagan stopped short of mentioning her part in trying to see that Briar Park got that land or that she opposed Trey's plan to lease a portion of it.

"So, how about that puppy for Alex?"

Macie ran a finger through the condensation on her plastic cup. "Let me think about it. I should also talk to Lane."

Reagan shifted her attention to solicit Jo, but before she could open her mouth, Jo waved her off. "Not a chance. Kyle's bullmastiff is dog enough for our small house." She paused, a secretive smile creasing her face. "Besides, the place will become even more crowded soon."

Reagan and Macie stared at her, Reagan mulling over the statement.

"Come on. Do I have to spell it out, ladies?"

"Yes."

"No."

Reagan and Macie answered together, then Macie squealed. "When are you due?"

Oh, that was her point. Reagan's face warmed. How clueless was she?

"Early December."

Macie lunged across the spread to hug Jo. "I'm excited for you and Lane."

Reagan added her congratulations.

"Thanks. Kyle's parents are over the moon. So is Gran. We can't wait. Before we were married, we dreamed of being parents one day, but never expected it this soon."

Over the past decade, Reagan hadn't allowed herself to imagine motherhood or marriage. But for the first time since Matt's death, a tiny seed of yearning sprouted in her to experience a happiness like Jo's.

Fifteen

For several minutes, Reagan's friends talked about babies. With little to contribute, she listened, interjecting a generic statement here and there.

"Less than a month until the wedding, Macie."

Macie's grin spread faster than spilled milk. "Yes, and I can't wait."

Always the bridesmaid, never the bride. The old saying flashed in Reagan's mind. Just as quickly, she dismissed it. "Have you finalized the plans for your honeymoon trip to the beach?"

Macie nodded. "We've rented a condo on Oak Island for five glorious days. Sutton has agreed to help Monte out around the ranch while we're gone. He comes across as grumpy sometimes, but he's a good man, and he cares for Lane."

Jo leaned back on her elbows and crossed her ankles. "What about Alex?"

"He'll stay in Charlotte with Eva."

Reagan met the mother of Macie's late husband at last year's event for the volunteers and sponsors of the Healing Springs Equine Therapy Center. She'd liked the woman, who was independent and outspoken—much like her. "He'll have fun with his grandmother, so don't worry about him."

"I won't. Much. Last summer taught me I can't control what happens to others, but I can place the people I love in God's hand. I try to remember that, but it isn't always easy." A wistful note saturated Macie's statement. "Sometimes, I want to snatch them back, even when I know they're better off in His care."

What Reagan wouldn't give to have snatched the letter she wrote Matt out of the post office box before it flew halfway around the world and into his hands. She couldn't recall a time when she'd worried—excessively worried—over Matt as Macie had done over Alex. Yes, she had prayed for him daily, but were there moments of crushing fear that, over time, had slipped her mind? Or had her feelings been shallow? Was she even capable of feeling deeply for someone—deep enough to agonize over their well-being?

But she worried about her family. If something happened to her parents or her sisters, it would devastate her. But with Matt? Over time, the lines of grief and guilt had blurred.

"As you see, I'm here after leaving my son in Monte's care, and I didn't bat an eye when Lane said he was coming to the lake to kayak." Two worry lines bracketed the bridge of Macie's nose.

Reagan laughed. "Hold out your palms. I want to see if you've snatched them from God's hand."

The frown went away, and Macie grinned. She held up both hands. "Empty."

Reagan wouldn't blame her if they weren't. Before Alex's

father died, her friend had led a thrill-seeking life. She was finally getting back on her adventurous feet after letting fear nearly ruin her relationship with her son and Lane.

"We're proud of you, Macie." Jo pushed her sunglasses to the top of her head. "This is nice. While the guys are working up a sweat kayaking, we have the luxury of relaxing on the lake shore, catching up on each other's lives, and eating gourmet sandwiches from Chef Macie."

Macie snapped her fingers. "I knew I forgot something." With Jo and Reagan's groans, she snickered. "Got ya."

"Maybe, but you came close to taking an involuntary swim." Reagan raised her face to the sun. "You're right. This is nice." A good chance to forget her problems.

Jo sipped her drink. "Who's going to the Blossom Bash?"

Macie raised her hand. "Lane and I."

Reagan would like nothing better than to dodge the question, but Jo's gaze zeroed in on her. "Yes, I'll be there."

"Who is your date this year?"

"A guy I met at the conference I attended. Scott Hendrix."

"Oh. I'd hoped—"

Before Macie's words matched the disapproval on her face, Reagan pasted on a cheery smile. "Will Kyle do a performance?"

Jo shook her head. "He wants to enjoy the dance. Gran and Bobby will be there."

Macie passed out sandwiches. "She's all right, isn't she? She hasn't had another heart issue?"

"Oh, she's doing great. But we don't spend as much time together since Kyle and I married. Besides, she has Bobby."

Macie unwrapped her sandwich. "I love seeing people their

age take another chance at romance."

The diversion had worked. On Macie, not Reagan.

Should she have told Trey of her date with Scott the day he saw them together in the parking lot? Had she blindsided him Thursday night? Then again, she wasn't obligated to inform him of her dates just because they went to the dance together last year after she'd broken up with Shawn. Or was it Mitch? Ugh! Bri was on target with her advice. She should stop dating random guys who meant nothing to her.

A splash and yell sounded nearby. Reagan wrenched around to see what happened as Macie gasped and ran with Jo toward the shore. Reagan sprang to her feet and followed with Quill at her heels. She stopped alongside her friends at the lake's edge.

Her heart jumped into her throat.

Stroke after stroke carried Trey through the water and closer to the panicked, flailing teen with a cat clinging to her head. Even with the bright sunlight skimming the lake's surface, the water cooled his skin. Thanks to his childhood swim lessons, he'd figured he could swim faster than paddle. Either way, he'd end up in the water.

Each second in the lake brought him closer to the girl. It also brought her closer to going under for the last time. He pressed himself to swim faster until he drew up behind her. "Hold on. I've got you."

Trey wrapped one arm around her middle as he tread water

with the other. She whirled to face him. Her eyes wide with panic, she screeched and thrashed, landing a wet blow that sent pain spiraling through his jaw. Trey lost his hold on the life vest.

Gripping his upper arms, the girl tried to climb on top of him, knocking the cat into the lake. She pushed his head under the water. Once. Twice. The third time, he struggled to free himself from her hold, and broke through the surface.

His chest heaved as he drew in great gulps of air. "Don't fight me!" Whether shocked by his command or too fatigued to continue, she stopped flailing at the water and him. "That's better."

Trey reached for the vest. The claws of the yowling cat dug through his tee-shirt and into his skin as it scrabbled to the top of his shoulder. He did his best to ignore the pain until he'd gotten the girl in the lifesaving vest.

The boy in the drifting canoe stood empty-handed. The current carried him away from Trey and the girl and closer to shore.

Trey turned his head, and the cat gripped tighter. His friends had almost reached him. A moment later, the cat disappeared, yanked from his shoulder. Sutton clutched it to his chest, stroking its wet fur and murmuring soothing words. Who'd have guessed the gruff farmer had a soft side for a feline?

Lane reached the canoe and calmed the shaking boy, while Kyle snatched the life vest from the water and tossed it to Trey.

Trey told the girl, "Slip this vest on." Once he'd buckled her in, they held to the side of Kyle's kayak as he paddled to shore.

Once they stumbled onto land, a worried couple met them—parents, he assumed—and took control of the teens and the cat, their appreciation effusive. Other strangers helped the guys pull the kayaks onto the sandy dirt and grass.

Kaine arrived with Trey's kayak and handed him his glasses. "You okay?"

"Yeah."

Sutton brushed wet cat hair from his bare arms. "I can't believe that kid just stood in the canoe and made no effort to save the girl."

Trey could believe it, but he said nothing, as the criticism cut too close to home.

The girl returned Trey's life vest and wrapped her arms around him. "Thank you, and Peaches thanks you, too. I'm so sorry I tried to drown you."

Trey glanced at the wet calico cat. Peaches looked irate, but none the worse for her experience. "You're welcome. Just do me a favor. Wear a vest next time, okay?"

"Mom already lost her cool about it."

"It's because she loves you and what happened scared her."

The parents also expressed their gratitude again before they all left in the canoe, the girl's dad rowing, and the cat held in a death grip by the repentant boy.

Sutton slapped his back. "I told you before. You're a hero, Trey. You not only saved the girl, but you saved the cat."

The words brought a certain amount of satisfaction. Today, God had placed him in a position to help someone who almost lost her life, and this time, he didn't fail to act. Because, unlike last time, he was confident in his swimming skills and never considered himself in danger?

If he'd had that confidence before, how different would

things have turned out?

"I'm no hero."

When a dog barked, he looked up. Reagan stood a few feet away, staring at him. Quill lunged on the leash, but her tight grip held him back. He took a step toward her, but stopped when she pedaled backward.

What was going on? Sure, he was dripping lake water, but it wasn't as though he planned to wrap his arms around her. He knew better.

No one else moved. Even Quill had settled down. A bird squawked from a nearby tree, joining the lapping of water against the shore as the only other sound.

"Heroes are overrated." After that quiet but stark pronouncement, she whipped around and marched away, dragging Quill behind her.

"Reagan!"

She kept walking.

Lane held Macie—whose first husband drowned—probably sensing her need for the comfort of his arms around her. He whistled. "What was that about?"

Jo shook her head. "Men."

Macie pulled back and squeezed Lane's arm. "Jo and I will go after her."

The two women walked away, leaving the guys standing dumbfounded.

Trey wiped the water from his face and smoothed his hair. His mind spun at the effort to comprehend those three words Reagan had shot at him. He'd thought she wanted a hero. Rather than being impressed, she glared at him as though he'd pushed the girl out of the canoe. He couldn't wrap his mind around her anger. Even though he hadn't jumped into the water to impress her, why express her lack of respect for him in front of the guys?

Nearby, a fish jumped, its splash creating concentric circles on the water's surface. Circles. Round and round, like Trey's thoughts concerning Reagan.

Sutton pulled him aside and lowered his voice. "If I had someone who feared for my safety like that, I'd do something about it."

"You saw. She isn't interested in me beyond friendship."

"You are thicker than my spring house wall, Vet Boy." He slapped Trey on his sore shoulder and walked away.

It's because she loves you, and what happened scared her.

What he'd said to the little girl came back to encourage him, and the stinging ache in his shoulder vanished as Sutton's taunt penetrated his *thick* skull. A slow smile replaced the confusion. Could Farmer Boy be right?

Sixteen

The incident with the kids, the cat, and Reagan's temper ended the guys outing. They paddled back to the boat launch. Little by little, with each stroke, the pleasure and confidence Trey had experienced over Reagan's reaction dwindled, and doubt swelled.

Today's action hadn't required true bravery on his part, and would never make up for the time he didn't act. He couldn't figure out why she would call heroes overrated, but he could imagine her scathing opinion if she knew of his previous cowardice.

After dropping off the extra kayak at Hidden Veil Hideaway, Kaine shifted on the passenger seat. "You saved someone's life an hour ago. Why so tense?"

Tense?

"You look like you did that time I hid your math homework, Trey."

"Hid it? You stole it." Trey's homework. Their father's respect.

"I rushed through redoing the work over in order to hand it in on time."

"It was a stupid math assignment. So you didn't get your normal A."

"No, I got a C." Trey blew out a breath. He shouldn't take his frustration out on Kaine. "Sorry. The stress is catching up with me, I guess."

"Yeah, that happens when you try to play the hero."

"I didn't see anyone else dive in."

Kaine whipped around in the seat. "What is that supposed to mean?"

Defensive again, bro? His brother might get on his nerves on occasion, but mainly, Trey had enjoyed their time together, even though he questioned the reason for the visit. "Look, someone had to keep her afloat until the rest of you arrived. I was closest, so . . ." He shook his head.

"I get it." Kaine sighed. "Are you stressed because Reagan is going to the dance with someone else?"

Trey took his eyes off the road and shot a glare at his brother. *What a way to twist the knife.* "How do you know that?"

"She told me."

"When?"

"I saw her yesterday." Kaine frowned. "I don't understand your problem, Trey. It's just a dance. You act like the guy who asked Reagan intends to elope with her. Why didn't *you* ask her?"

Even Kaine had discovered his obsession with Reagan. "I did. Too late."

As he rethought his conversation with her the other night,

Trey realized he hadn't done that hard thing. He hadn't clarified his invitation to mean a date—his romantic date. He'd suggested they go together, having fooled himself into thinking he could slide into her heart like some runner stealing second base. Did he really want to win her love that way? Didn't seem very courageous.

"You've obviously never told her how you feel. Why not?"

"I never told you either." Trey spoke about Reagan's engagement to Matt Becker. "How am I supposed to measure up to a man whose death she mourns every year?"

Kaine rubbed a hand down his beard. "If it helps, she thinks you're a terrific guy."

It didn't.

"Take someone else to the dance."

Trey's anger deflated like a blood pressure cuff. He was ready to lighten the mood. "Who? Mrs. Schutz?"

Kaine spurted a laugh. "I can see you fighting some old man for the chance."

Trey grinned at the mental imagine of a boxing match with Monte Becker. "Why don't you ask Shaina to go with you?"

Kaine clenched his fists, the humor long gone. "No way."

"What's wrong with her? She's fun. Pretty."

"You have no clue what some people are hiding . . . people right under your nose."

Trey glanced his brother. "People like you?" He may as well drag the elephant in the backseat up to the front. "What are you hiding, Kaine?"

His brother turned his head and stared out the window.

"Look, if I need to know something—"

"One day. Not now."

They rode the rest of the way in strained silence until Trey pulled into the garage at his house. Thirty minutes later, after a soothing shower, he came out of his room in clean shorts and a T-shirt. Kaine trotted down the stairs in jeans and a button-down shirt, his hair damp and freshly brushed—a little too cleaned up for an evening at home. "Going somewhere?"

Kaine twirled his keys—Trey's keys—in his hands. "Figured I'd discover the Saturday-night hot spots around here. Come with me."

Ha! There were no hot spots, not the kind his brother sought. "No thanks. I plan to thaw a pizza, watch a movie, and relax."

Kaine's hardened jaw twitched with obvious frustration. "Then I'll see you later." He slammed the door going on the way out. The garage door went up, then down, and Kaine was gone, leaving Trey in peace.

Peace? He felt like a dump truck had run over him and unloaded the contents of the dump bed on him for good measure. There was no peace.

Reagan dropped her purse on the kitchen table and flopped into a chair. What was wrong with her? She'd acted as though Trey should have let that girl drown. While she hated the risk he'd taken, she truly admired what he'd done and was grateful that he'd saved the teen's life.

But it wasn't uncommon for a rescuer to drown while trying

to save a panicked person in the water. As she stood on that lakeshore with Macie and Jo, all she saw was the terrified girl pushing Trey underwater. Each time, Reagan had held her breath, trying to blink away the vision of rescuers pulling him from the lake, dripping wet and lifeless. In reality, each time, he reappeared to start the process over until he'd finally calmed the battering teen.

What brought on the intense reaction? No one else had lost it. Not even Macie, who had every right to burst into tears. With Macie's background—

Of course, Lane wasn't the one struggling in the lake, trying to save a frightened teen and an equally terrified cat with sharp claws. Clearly, Trey was a fine swimmer, but her insides had done flip-flops while watching his effort to stay afloat until the guys arrived. She thought she'd be sick right there in the grass.

Heroes. She hadn't exaggerated when she told Trey they were overrated—for her, anyway. She had always respected him for his everyday quiet and *safe* heroics. Until today, Trey seemed content to save the world, one puppy and iguana at a time.

God, I can't go through another loss.

Reagan bolted upright in the chair. Quill, lying at her feet, yelped in surprise. Losing Trey. That was the bottom line, wasn't it? But was her fright based on the possibility of losing a friend? Or someone more important to her?

A nagging voice inside said it was more. If true, what did that imply for the future? What was the most selfless path she should take? Ignore it? She released a grunt. Try putting that genie back in the bottle.

Yet if Reagan gave in to this love or whatever it was, would history repeat itself? And if Trey found out about her call to Marshall Burnside? There would be no more concern over his feelings for her.

A little pain now was better than deep hurt inflicted later. Right?

But what about this pain she had already inflicted on herself?

Trey slid a thin crust frozen pizza into the oven. Twenty-five minutes later, he pulled it out and dropped the pan on the stovetop. The metal clanged on the burners. He grimaced at the crisp, blackened pepperoni and scorched cheese and thought of chucking it in favor of a meal out. It looked as appetizing as his evening alone. He should have gone with Kaine.

The only saving grace to this week had been Sutton's hope-inducing words after Reagan walked off. He closed his eyes, reliving—over and over—those few minutes by the lake. He had two choices. Either get over Reagan Hartwell, or man up and tell her he loved her.

Heroes were overrated? That, in itself, gave him some hope.

Standing at the island in the kitchen, he said a short blessing over the unappetizing food and added a plea for God to protect his wildfire-fighting, woman-chasing hero of a brother—the one who had what appeared to be a soul-crushing secret he refused to share.

Trey's phone trilled. Although in no mood for an emergency call, he grabbed the cell phone from where he'd laid it on the counter near his plate. He eyed the screen, and his pulse ticked faster at seeing the number. This wasn't a call for his services. Far from it.

His finger swiped the screen. "Dr. Abbott." Somehow, he could not stop himself from getting the dig in.

"Trey."

His spine stiffened, a common result of hearing the voice on the other end, even though he'd expected it. "Dad." His father never said much on the phone and rarely initiated a call. That task normally fell to Trey's mom. He pushed away the pizza, his appetite gone. "Is Mom okay?"

"We're both fine. We've tried to reach Kaine, but he isn't answering or calling us back."

Trey breathed a soft grunt. Of course. Why think Dad called to see how things were going with him?

"I talked to someone in the Forest Service office who said he took a leave of absence. Have you heard from him?"

Leave of absence? "I think you misunderstood. He's on vacation and visiting me for a while."

"He said nothing to us. Your mother is concerned about him. I told her he's fine, but he's never returned our calls."

Trey had no intention of inserting himself between his parents and brother. "I can't say why he hasn't called, Dad, but he's safe." Safer than he'd be fighting a fire.

The recollection of a body blackened and motionless rampaged through Trey's mind, and the burned smell of the pizza turned his stomach. *Man up, Trey. You're an Abbott. Abbotts aren't afraid of the smell of smoke!*

"Let me talk to him, will you?"

Trey swallowed. "He isn't here right now, Dad. He's exploring the area." If he knew his brother, Kaine probably occupied a seat in a little bar somewhere.

"Well, tell him we called, okay?"

"Sure."

"I'll put your mom on the phone."

Before Trey could say goodbye, his mother began talking. "How are things with you, sweetheart?"

Do you have an hour? "Fine, Mom. Busy at the clinic."

"You work too hard."

He couldn't argue with that. "A new vet will start working for me soon. It should take some of the load off me and allow for more downtime."

"Good. I worry about you. How is Reagan?"

His mother never failed to ask that question. Did she know, too? Did anyone *not* know, except Reagan? "She's good." *She's also mad at me.*

They spoke for a few more minutes, then she said, "You take care, Trey. Love you."

"Love you, too, Mom."

An hour later, he slouched in his recliner, half asleep and with Mocha sprawled across his lap. On the TV, the long-gone actor John Wayne brought justice to the bad guys in a movie he'd seen too many times to count.

He stirred when hearing the garage door open. With the sound of keys sliding across the kitchen counter, Mocha jumped off the recliner and sashayed into the kitchen. Trey muted the TV as Kaine walked past the cat and into the den. "I smell burned pizza."

"You'll find what's left in the fridge."

"Nah. I went to that cafe for one of those hamburgers you've raved about. I guess I should have called to see if you wanted me to bring you one." Kaine jerked a thumb over shoulder, pointing behind him to the door. "I can go back."

"Don't bother." Although it would be a one hundred percent improvement on the pepperoni cardboard he'd eaten.

His brother frowned at the TV. "Have you ever seen a movie from this century?"

Trey shrugged. "You have a problem with the fact that I prefer the old flicks?"

Kaine raised an eyebrow at the sourness in Trey's voice. He raised his hands in surrender and headed for the stairs. "Hey, who am I to judge your taste in entertainment?"

"Dad called and expects you to call him back."

Kaine's feet froze in the center of the den, shoulders tense and posture stiff. It brought Trey fully awake and raised alarm bells in his brain.

Seventeen

Kaine peered over his shoulder at Trey. "Dad called you, looking for me?"

"He tried your phone a few times. You never answered or called back, so he took a shot."

The wince on Kaine's face told Trey that his brother had seen their dad's calls and ignored them. "Did he say what he wanted?"

"I am not your personal assistant. If you want to know what he wanted, call him back. Or not." Okay, maybe anger at his father still bubbled under the surface ... or spewed like a volcano.

"I choose not."

Trey bit the tip of his tongue to keep from asking. Nope. He definitely didn't want to land in the middle of whatever was going on between his brother and father. Still, the curiosity itched like poison ivy.

Kaine dropped onto the couch and studied the opposite wall as though another movie ran on the pale gray-painted drywall, one that confused him, judging by the furrowed brow. "I should have mentioned this before. I'm leaving the Forest Service. To be honest, I'm leaving firefighting altogether."

Trey sank back in the chair to digest that out-of-left-field confession. Kaine loved fighting fires. It's what he'd always claimed, anyway. "Leaving? Why? I thought you thrived on what you did."

"I do. I did. Now I'm ready for a change."

"What kind of change?"

"More money, for one thing."

Trey chuckled. "More for the guy who's always claimed money corrupts people?"

"Yeah, well, I've discovered it also opens doors."

Taken aback by Kaine's glower and reasoning, Trey sensed that, if he dug a little deeper, he'd learn the answer to the mystery behind his brother's visit. "What doors?"

"Doors that never close to the privileged."

"You can't find what you want at a regular fire department? With your experience, Dad can pull some strings and get you on in Raleigh."

"I won't fight fires anymore." Kaine jumped to his feet. "You may want to be a hero, but I've already told you. I won't be responsible for someone else's life."

Wow. There was more to this story than he knew so far. "What happened, Kaine?"

His brother stood silent. As he'd done since his arrival in Hidden Veil, Kaine put up a wall that blocked any further explanation.

"What do you have in mind to do for a living?"

Kaine's tense body relaxed some. "Can't say yet. It's why I came here. I needed time to think. And we both know Dad will freak."

That was a problem. "Which is why you haven't called him back."

Kaine nodded. "I'm dreading the argument."

"It's not his life, Kaine." At his brother's you're-kidding-me expression, Trey shook his head. "Fine. I get it."

"How did you approach the subject?"

With a naively honest dialog that turned into an inferno of tempers.

Trey thought back to the day he informed his father he intended to be a veterinarian instead of a fireman. He saw again the fury and disillusionment on his father's face. Dad had expected his oldest son—his namesake—to follow in his footsteps as he had followed in *his* father's. The argument opened a bottomless chasm between them, something he hoped Kaine wouldn't experience.

His dad had mellowed some over the years, but their relationship continued to suffer. Even so, Trey had never regretted his choice of career. "You're an adult. Be candid with him."

Kaine closed his eyes and seemed to count to ten before opening them again. "You're right. I'll call him tomorrow, but I'm not ready to tell him about quitting firefighting. Not yet. I can't talk to him about it until I've decided what I'll do."

"I understand, but you can't put it off indefinitely."

Like you've put off making it clear to Reagan how you feel about her?

Kaine headed for the stairs. "I'll see you in the morning."

Trey leaned his head against the back of the recliner. He hadn't intended to pray, merely rest his eyes, but it happened. Not so much in words, but in that groaning in his spirit described in the Bible. Incoherent to anyone but God, the pain, the questions, the insecurities poured out of him, little-by-little draining him of the gloom and filling him with the sense of hope and calm he'd been missing lately.

It was true. God's grace was sufficient and His power made perfect in Trey's weakness.

Which left him with a problem. The longer he sat there, the greater the compulsion to change his mind about going to the dance—to show himself, his brother, and others that he was a mature adult and not a tantrum-throwing two-year-old.

To earn the respect he desired, even if it came solely through self-respect.

Sunday morning, Reagan walked from the bedroom into her living room. Quill whined from his crate. She flipped the gate open. "You ready to go out?" The puppy ran to the kitchen door and sat like a gentleman. He stared back at her, pleading with soulful eyes. Yes, he was a work in progress, but he'd come a long way in his training. "I'll take that as a yes."

A few minutes of playtime in the yard, and they returned to the house. Reagan glanced at the empty coffeepot on the kitchen counter. Almost eleven a.m. and church attendance was out of the question. She couldn't face her friends this morning. Having Jo and Macie surround her yesterday like mother hens was awkward enough. She wanted no more pitying looks from anyone.

Reagan took her coffee to the sofa and pulled up the list of dogs still in need of homes. Steam swirled in the air and she breathed in the aroma of the brewed beans. Quill squiggled next to her, resting his chin on her lap.

After a few sips, she set the coffee cup on the side table and made a list of more places to contact tomorrow. Word had reached a few breeders who got in touch with her. It wouldn't be long before all of Oren's dogs were gone from his kennel.

Nearly an hour passed. Quill jumped off the couch and ran to the front door a couple of seconds before someone beat on it.

"Reagan? Are you in there?"

"I'm here, Bri." She set aside the tablet and crossed the room to open the door.

Her sister studied her from head-to-foot, then pushed past her. "Thank goodness."

"Thank goodness for what? Why the panic?"

"When you weren't at church, I got worried."

That was the trouble with living in a small town with family close by. One little deviation in routine and they imagined you in the intensive care unit of a hospital. "It's no big thing. I overslept and stayed home this morning."

"You aren't meeting everyone for lunch, either?"

Wrapped up in the dog situation, Reagan had forgotten about lunch at the barbecue restaurant. How could she join the group until she could look all of them in the eye without feeling foolish? Especially Trey? She had better figure it out soon. He expected her at work tomorrow. She couldn't dodge her job like she had church this morning. "I'm busy right now."

"Then I guess you wouldn't want to go to Ricardo's with only me."

Not even the imagined taste of the restaurant's food enticed Reagan to say yes, and she would have declined the invitation if her hollow stomach hadn't overruled her—loudly. "Okay. I haven't eaten since last night's supper, and I'm starved."

Besides, disappointment in Bri's voice and the downcast look on her face said she wanted to share more than a meal with Reagan. What did her sister have up her sleeve?

Brianna brightened. "Are you sure?"

"I'm sure. Give me a few minutes to get ready." Once she returned to the living room, she signaled for Quill to enter to his crate, then grabbed her purse. "Let's go."

Trey entered the noisy barbecue restaurant and looked around the dining room, crowded with a slew of after-church customers like him. He spotted Sutton seated where the staff had pulled together two tables for their group. His friend nursed a glass of iced tea.

He had debated attending church and this lunch after the incident at the lake, but he had to work with Reagan, and he couldn't let her drive him away from a time of worship. Plus, he'd see her tomorrow, so why hide today?

Turned out he didn't need to hide. She was the one who

didn't show this morning. Was *she* avoiding *him*? That didn't sound like her. Before heading to the table, he shot off a quick text to be sure she was all right.

Missed u @ church. OK?

Trey dodged a waitress and took a seat across the table from Sutton, who asked, "Where's your brother?"

"I invited him, but he had other things to do." Kaine had found quite a bit to do on his own since his arrival. Despite his brother's current outlook about God, Trey had half-expected Kaine to choose church over calling Dad this morning as he'd promised.

His phone vibrated on his hip. Pulling it out, he read Reagan's text and frowned.

I am. See you tomorrow.

Short and sweet. Trey set his phone on the table, determined to not ask for more information. Knowing Reagan as he did, she had probably bristled at his inquiry, anyway. Independent. Stubborn. Strong. Competent. The woman drove him crazy— usually a good crazy. Right now? Just crazy.

"Looks like I got here before the others." For good measure, he added, "Early."

"For once." Sutton opened his menu. "I'm hungry. Next time, try to hurry your pastor along."

The smell of smoked meat and tangy sauce stoked Trey's hunger. "Next time, come to the service and hurry him along yourself."

Sutton scoffed, then crossed his arms, resting them on the table. "While we're alone, tell me what you'll do about him."

"Do?"

"If you want, I'll work him over for you."

Ah, they were no longer talking about Pastor Jim. "Is this about Reagan's date for the dance? I don't need you to work anyone over for me."

"Lighten up. I'm joking." Sutton winked. "You should be the one to work him over."

Trey sank against the back of his chair, unable to stop the laughter. "You are one crazy dude."

"Probably." Sutton sobered. "Did you know before yesterday?"

Trey grabbed a menu, paying no attention to the entrees listed. "I found out from Reagan Thursday night ... after I asked her to the dance."

Sutton dropped the laminated menu on the table. "So you were too late, and she didn't just say no."

"Too late."

"Good."

Trey had tried his best to forget that moment. The only saving grace to that fiasco was seeing the regret on her face. Maybe he'd chosen delusion over reality, but he'd talked himself into believing she was sorry she'd accepted Blondie's invitation. He could easily talk himself into thinking she'd rather go to the dance with him ... if only he'd asked her first.

Today's sermon had reminded Trey of his prayerful request to accept the person God created him to be, no matter what others thought of him. How influential was his witness, especially to the unbelieving man across the table, if he didn't trust God to have his best interest in mind?

"Don't count me out yet, Farmer Boy."

Sutton let out a howl of laughter that drew the attention of customers at the tables around them. "Now you're talking. Proud of your backbone, son."

God's grace is sufficient, and His power made perfect in my weakness.

If he were sitting next to Sutton, Trey would have expected a hearty slap on the back. "Thanks, Dad."

Eighteen

Walking the two blocks to the restaurant shored up Reagan's energy—that and suspecting Brianna had something important to discuss.

They entered Ricardo's, and Bri glanced around the main room. "It's crowded."

"It's Sunday lunch and there are only two sit-down restaurants in town. That may soon change."

Brianna's eyes widened. "What have you heard?"

"Macie is considering opening a restaurant next to All That Blooms."

"Where the shoe store used to be?"

"Yes. She hasn't worked out the details yet, but I think she's considering dinner only, along with catering."

"When?"

"It isn't certain. Right now, she's focused on the wedding."

Bri sighed. "Two sets of friends married this year."

Her sister's comment left Reagan feeling old and depressed.

Had Matt lived, they might celebrate a decade of marriage this year.

Reagan's phone dinged with a text from Trey.

Missed U @ church. OK?

Could she not miss one Sunday without the settlers calling out the cavalry? Though she tried to dredge up annoyance at the well-meaning interference in her life, a pleasant warmth surged through her, washing it away. Anger made no sense when others showed they cared, especially Trey.

Her thumbs skimmed the keys, then Reagan slid the phone into the back pocket of her jeans. No, he hadn't annoyed her, but neither would she tell him the truth of why she'd skipped the service this morning.

Even with the after-church rush, they were seated in no time and ordered their food. Brianna broke a chip in two and dipped it in the salsa. "I called Paige yesterday."

"What is she up to?"

Bri leaned over the table and lowered her voice. "She's thinking about selling her house and moving back to Hidden Veil."

Reagan paused while dunking her chip in the bowl of melted queso. "What? Why? She said nothing to me. Not that I'm not happy, but she's been gone for years. Why return now? At all?"

The waitress brought Reagan's chicken enchiladas and her sister's arroz con pollo. After she left and they said a short blessing, Brianna sliced into her chicken. "It's been tough. I think she needs more family support."

Paige's husband had walked away from their marriage

eighteen months ago, two months after Paige's best friend, Marissa, passed away, leaving her children in the care of Paige. Now, Reagan's older sister was a divorced mom and guardian of three children.

"Don't mention it to anyone. She hasn't decided yet and wants to tell Momma and Daddy herself."

"I won't." Reagan sipped her iced tea. "What about the kids? I wonder if they'll put up a fight at leaving their friends."

"She hasn't told them either." A frown pulled at Brianna's lips. "I can't imagine what those kids have gone through. First the death of their dad in the line of duty, then their mom from cancer."

"At least they have a good home with Paige. They aren't in foster care or separated." Liam was now nine, close to Alex Newman's age, and Leyla was five. Cassie had just turned three.

"She has a good heart."

"Every time I think about Dustin leaving Paige, it makes me so mad." Reagan tried to imagine being thirty-three and raising young children by herself. Then there was little Leyla with her hearing loss. That added an extra complication for her sister. "Such a stand-up guy."

Bri giggled.

"It's strange how things work out. Paige has the children she always wanted, even though I don't envy her situation. And her pottery business has taken off. Most of her orders come through her website and shows. As long as she has her kiln and other equipment, she can live anywhere."

"You know it will thrill Momma and Daddy to have their daughter and new grandchildren available anytime."

"I can't imagine how spoiled those kids will be with grandparents and—"

"And two aunts to dote on them." Bri bit into a tortilla chip. "I'm sure Paige hasn't forgotten the elephant on the farm. I think she's a little worried about how Sutton will react when he finds out."

Their older sister had left town—the state—thirteen years ago after breaking up with Sutton Vance over her desire for a large family and his fatherhood phobia. He remained bitter, especially after none of the Hartwells would reveal her location. They only followed Paige's wishes, but Sutton had never forgiven them. He didn't know Paige had married and divorced, something else they'd kept from him and everyone else.

"Sutton stopped asking about her years ago. I'm sure he's over her."

"Then why is he still angry with us?"

Macie had called him a good man. That may be true, but what will happen when he learns of Paige's plan to move back to Hidden Veil? Although they shared friends and attendance at social events, Sutton avoided being alone with Reagan and Brianna. "Men have fragile egos. They don't enjoy being rejected."

"Who does?"

True. And she had contributed to her share of battered egos.

A shadow passed over the table. Reagan glanced up, thinking it was the waitress. Instead, Blaine Simmons stood next to the booth, wearing that lazy grin that most women adored. Speaking of rejected men. She hadn't seen him in several months, not since the Thanksgiving celebration at Jo E's with her friends, the day Trey left early with the excuse of work waiting at the clinic. That night, Blaine had gotten too cute with his hands—again—so she dumped him. Fortunately, he was the exception to her "fragile ego" comment and not the type to hold a grudge.

"Hey, y'all."

"Hey, Blaine."

Brianna pulled another chip from the basket. "How's the dairy business?"

Reagan almost spit out the tea she sipped. *Sly, Bri.*

Since high school, Blaine had worked for Johnson's Food Mart, their local grocery store. He'd worked his way up to the position of manager of the dairy department, but to hear him tell it, he now managed the whole store and their dairy suppliers.

They talked for a couple of minutes, then he went back to the tattooed, fake blonde whose eyes shot daggers at them. Reagan smiled at her until Blaine's date looked away.

Brianna cut into her chicken. "He's a nice enough guy, but I cannot believe you went out with him."

"For an entire month."

Her sister laughed. "That's even harder to believe." She sobered.

Reagan grabbed a tortilla chip. She dunked it in the salsa and prepared herself for the heat of the jalapenos. *Delicious.*

Brianna glanced around the restaurant, crowded with after-church diners. "Maybe I should have suggested going somewhere else."

"Why? I like this place. I thought you did, too."

"I do, but I think we're in a rut. We need something different to keep life from becoming too boring."

Reagan wiped her hands on her napkin, then folded them on the table. "Okay, what's up?"

"What do you mean?"

Her sister avoiding eye contact confirmed Reagan's suspicion. "You didn't invite me out to eat so you could question the choice of restaurants. Now give."

Brianna settled against the booth's seat. Her shoulders fell. "I'm in love."

Reagan froze. As far as she was aware, her sister wasn't dating anyone seriously. Brianna and Lee Culver dated off and on, but like Shaina and Chase, the relationship was more a friendship than romance. How could she be in love? "With who?" She blinked. "Whom?" Whatever.

Her sister concentrated on swishing a tortilla chip through the salsa until Reagan imagined it soggy and unappetizing. "Maybe infatuated is a better term, because I've never met him."

"You think you're in love or infatuated with someone you've never met?" And Reagan thought her love life had turned weird.

"We've never met in person."

"I see." She pulled her sister's hand away from the salsa bowl. "No, I don't. Bri, start at the beginning."

"You've met Tara Fleming, my friend from school, right?"

"From college?"

"Yes."

Reagan saw the woman in her mind. "Dark hair, blue eyes, tall? I've met her."

"She has a twin . . . a fraternal twin."

It took only half a second for that statement to register. "You're infatuated—possibly in love—with her twin?"

Brianna nodded. "Tucker."

They were getting somewhere, but Reagan rolled her hand, encouraging her sister to spill the rest.

"Last May, when Tara graduated, Tucker sent me a text asking what I thought he should give her as a graduation gift. I suggested something that went over well. Ever since, we've communicated through texts and emails and a few video calls."

Reagan grinned. "Why haven't you mentioned him before now?"

"I don't know." Brianna groaned. "Yes, I do. He's in the Army, stationed in Texas. I didn't want to bring up bad memories for you."

A soldier? Reagan's stomach plummeted, taking her appetite with it.

"He'll come to Fort Bragg in a few months for a class. I mean Fort Liberty. Or is it Bragg?" Bri shook her head. "Anyway, he said he wants to meet me, face-to-face. The two of us. In the same room."

"I get it." With the base in Fayetteville, a couple of hours away, the two of them probably wouldn't see each other regularly. And once they met, they might not like one another. "How long will he be in North Carolina?"

"At least six weeks."

"Then what?"

"I don't know."

Six weeks wasn't long. Afterward, he'd return to Texas or somewhere else. Long distance romances were notorious for not working out. She and Matt were a perfect example.

Thinking that way wasn't fair to Brianna. She deserved the

chance to decide for herself who she'd fall for. "Be happy to get to know him."

"I should, shouldn't I? But I'm not sure I want to meet him."

The waitress chose that moment to arrive and ask if they wanted more tea, giving Reagan an opportunity to try to understand her sister's hesitancy. Once the waitress left, she asked, "Why don't you want to meet Tucker?"

"What if his feelings for me aren't the same as mine for him? We've never mentioned dating one another. He's never asked."

"But he asked to meet you. For that to happen, he'll need to drive here from the base. That says something, doesn't it?"

"I suppose." Brianna's rice-filled fork hung over her plate. "I guess I'm afraid."

"That he won't like you?"

"That he will. He's the brother of a good friend. What if things don't work out? I'll risk my relationship with Tara."

Her sister had a good point. "It's up to you, but you can talk yourself out of anything."

"Okay, but what if history repeats itself?"

Reagan looked up to find her sister studying her. She set her fork down and, for once, thought before speaking. "No one can promise you—"

"A rose garden?"

Reagan chuckled at the reference to the old country song their mother sang around the house years after its popularity faded. "I was going to say tomorrow, but that works. Don't borrow trouble. If you like this guy, take a chance. Isn't that what you've been preaching to me?"

"Has it done any good?"

She sighed. "Maybe a little."

Brianna perked up. "Has he asked you to the dance?"

No point in pretending she didn't know who her sister meant. "Yes, but I told him no."

"No?" Bri's eyebrows slanted with confusion. "What is your problem?"

While she enjoyed all the community gatherings, the Blossom Bash was Reagan's favorite. It celebrated an end to the barrenness of winter and the beginning of green new life. Something she desperately needed. Just not with someone like Scott.

In the interest of fair disclosure, the words itched to dance off the tip of Reagan's tongue, to tell her sister about yesterday's episode at the lake. If she set those words free to pirouette through the air, she could end up telling her sister everything, including her fear Kaine would tell Trey about the conversation he overheard with Marshall Burnside. No one should know about that. It was one more secret she'd keep from everyone, especially Trey.

"He asked too late. I'd already agreed to go with someone else." At seeing the pit of her sister's open mouth, she said, "Flies, Bri."

Brianna snapped her mouth shut. "Not his brother, I hope."

"Why would you think I'd go with Kaine? And what's wrong with him?" Other than he could sink her relationship with Trey.

"He's such a . . ."

"A what?"

"Shaina called him rude, grumpy, and a jerk."

Over the past two years, Shaina had become Brianna's closest friend in Hidden Veil, so Reagan could imagine the two of them talking about Kaine and his visit to the clinic. She had to agree that Trey and his brother had unique personalities. So did she and her sisters. "I don't know why Kaine and Shaina don't get along, but he isn't my date for the dance."

"You're going with another loser."

"One who asked me first. End of story. Are you going with Lee?"

Brianna's brown eyes lit with a wicked glint. "I hadn't planned to go at all. Now, I think I should, if for no other reason than to see how the night turns out. But, no, not with Lee. He's dating someone else."

"I'm done talking about men. Let's finish eating."

Brianna pointed her now-empty fork at Reagan. "Oh, no you don't. Your face lit up a few minutes ago. We're not done talking about—"

"Shh." Reagan glanced around the restaurant. She and Trey didn't need their story floating around town. "We'll discuss it when I'm ready. I'm not ready."

She may never be ready to face, or even talk, about her conflicting feelings for Trey Abbott.

Nineteen

"Reagan, I need you." Trey strode into the clinic with his cell phone pressed to his ear.

"What's wrong?" Her sleep-roughened voice added fuel to the pang of guilt over calling her at almost two o'clock in the morning—Monday morning.

"Mrs. Marlow called. A dog attacked Lucy tonight. She thinks the cat has a broken leg. They're on their way in."

"I'll be right there." She clicked off before he could say thanks.

He had suggested Lucy go to an emergency clinic, but the woman begged Trey to treat her cat. If the injury required surgery, he would need Reagan's help. Dedicated to the welfare of the animals they treated and to their owners, she never complained about receiving a late-night call to duty. As her employer, it was one of things he appreciated about her.

But he counted the days until Carolyn—and a new vet tech— came aboard to share some of the after-hours burden. He hoped the additional payroll wouldn't sink him. And he still had the expenses of the boarding kennel, should that become a reality.

Reagan rushed through the back door while Mrs. Marlowe pushed through the front, carrying a cardboard box. Reagan pried the box from the teary-eyed woman.

"I didn't even know my girl was outside." Mrs. Marlowe wrung her hands. "I don't sleep well and busied myself around the house. When I took out the garbage, she must have sneaked outside. My poor Lucy."

"Don't worry, Mrs. Marlow. We'll take care of her."

In the treatment room, Reagan pulled on gloves, then gently lifted the mewing Lucy from the box the woman had placed her in and laid her on the table. As direct and matter-of-fact as she was about most things, when it came to hurting animals, Reagan had a heart as soft as a down pillow, even if she would scoff at the description.

With the cat sedated for Trey's exam, he hadn't needed the x-rays to agree with Mrs. Marlow about a broken leg, but the films showed the extent of the damage. Fortunately, brave Lucy hadn't fallen into shock.

He approached Mrs. Marlow in the waiting room. "Besides the punctures in the skin, she has a clean fracture. We can splint it, but I don't advise it. Lucy will heal better with surgery."

The woman wrung her hands. "Are you talking about pins and metal plates?"

"In this case, a pin. Then she'll require confinement. I'll stabilize her, but you really should take her to a veterinary orthopedist."

After a resigned exhale, Mrs. Marlow asked, "Have you done

this type of surgery before?"

"Yes, but—"

"Then I want you to do it. Lucy would want you to do it."

Trey rubbed his forehead, thinking, then asked Reagan to prepare Lucy for surgery. He'd gotten some sleep before being awakened by Mrs. Marlowe's call and should be all right.

"There's nothing you can do here, Mrs. Marlow. Why don't you go home? We'll call you when she's awake."

In the meantime, he'd spend the next few hours alone with Reagan and, maybe, share his thoughts about more than an injured cat.

Monday dawned when Reagan tucked Lucy in a cage to recover. Reagan trudged into the treatment room. "I've cleaned the surgical room."

"Thanks for your help. It's been a long night. Go home and get some sleep. I'll stay and monitor her."

Poor Lucy's injury had provided a private time to talk with Trey. "I'm wide awake now."

She rolled up a stool and plopped onto it. Over the past couple of hours, they had discussed surgical matters. Now, with the emergency over, the clinic possessed a calming silence, or an unnerving stillness. Not even the dogs in the two cages under Lucy spent the energy to bark. One of them shifted position in the cage, drawing the attention of both Trey and Reagan. When the animal settled down again, Reagan tried to relax, but her thoughts swirled with the way she'd behaved on Saturday.

"Have you heard from Carolyn?" Reagan rolled the stool back and forth with the toe of her shoe. She'd ease into the apology she owed Trey.

"She has the employment agreement and wanted the weekend to talk it over with her fiancé."

"Fiancé?" Reagan's toe scuffed the floor, stopping the stool. "I didn't know. I mean, she's pretty, so it shouldn't surprise me." If she joined the clinic staff, Carolyn would be the only married employee. A wisp of envy, like smoke, clouded Reagan's vision. She mentally waved it away, dismissing it as a reaction to the number of weddings taking place this year. "Do you believe she'll be a good fit?"

"I do. Her knowledge and willingness to move to a small-town impressed me, especially when her fiancé will need to relocate."

"What does he do for a living?"

"He's a marketing manager for a group of car dealerships. Fortunately, he can do his job remotely."

Trey leaned back against the counter, his palms pressed to the surface behind him. He'd removed the glasses that gave him a studious appearance, but with or without them, he could turn any woman's head. More and more, he turned hers. Why the change? Could a concussion affect emotions? She would do some research into it, because this new affection for Trey Abbott scared her.

"Reagan?"

She blinked at the vocal intrusion into her thoughts. "Yes?"

"You disappeared on me."

"I'm sorry. What did you say?"

"I want to know what you really think about Carolyn. It isn't too late to change my mind."

She poked a finger into Lucy's cage and ran it over the sleeping cat's dark fur. "I liked her, Trey, and I believe she'll be a wonderful addition to the clinic."

"Good. I'm glad we agree. Her wedding is a week before Lane and Macie's. If she accepts the position, at the earliest, she'll start in mid-June."

"We need her as soon as possible. Shaina has received applications for the new tech position."

"Has she set up any interviews?"

"Two for next week."

"I'm glad you suggested promoting her to office manager."

"Me, too. She's doing a great job." Reagan adjusted on the chair. "There is one issue we should discuss."

"What is it?"

"It involves Kaine."

Kaine? What now? "What's the problem?"

Reagan shook her head. "Nothing serious. Puzzling, really. On Kaine's first visit to the clinic, he and Shaina took an instant dislike to one another. When he brought in the pastries the day you met with Carolyn, he offered Shaina one, saying she looked like she could use something sweet. It wasn't a courteous remark."

"Ouch." Like everyone, Kaine had his faults, but he got along with most people. Even those he didn't like, he charmed. Trey had witnessed it time after time and envied his ability.

"He also called her Shayla."

"Shaina. Shayla. They're not so far off. I'm sure he meant nothing by it. He may have misunderstood or forgotten her name. It happens."

Reagan shook her head. "The way he said it was subtle, but I got the idea he meant to rile her, which it did. She reacted as though he'd called her something vulgar."

"That doesn't sound like him." Then again, Kaine had acted weird since the day he arrived in Hidden Veil. With their talk Saturday night, Trey had gotten a better idea why. "What did she say to him?"

"Just that her father thought she was sweet enough." Reagan shrugged. "They stared at one another for a minute, then Kaine left. Overall, it was a strange visit. I felt like I watched a win-or-die ping-pong match."

"I'll talk to both of them. I can't have Kaine disrespecting my employees, and I can't have my employees disrespecting my brother."

"Don't worry about it. I've already talked to Shaina. She's said she'll avoid any issues in the future. I only mentioned it, because I thought you might have some insight into the reason for the way they're acting."

"Kaine is making some changes in his life. It could be stress. Let me know if it happens again."

In the quiet that followed, Reagan sat on the stool, picking at the chipped nail polish on her thumb—a neutral color that barely showed on her nails. She stopped, drew in a deep breath, and released it. "I'm sorry about Saturday. How is your shoulder?"

"The scratches will heal." Trey rubbed his shoulder and grinned. "I almost offered to declaw Peaches for free."

"Why doesn't that surprise me?" She rubbed her eyes. "No matter what I said to you, jumping into the lake to save someone was a heroic move, Trey."

Heroic. It was the way he'd wanted her to see him, right? Still, her voice flattened with the word. And what he had done wasn't him, was it? Not the everyday Trey Abbott. "What I did was pure reaction, nothing I reasoned out."

He eyed her for a moment. "Can I ask you a question?" The last time he used those words with her, she turned down his invitation to the dance.

"Okay." Reagan stiffened, as though she braced herself for what was coming.

The way she'd acted around him lately, he wondered if that concussion had changed her personality. "Me jumping into that lake really upset you. Why?"

Under his intent gaze, she squirmed and turned on the stool toward Lucy's cage. She poked between the wires to rub the sleeping cat's fur with her finger. What did he want her to say? That the idea of something happening to him would be her undoing? Truthfully? Yes.

Finally, she looked at him. "I think—" Lucy stirred, and she pulled her finger from the cat's cage. "She's awake."

And had lousy timing.

Reagan thought what? That it was only by God's grace that

he survived his venture in the water? With the unexpected way the teen had fought, he could agree with that.

Trey neared the cage. "Let me take a quick look, then you can call Mrs. Marlow. I doubt she'll be asleep."

"You'll give her a discount, won't you?"

His face warmed. Reagan probably knew him better than anyone. "Maybe a small discount. Ever since her husband passed, except for Lucy, she has no one else at home."

"You are a marshmallow, Dr. Abbott."

She'd said it with a smile, but Trey couldn't summon a smile in response. He'd heard the term as anything but a compliment. *Marshmallow: A pushover. Feeble and powerless.*

"Kindness is one of your best character traits."

Okay. That took the sting out of her previous description of him. "Thanks."

Once he'd examined Lucy, Trey placed the still-sleepy cat into the cage, taking care with her leg.

Reagan hung up the phone. "Mrs. Marlowe will pick up Lucy on Tuesday."

"Good." He shut down the computer. "You never answered my question. What upset you at the lake?"

She turned away from him and straightened Lucy's file on the counter. "I saw you go under multiple times. I don't want to add to memories that already haunt me, Trey."

The answer fanned another of those sparks of hope inside him. She cooled it by adding, "I'm ready to head home."

"Me, too." He could use a shower and shave before starting his normal workday.

Trey cut off the lights and walked out of the building after

Reagan. Near her car, she stumbled over a slight dip in the gravel lot and went down on one knee. He caught her around the waist, keeping her from falling face first on the stones. Once she'd settled on her feet, he turned her around to face him. "Did you hurt yourself?"

"Only my pride."

She peered up at him, one palm planted on his chest as she gained her balance. Heat penetrated his T-shirt, and a shiver ran up his back. He preferred to think of it as a reaction to the morning air, as opposed to a reaction to her touch.

The rising sun had turned the sky into shades of cobalt and gold. The nearby dusk-to-dawn light still glowed, bringing a shine to Reagan's dark hair, gilding areas in buttery shades. Trey couldn't stop himself from running his hand over the long strands. *Soft.* Unlike in the hospital, this touch didn't shock him with its unexpectedness. This touch felt right. As though it was meant to be.

His thumping heart roared in his ears. Surely, she felt it through her palm. He lifted the hair on her forehead, studying the red line running across her skin. "The stitches are gone."

"As of Wednesday." She stared at him with an un-Reagan-like sedateness and laid her other hand over his, curling her fingers. Okay, that touch warmed his skin like a roaring fire on a January night. "I'll have a scar."

"Scars are reminders of having lived life."

A slight smile lifted her lips. "You're a philosopher now, Dr. Abbott?"

"I probably read it somewhere." Actually, it was one of his grandfather's favorite sayings.

"On a cereal box?"

He grinned. "Probably."

His gaze fell to bare, rosy lips that parted with an invitation—an invitation he accepted. One step from her brought those lips closer, so close he could feel her breath on his cheek.

Before he realized his dream of kissing her, she ducked her head, dropped her hand, and backed away. "I-I must be more tired than I thought if I can't walk."

Or if she considered kissing him?

Trey straightened. "Would you like me to drive you home?" The question came out low and gravelly, but he resisted the urge to clear his throat or apologize.

Reagan opened her car door. "No, thanks. I can make it. I'll see you later."

Trey waited until she'd driven off, then ambled the couple of hundred feet to his house, hands in his pockets and shoulders slouched. Fist around the doorknob, he relived their last few minutes together. He'd almost kissed her. Hope fanned again. Better yet, she had almost kissed him. He called that progress.

Twenty

With his elbow planted on the arm of his office chair, Trey rested his cheek on his palm and closed his eyes, ready for a lifelike dream.

Not that he hadn't daydreamed since the moment Reagan drove off this morning. He'd daydreamed about that near kiss and the future it foreshadowed until he'd almost convinced himself of the reality of that future. Then Reagan returned to the clinic this morning and all but ignored him.

Still, something had changed between them. He intended to take advantage of that change.

He opened his eyes and sighed as he straightened in the chair. His loaded schedule showed too many appointments today to play hooky.

The desk phone rang. The light showed an inner-office call. He picked up the receiver. "Yes?"

"Dr. Abbott, Marshall Burnside is here to see you," said Shaina.

Though polite, her voice sounded strained. The younger

Burnside had that effect on people, so he didn't blame her. Yet it reminded Trey of his conversation with Reagan in the early morning hours. He should ask Kaine about his treatment of Shaina. But he'd approach the discussion with kid gloves. After their talk Saturday night, his relationship with his brother already stood on shaky ground.

First, Trey had to tackle a bully. "Tell him to come on back." He'd let Burnside come to him. Having an inkling of the reason for the man's visit, he didn't relish the idea of a confrontation taking place in his waiting room.

Not thirty seconds later, his office door opened—no polite knock first—and the big man filled his doorway, a scowl marring his middle-aged face. He raised his voice. "We need to talk."

Trey had expected this visit at some point. Maybe he should stand and shake the man's hand, but Marshall didn't appear amenable to cordiality and, in his mood, Trey couldn't care less. "I'm happy to talk with you, Mr. Burnside, but only if you come inside and shut the door. I don't want my patients disturbed."

Burnside shut the door behind him and approached the desk. He leaned forward until his face loomed only a foot from Trey's.

Trey indicated the chair by the wall, refusing to be intimidated. "Pull up a seat."

"I'll stand." But he backed off, standing ramrod straight, his legs spread and arms crossed. "You want to lease my father's property?"

Had he used this browbeating tactic with his father? Probably. "Oren and I have talked about it." He wouldn't offer any more information than necessary.

"Have you signed the lease yet?"

Odd. If Oren told his son about their potential agreement, Marshall should also know whether they had signed a lease. "Not yet. We're to meet this week to discuss it again."

"Cancel that meeting. My father's property is not for lease."

Trey studied the man, trying to decide whose interest he represented, Oren's or his own. He concluded that if Marshall truly wanted what was best for Oren, he would support his father's decision. "Do you have a power of attorney over your father's estate?"

Rather than answer, Marshall relaxed the scowl, putting Trey on edge. "If you want to buy the property, then we might work out a deal. Otherwise, it's in Dad's best interest to sell to someone else."

Like the company wanting to build a nursing facility? "Mr. Burnside, your father isn't ready to move out of his house. That property has sentimental value to him, and since he owns it—"

"Dad doesn't know what's best for his future."

And you do?

Could he be doing Oren a disservice? The man wasn't getting any younger. What if Oren's health took a sudden turn for the worse?

"In all my conversations with Oren, I never noticed any mental concerns." Physical, yes, but he still got around. Slowly. His mind was sharp, as were his opinions. And the last he'd heard, Oren held the opinion that his son wanted to shuffle him off into an assisted living apartment somewhere against his wishes.

Trey was in no mood to spar with anyone today, especially

Marshall Burnside. "If Oren disposes of his property or leases it to someone else, that's his choice. I won't put up a fuss. But I expect him to tell me himself."

Burnside's jaw tightened and his face turned as red as the shirt Reagan had worn during the night. "You'll be sorry you got mixed up in my father's business."

Trey rose from his chair. "Is that a threat?"

"I don't threaten, Dr. Abbott. I state fact."

Stepping around the desk, Trey went to the door and opened it. "We're done here."

The man drew in a deep breath and released it, like a bull preparing to charge. He stomped to the doorway, then stopped and turn. "We're done for now. Don't think I won't get my lawyer involved, Dr. Abbott. You sign that lease and you'll regret it."

Trey's mind conjured the day in college when he'd happened upon a robbery. That man had made loud and menacing threats, too. Threats he could have carried out while Trey stood frozen and indecisive.

Burnside's stomping feet were the icing on the cake of his anger. Would Marshall accuse him of taking advantage of an elderly man and tie everything up in court? It would drain Trey's finances and his excitement over the project with Zeke's organization, as surely as his father and the thief during his college days had drained Trey's faith in himself.

That would stop. From now on, he would allow God to work in his weakness.

Reagan stepped into the hallway at the sound of a loud voice coming from Trey's office. What on earth? Before she could make out the words bleeding through the closed door, the voices settled into a low volume.

Maybe she misinterpreted it as anger. It wouldn't be impossible. Her emotions were in overdrive after this morning. How could she have been so stupid as to have almost kissed Trey? After tripping over her feet, he'd caught her and held her and . . .

She'd only placed her hand on his chest until her balance steadied and she could—

Oh, give it up, Reagan Hartwell. Admit it. You wanted that kiss.

With Trey's arm around her, she'd let herself imagine that the way he held her meant something more than a simple catch to keep her from falling on her face. That his fingers running through her unruly hair implied a purposeful intimacy, rather than an attempt to clear her vision. That she fantasized leaning toward him, a kiss on her mind.

The door to Trey's office opened. Reagan ducked back inside the exam room to keep from being found spying. She pushed the door semi-shut, leaving it open an inch or two to see and hear. Normally, she wasn't nosy, but she hadn't liked the tone in the visitor's raised voice.

"We're done here." Trey's own voice had deepened with anger.

"We're done for now. Don't think I won't get my lawyer involved, Dr. Abbott. You sign that lease and you'll regret it."

She sucked in a breath at hearing Marshall Burnside's threat. What was he doing at the clinic? She hadn't expected him to confront Trey in person. She'd expected him to use his influence with Oren. And why didn't Trey respond?

Her nerves buzzed like an electrical line. Not only her nerves. Her conscience zinged as she waited for Burnside to mention her name. Maybe he already had, and she'd missed it. Had that raised Trey's anger?

She opened the exam room door, ready to interrupt them, to head off more trouble for her boss.

Burnside stepped into her path, almost knocking her down. He glared, then his expression softened a bit. "I hope I didn't hurt you, Ms. Hartwell."

"I do, too, Mr. Burnside."

He paused a moment before comprehension lit his eyes. "You'll be fine."

Reagan tried to relax. Why should she feel guilty? She'd acted for the good of the community.

Marshall nodded a goodbye and walked away before she could say good riddance. Could anything worthwhile ever come from linking herself with a devil? The one time she'd chosen the right path—the unselfish path—and she doubted herself.

The need for reassurance drove Reagan to knock on Trey's door. After a few seconds of silence, she heard, "Come in," and she entered Trey's office. He sat behind his desk, his eyebrows drawn down, mouth tight. When he looked up, seeing her, he leaned back in his chair. His casual look didn't fool Reagan. She saw a man struggling to bring himself under control, to keep her from witnessing his anger. Why not let go sometimes? Why button himself down like a straightlaced spinster?

"I saw Marshall Burnside in the hall. What did he want?"

"Evidently, he talked to Oren. He wants to stop me from leasing his father's kennel."

So, Trey didn't know of her involvement. He thought Oren spilled the beans. She should tell him the truth. The confession stuck in her throat. "Why don't you give up that plan and build a boarding kennel here? You don't need Oren's property."

"You're wrong, Reagan. There's more at stake than my business."

"Oren will be fine once he's out from under the responsibility of keeping the place up."

Trey opened his mouth as though he planned to say something, then shut it again. He glanced at his watch. "Did you need something? If not, I have appointments. *We* have appointments."

In his present mood, continuing to push the sale of the land wouldn't end well. "Nothing else. I wanted to be sure everything was all right."

"It's fine." He grabbed the stethoscope laying on top of the leather portfolio she'd given him last Christmas, the one she'd had imprinted with his name. "Then let's get to work."

It seemed whatever connection they had shared in those early morning hours had dissolved. Or she'd imagined it.

Reagan followed Trey out the door and watched as he strode down the hall. Once he reached the waiting room, she turned and pressed her forehead to the wall, breathing in and out several times. She tried to reassure herself that her effort to see the Burnside land sold to Briar Park was for the best of everyone involved, even Trey.

Given Marshall's threat, especially Trey.

Trey made it through the rest of the day without another incident, even with the conversation with Burnside on his mind. Unless Oren had appointed his son as his guardian, there probably wasn't much Marshall could do to stop either lease. The older man's physical limitations contrasted with his sharp mental faculties.

Reagan popped her head into the treatment room. "Unless you need me, I'm headed home."

He needed her, all right. Just not how she had in mind. "No. Go home and get some rest. It's been a long"—he consulted his watch—"sixteen hours."

"True." Still, she didn't move.

"Is there something else?"

"I heard Marshall Burnside threaten you with legal action. I don't think he was bluffing, Trey. Be careful."

How weak did she see him? It was in her voice, her earlier suggestion that he drop his plan for the kennel property. She thought he couldn't hold his own against a bully like Marshall Burnside. "He's all talk. Oren still controls his property, so there isn't anything he can do."

Experience had taught Trey to let people like Burnside talk themselves out without responding in kind. Two bulls in the same pasture often brought unnecessary trouble. Disappointment over an unfulfilled kiss and the unforeseen threat from a blowhard had tested his patience. Now, the woman he loved had decided he couldn't take care of himself. He shook his head. "Go on home, Reagan."

"But, Trey—"

"Go home."

She hesitated, then turned on her heel and walked away.

Trey ran a hand down his face. What if she was right, and he hadn't taken Burnside seriously enough? Was his hope for the property worth losing everything?

Twenty-one

At a nudge to her hand, Reagan's eyes batted open. Quill sat at the side of the recliner, peering up at her. In a low volume, the TV weatherman rattled off something about rain. Obviously, she'd fallen asleep in her recliner, her body telling her it needed to recoup some of the sleep she'd missed the past few nights. Conflicting emotions and the stress between her and Trey kept her dozing and waking up.

It still stung to have had him snap at her Monday when she'd only tried to warn him about Marshall. For the past two days, they had tiptoed around one other. He would look repentant. She would feel repentant. In the end, they said nothing.

She glanced at the clock on her phone. Nine-twelve. She couldn't remember the last time she'd fallen asleep so early.

Her phone buzzed with an incoming call. She groaned at the name. "Hello, Scott."

"Hey, Reagan. Hope I'm not calling too late."

"No. It's okay." It would have been more okay had he not called at all.

"Good. Listen, I have some bad news."

"Oh?"

"Yeah. I'm going to have to cancel our date for Saturday."

The fatigue of a moment earlier vanished with the best news she'd heard all week. "That's a shame. No problem, I hope."

"No, nothing like that. Something came up."

"I understand." She understood that he probably got a better offer. Not that she'd never been rejected. It just hadn't happened in years. This one, though, brought joy rather than tears.

"We'll see each other again sometime."

Not if she could help it. "Bye, Scott."

After ending the call, she pushed out of the recliner and stretched. Quill whined, ready to go outside for the last time. "Let's go." She laughed as her silly puppy galloped to the door.

They played outside until Reagan ushered Quill back to the house. She squinted at headlights from a large vehicle pulling into her drive. Although she shaded her eyes with her hand, the lights and the moonless night left her unable to identify the vehicle. Quill stood at her side and barked. She opened the side door and flipped a switch, turning on the outside light. The glow illuminated what looked like Trey's SUV. What was he doing here this late?

Her hand shot to her hair, smoothing the back of it, mussed from the nap in the recliner. She dropped her arm to her side. She'd never worried much about her appearance around him before landing in the hospital.

The headlights went dark, and the driver's door opened. Quill ran to greet Trey. Only Trey wasn't the one to step out onto her driveway. *Great.* What did Kaine want?

Reagan approached the SUV. "What are you doing here?" That sounded rude, but his presence reminded her of Marshall

Burnside, which then reminded her of Marshall's threat.

Kaine leaned with his hip against the front quarter-panel of the vehicle, relaxed, as if he visited her every night. "I know it's late, but I saw your light on, so I figured I'd stop."

A sudden fear clutched her heart in its tight grip. "Is there something wrong? Is Trey okay?"

When his curious gaze bore through her, she realized how frantic she'd sounded. Why would he appear calm if something had happened to Trey? Why, also, did he stare at her with a knowing smile on his lips?

Quill jumped on Kaine's legs, begging for attention. The puppy never met a stranger. Kaine picked him up and ran a hand over him from head to tail. "Cute." He took a few steps forward and handed Quill off to Reagan. "Funny that you asked about Trey."

She'd considered inviting him inside, but that cocky grin irked her. "I'm exhausted, Kaine. If you have something to tell me, I'm all ears."

"Okay." He shoved his hands in the front pockets of his cargo shorts. "You acted like you were worried about my brother at the lake Saturday. Was that only an act? Because, you know, I got a different vibe from that phone call I overheard last week. Where do you stand with my brother."

"I stand with Trey. Always." She restrained a wince. *Almost always.* "What did you think you heard from that call?" She'd asked a risky question, but she had to know how dangerous Kaine Abbott actually was.

He crossed his arms, and she could see doubt rolling through his mind. "How would I know when I only heard your side of the conversation? It was the look on your face, like I'd caught you coming out of a bank with a bag full of stolen money."

A soft snort escaped. "You're calling me a thief?"

"No. Just someone with a secret. What's Briar Park?"

Her body froze as though he'd dumped a load of ice water on her. He had overheard more than she'd hoped that day.

He grinned. "Yeah, that's the look I saw."

Why not tell him? He could find the answer to his question from almost anyone in town. "It's a company."

"I got that."

She frowned at his sarcasm. Shaina was probably right about him. He was a jerk. "Hidden Veil needs a nursing and rehabilitation facility. They want to provide it."

"And?"

Quill squiggled in her arms, so she put the dog down while she mulled over the wisdom of total honesty. In the end, she chose a partial relief for her conscience. "And they want the land he has in mind to lease."

"So you want to stop that lease?"

Reagan didn't enjoy playing defense, but she worked hard to keep her cool. "I wouldn't be unhappy if it fell through, something Trey knows."

"Does he know you're working against his interests? How do you think that will go over when he learns the truth?"

"When you tell him, you mean?"

"I didn't say that. I'm only suggesting you think about what you're doing."

She had thought about it, especially since that fiasco at the lake and in the clinic parking lot. She'd thought about it over and over. "You don't know me, Kaine. You know nothing of my friendship with Trey or what I have or haven't done."

"I know more than you give me credit for." One eyebrow quirked upward as Kaine studied her. "I didn't come here to argue with you, Reagan. What happens between you and Trey is for you two to figure out. I have enough problems of my own. But I recommend you tell my brother the truth before he finds out some other way."

Reagan rubbed her forehead and tried to stretch her lips into something that resembled a smile. She couldn't promise that, could she? "Look, it's late. I'm going inside." She turned, Quill at her heels, leaving Kaine standing alone in the driveway.

As she approached her side door, he said, "One thought to keep in mind."

She stopped so fast she could have gotten whiplash. Quill ran into her, then dodged to the side. She rotated on the balls of her feet, cocking her head as she eyed him. "What?"

"Don't play with fire, Reagan. It can lead to losing what you want most." After those cryptic words, he settled into the SUV and started the engine.

She stared, dumbfounded, as he backed out of her driveway. What a weird thing to say.

Her temple throbbed. Kaine had assured her he wouldn't tell Trey of the conversation he'd overheard. Although it boiled down to her word against his, she couldn't see herself lying to Trey, not in words anyway. But there was that pesky little lie of omission.

As she readied for bed, Kaine's last statement played in Reagan's mind. He'd spoken as though his advice came from experience. Who had he lost, and what were his ample problems?

Trey arrived home from the clinic to find Kaine in the backyard.

As he'd done on other occasions, his brother had carried a patio chair to the center of the yard where he sat holding Lulu by the rope Trey stored in his garage.

Grabbing his own chair, Trey eased across the yard, not wanting Lulu to freeze in fright. He settled the chair in the grass, then reached out and ran a hand over the rough hairs on her back. He really should look harder for a new home for her, preferably with other goats. But he'd grown used to having her here.

"When you leave, you're taking her with you." He couldn't help teasing his brother.

Kaine glanced up. "What would I do with a goat?"

"What are you doing now?"

His brother exhaled. "I do need to leave Trey, but I have nowhere to go. I can't go back to Idaho." Trey had taken a breath and opened his mouth, ready to mention his idea, when Kaine cut him off. "And I'm not going to Raleigh."

"Not my suggestion."

Kaine drew in the rope until Lulu stood at his feet. She closed her eyes as he ran a knuckle from her bony forehead down to her muzzle. "Then what?"

"Stay here." At the dubious look on his brother's face, Trey waved a hand, encompassing his property. "Not here. Around Hidden Veil."

Not that Trey didn't love Kaine, despite the difference in their personalities, but his brother needed to straighten his life out. If he was serious about quitting firefighting, he needed a strategy for his future. Trey hoped to be close by to help without having a permanent roommate. Maybe he'd grown too solitary and independent over the years. Too solitary to share his life with anyone else? Hopefully not, because despite the week's strain between Reagan and him, Trey had his own idea for the future.

"And do what, exactly?"

"There's a county airport, a small one about twenty minutes away. Maybe you can teach skydiving."

"No!" The emphatic reply scared Lulu. Her legs stiffened, and she fell onto her side in the grass, jerking the rope from Kaine's hand. His eyes widened, and he stared at her. "Did I kill her?"

Trey laughed. "Three. Two. One." Lulu pushed to her feet. "It doesn't last long."

Kaine stood up and grabbed the rope. "Time to go back in your pen, silly goat." He tugged her to the gate and locked her inside, returning with the rope. "That's too weird."

"So was your response to my suggestion. What's going on, Kaine? I'm tired of the mystery. Let me help if I can."

"I can't talk about it. Not yet. Maybe never."

Both frustrated and concerned, Trey accepted his brother's lack of readiness, and they sat in silence for several minutes before Kaine stood up. He took several steps toward the house, then turned. "Trey, go to the dance and tell Reagan how you feel."

"She's going with someone else, remember?"

"Forget that guy. She isn't serious about him." Kaine shook his head. "Don't be me, Trey. Don't wait."

Don't be him? What did that mean?

After his brother walked away, Trey remained in the chair. A warm May breeze blew around him, carrying with it Kaine's advice. *Don't wait.*

Once more, he saw Reagan's car smashed against the pine tree. He saw her behind the wheel, the blood dripping from her injured head, then in the hospital, weak and dazed. Did he have time to wait?

Trey had known how he felt about Reagan for ages. But her?

Heroes are overrated.

Only recently had he'd thought he might stand a chance with her. That she wouldn't care if he couldn't compare in the hero department to men like Matt Becker. Maybe being her hero was a simple matter of showing her he loved her.

What kind of chance did he have of winning her if he waited or didn't even try? None.

Twenty-two

Reagan entered the packed high school gym with Brianna. Her sister leaned close to her ear. "There must be a hundred people here."

"Not counting those wandering the halls."

The area echoed with the sound of country music coming from the band stationed at the far end. The original plan had been to hold the dance in the park, but a day of rain had caused the town to enact Plan B—holding it in her old high school gymnasium.

Reagan nodded. "A good turnout, considering the weather." Thankfully, the rain had stopped an hour ago, so they hadn't gotten wet on the way in.

"I'm glad that Scott guy bailed."

When Reagan asked Brianna to come with her to the dance, she'd had to tell her sister Scott canceled their date. It didn't endear him to Bri any more than Kaine had endeared himself to Shaina.

"Why didn't you ask Trey to come with you?"

Reagan scrambled for an answer. "How would you feel if I asked you, 'Would you like to be my second-choice date to the Blossom Bash?'"

"You did."

"Bad example."

"I see your point, but it didn't stop you last year."

"This year is different." Way different. "Let's see who else is here."

People of all ages looked as though they were enjoying their evening—laughing, talking, dancing. She recognized many who attended every year. And one first-time attendee.

Kaine Abbott stood alone near the folded-up bleachers a few yards away. She would prove to him his visit to her house hadn't bothered her. "Would you like to meet Trey's brother?"

Her sister's nose wrinkled. "Do I have to?"

"Come on." Reagan grabbed Bri's arm and tugged her over to Kaine. "Hey."

"Glad to see you."

"I wouldn't miss tonight for any reason." She pulled Bri closer. "This is my sister, Brianna."

Kaine held out his hand. "Nice to meet you."

Bri's return grin looked more like she realized she stepped in something soft and smelly but wanted to pretend it hadn't happened. When Reagan cleared her throat, Brianna took his hand and said, "You, too."

Reagan looked around for Trey, but he was nowhere in sight. He hadn't actually said he'd be here, but he didn't say he wouldn't either. "No date for tonight?"

Kaine's smile couldn't overcome the sudden sadness in his eyes. "No. I'm here to observe."

"Observe what?"

"Small town life." He gestured to the crowd. "I thought you had a date."

"He had something come up."

"Too bad. Looks like everyone's having a good time. Is it always this crowded?"

"Yes." She raised her voice to be heard over the noise. "People come from all over the county. It's a great way to meet neighbors."

"Where is Trey?"

Leave it to Brianna to seek an answer to the question on Reagan's mind, the one she'd pressed her lips together to keep from asking. She came tonight to prove to herself Scott's last-minute rejection hadn't affected her. But the real reason may have been to spend time with Trey outside the clinic.

Kaine's face grew hard a second before someone tapped Reagan on the shoulder. She spun to find Shaina grinning at her.

"You finally showed." Shaina wrapped her arm around Brianna and drew her in for a side hug. "Hey, Bri."

"Hey, girl. Quill ran off, and Reagan had to chase him down."

"That little stinker." Shaina eyed Kaine from head to foot, her smile looking more like a dog's snarl. "All alone tonight?"

With the dig, Reagan saw the wheels turning in Kaine's head, churning up an equally snarky comeback. Before a verbal war broke out, Reagan introduced him to Shaina's date, Chase Taylor, and the two men shook hands.

Shaina stood on tiptoe and looked around the decorated gym. Everywhere, the spring pastels of yellows, pinks, purples, and greens dominated table coverings, crepe streamers, and balloons. "I haven't seen Trey yet."

Kaine glanced toward the door Reagan and Brianna had entered. "He said he didn't think he'd come."

That answered Bri's question from earlier.

"I'm sorry to hear it." Shaina's sympathetic glance bounced off Reagan, then scanned the gym again as though she wouldn't believe Kaine unless she saw for herself evidence of Trey's absence.

The five of them wandered farther into the gym, joining Lane and Macie. Sutton and his date, Miranda, a tall, curvy blonde, also stood with them. Looks-wise, she was the complete opposite of Paige. While she didn't know Miranda, Reagan suspected she also differed in personality. It hadn't occurred to her before, but Sutton's dates never resembled her sister. Had his taste in women changed, or had he never gotten over Paige and couldn't bring himself to date someone who resembled her?

The group tried to talk over the music, then decided not to fight it. Within thirty minutes, Reagan had danced with Chase, Harley Whitman, and Kaine—who was almost as smooth on his feet as Trey. Although Harley was a plump teddy bear, she was thankful not to see that familiar lump of tobacco in the mechanic's cheek. It was bad enough to smell it on his breath.

Normally, she enjoyed being with her friends and socializing, but this year, the dance held little appeal for her without Trey's presence. If he'd known she wouldn't come with Scott, would he have invited her again? He'd seemed eager for her to accompany him. And that near kiss Monday morning? Her stomach fluttered with the memory of the beating of his heart under her palm, the warmth that seemed to seep from his body into hers.

Reagan lifted her gaze to peek at the clock on the gym wall. She'd stay another fifteen or twenty minutes, and then make an excuse to leave. Brianna could leave with her or catch a ride home with Shaina and Chase.

While Macie danced with Kaine, Lane swept Reagan across the dance floor in a Texas two-step. "Macie and I have been cleaning out the attic at the house. We ran across a box of things the Army returned to my parents after Matt died. They stored it up there without going through it. We found letters I thought you might want. When I get a chance, I'll bring them to you."

She wanted to tell him not to bother, to throw them away. She had no need for them. But all she could do was nod. Did that collection of letters include THE letter? Although it might be safer in her hands, she didn't want to see it again.

They danced halfway around the gym floor when Lane's feet slowed and his gaze settled on something over her shoulder. "It's about time you got here."

"Running a little late."

Reagan's breath caught, and her palms moistened with a nervousness foreign to her. Hopefully, her dance partner didn't notice. She turned her head to stare over her shoulder at Trey as if she hadn't seen him in ages.

"Mind if I take over?" Trey stared at her, too, sparks of determination in his eyes. Those sparks swirled around her like an electrified tornado.

Unprepared for the energy that arced between them, she sought to lessen it with a joke, asking if he was talking to her or her dance partner. For once, her mouth refused to spit something out that cemented her control.

She could stay here a little longer.

Lane stepped back and placed her hand in Trey's. "I'll take back my bride-to-be from your brother."

He left Reagan clutching the man who had occupied her thoughts all week. The one who looked at her now as if she were the only person in the room. "Kaine said he didn't think you'd come."

"No. I intended to get here earlier but—"

"Don't just stand there, Doc. Give her a whirl." Monte Becker shuffled past them in a combination limp and skate, leading Hidden Veil's librarian, Nadine Schutz, across the floor.

Trey chuckled. "We'd better move or prepare to be run over."

She placed her hand on his shoulder but stumbled in stepping back as he stepped forward. Rather than laugh, Trey tightened his grip on her back. "Sorry. I should have given you another second to get ready."

"No. My fault." Her voice shook.

Why was she so nervous? In the past, she had admired the way he danced. His movements were smooth, light, and precise. Last year, she'd told him that if he weren't a veterinarian, he could teach at a dance studio. He'd laughed and said his mother made her boys take dance lessons at one of those places.

As they fell into a rhythm, her nerves settled some and she fought a grin when she inwardly compared Trey's dancing to Matt's. Matt's feet never moved in the same direction at the same time, and they always found the tops of her feet.

So much about Trey differed from Matt, yet they were both

quiet, sturdy men. Unlike many of her dates these last years, they were men to be counted on. And she really didn't deserve someone like Trey any more than she'd deserved Matt.

But, oh, how she wished she did. Would it really be so dangerous to encourage these growing feelings for him?

Trey had danced with her before, of course, but not like this, not under these circumstances. Not with a realistic hope that he might finally achieve his dreams for them.

Years past, at the Blossom Bash, he'd played the role of an extra, a guy who led her around the dance floor, then handed her off to another man. Tonight, Trey had come determined to be more than an extra. Tonight, someone else had handed her off to him, and he would savor every moment of having her near him. Basking in her warmth. The fragrance of a perfume that reminded him of the gardenias dotting his mother's garden. The touch from her hand in his.

His feet shuffled forward along the polished gym floor in basic steps, guiding her backwards with the quick-quick, slow-slow rhythm of the Texas Two-step. Their spin was as smooth as the shakes served at Gene Locke's soda fountain.

Reagan looked up at him. "I didn't think you were coming."

"I got a call from Carolyn. She's agreed to take the position."

Her hand squeezed his. "That's great, Trey, and a relief. I can't wait until she starts."

"It'll take off a lot of pressure." And, hopefully, give him more time to devote to getting the Burnside property ready.

Trey spotted Kaine on the dance floor ahead of them, partnered with Pastor Jim's wife, Celia. "I'm glad to see my brother having fun."

"He's a great dancer. But not as good as you."

"Thanks." Trey had entered the gym, and like a missile, his gaze had homed in on Reagan dancing with Lane. One by one, he picked out their friends and noticed that none of the women danced with that blond-headed stranger he'd seen in the parking lot. "I thought you had a date for the dance." He couldn't deny the note of jealousy in his question.

"Last minute cancellation. Thankfully."

"His loss." Relieved, Trey moved them forward with the rest of the dancers in the counterclockwise direction. The coy grin she'd tacked on to her answer assured him the broken date hadn't upset her. "I'm sorry I was a grump this week."

Her smile fell away. "Dealing with Marshall Burnside is enough to turn anyone into a grump."

"True."

When the dance ended, he continued to hold her hand. Rather than leading her to their friends, he walked them in the opposite direction, toward the refreshment tables. "I can use something to drink. How about you?"

"Yes. One dance does work up a thirst." She waved a hand in front of her face, exaggerating the need to cool off.

Vera Bevins, Jo's grandmother, stood behind the drink table, ladled a fruit punch into two small plastic cups, and handed one to each of them. "Here you go."

Reagan took a sip of the drink. "Where's Bobby?"

Vera kept company with Bobby Goodwin. Rarely was one seen in public without the other. Yet they claimed to be too old and set in their ways for marriage.

"He's around here somewhere. Probably with those checkers buddies of his."

Trey spotted the men standing in a corner. Bobby and his retired friends, Ray, Gerald, and Walter, gathered many mornings at Jo's coffee shop to play checkers and gossip. Great guys, all of them. "Make sure you get at least one dance out of him."

"Oh, he says he's waiting until they play something nice and slow. We don't move fast at our age and don't want to get run over by more energetic youngsters like you." Vera winked at them.

They moved away, allowing Vera to serve others in line. Hoping to get Reagan alone—as alone as possible in a school filled with people—Trey led them along the edges of the room, almost brushing against the retracted bleachers. They guarded their drinks while dodging dancers and people standing around talking.

"It's crowded in here. Want to walk the halls while we finish these?" Trey held up his cup, in no hurry to finish the drink.

She stared into her cup, saying nothing, as if she realized his true purpose and had to mull over her response. Finally, she looked up at him. "Sounds good."

They left the gym and sauntered down the hall. People stood around in small groups, chattering like high schoolers in their cliques. A trophy case with awards representing various sports occupied a space down the hall. The building smelled of cleaning products, the tile floors polished to a mirror sheen.

They turned a corner in sync and entered another hallway, leaving behind those who lingered around the edges of the dance. The lights shone dimmer in this section, though he could see that the walls contained posters, announcements, maps, or emergency instructions. Not a large school, but large enough he didn't know where they headed. He'd never made it this far. "You went to school here. Where are we?"

Reagan peered around a corner and pointed down the hall. "This way leads to my old science class." She walked ahead of him and peeked in the small window in the classroom's door. She tried the handle, but someone had locked the door. She shrugged. "I really didn't expect it to be open."

Trey sidled up to her to examine the room through the glass. Large tables and high stools rather than desks. Microscopes. Beakers. His cheek came within a whisker's breath of brushing hers. Science was as far from his mind as the pile of laundry sitting on his washer.

If he turned his head even a quarter of an inch, he could brush her cheek with his lips. Leading her here, away from the dance, away from everyone, was a bold move. Not one he regretted, but neither would he push his luck. Not after she'd slipped away from their near-kiss last Monday morning. "It's a science room, all right."

Reagan laughed. "You should see the cafeteria. It really looks like a lunchroom."

"Can't wait."

They tossed their empty cups in a trash can and continued down the hall. Outside the cafeteria, drawings on the wall caught Trey's attention, and he stopped. Obviously done by talented art students, they depicted various scenes that had to do with the upcoming Memorial Day. The rows of white markers planted in a neat green carpet of grass. Symbols representing the various branches of service. Poppies and American flags and red, white, and blue. "These are amazing. The school has some artistic kids." As much as he appreciated the work, they triggered his sense of inferiority. He fought to regain the confidence that brought him here tonight.

It wasn't until he glanced at Reagan's pale face that Trey could have kicked himself for his mistake. He touched her arm. "Hey, I wasn't thinking. These have to be tough for you to see." Even tougher than it was for him. "I know I'm not Matt Becker, Reagan, and I never will be, but—"

Her eyes widened, then narrowed to slits, stopping what he'd hoped to say. "You think I want another man like Matt? Are you out of your ever-loving mind?" The words snapped in the air, but her eyes glowed, shiny and tortured.

While he scrambled for something to say, her gaze fell, and she whispered, "I killed Matt."

Those words sucked the air from his lungs.

Twenty-three

What have you done, Reagan?

Now Trey would want to hear the whole sordid story. When she told him, he would lose whatever good opinion he'd had of her. She would lose him as a friend . . . or more.

She'd sensed his purpose from the moment he suggested this walk through the halls. It was time he discovered the real Reagan Hartwell before things went too far.

Trey's shocked stare never left her face. Disbelief and the pitying look of sympathy. "Why would you say you killed Matt?"

She pressed her palms against her eyes, unable to bear looking at him. He gripped her hands, easing them down until she saw him. Leading her through the double doors into the cafeteria, he sat her at a round table and took the seat next to her. "Reagan?"

"You know that for years I blamed Lane for Matt's death."

"I do."

"It was a lie. I knew it was a lie. I used him as a scapegoat to ease my own guilt. I've spent over a third of my life regretting the past."

His hands squeezed hers. "Honey, Matt died from a sniper's bullet a world away from here ... away from you and Lane. How are you responsible for what happened?"

His soft voice and that "honey" threatened what little composure she maintained. She shook her head. "I killed him with my words."

He cocked his head, waiting for an explanation Reagan dreaded giving. Between his hands, her fingers curled into a tight fist as she prepared to reveal the hard part, the part that would brand her a merciless narcissist in his eyes.

On the last breath of an inner groaning for wisdom, she battled forward. "Do you know what it's like to live knowing someone you love faces death every day?"

"My family faces the possibility with every call out."

Of course. "I'm sorry. I wasn't thinking."

"No need to apologize. The tension and fear heighten with a spouse or fiancé. I saw it with my mom."

"Matt enlisted without discussing it with me first."

Trey's eyebrows rose above the frame of his glasses. "Why?"

"He believed I'd try to talk him out of it. For as long as I'd known him—since elementary school—he'd enjoyed video games that involved battles and strategy. I should have realized, shouldn't I? But he never told me he wanted to enlist. Not even his family knew. Matt wasn't as tall and athletic as Lane, and he didn't have his brother's sense of adventure. Sometimes, he could be a geek." Images bombarded her, bringing first a frown, then a smile, then another frown. "I guess none of us saw him as the type to join the military. I think he did it in secret because we didn't take him seriously."

"It caught Lane by surprise."

She nodded. "After a while, Matt started talking about re-enlisting when his time came up. One day, I'd had enough, so I wrote him a letter. I told him that if he remained in the Army, I wouldn't marry him. I wouldn't wait at home while he played soldier somewhere far away. Among other things, I accused him of being selfish. I was the selfish one."

Distant, muffled music from the gym overrode the quiet while Trey appeared to think over what she'd said. His chin dropped, and his eyes closed. Was he praying? He was that type of man. But was it for wisdom or a way to extricate himself from their discussion? Their friendship?

He opened his eyes, revealing a gentleness she hadn't expected. Knowing him, why wouldn't she? "Matt's decision was a serious commitment that involved both of you, Reagan. A woman deserves a man who'll share with her his dreams and plans, not make them without consulting her. He should have given you a say in your future with him."

Reagan pulled her hands free. "Please stop being so understanding. You don't know the whole story yet."

"Tell me."

Her throat tightened and tears welled, but she was determined not to let them fall, not to appeal to his compassion and protective instinct. "I took the coward's way out. I could have called him. I could have waited until he returned." Reagan's body shuddered at that admission. She and Paige had more in common than sisterhood. Both had given up on men who loved them in order to gain their own way. She peered through her wet lashes at Trey, surprised by not seeing his disgust. That would change, because she hadn't finished yet. He would give up on her.

"It took him a week or two to get my letters. After almost two weeks, he called. I didn't answer. The next day, his father called me to say . . ." She gulped away the rest. "Two weeks later, I received a letter from Matt. He said he was coming back and wanted us to get married." A sob broke through the brick wall of willpower she'd erected against the tears. She turned her head away from Trey before he could turn away from her. "Every year on the anniversary of his death, I-I want to crawl up in a ball and die for the things I wrote to him, for what I said, what I did and didn't do."

An aggravating trail of wetness streaked down her face. Oh, how she hated crying in front of others. She shook her head. "Matt might have lived if I hadn't written that letter, Trey. If my words hadn't distracted him."

"Hey, now." Trey turned her to face him and laid his hands on her shoulders. "You can 'if' until Jesus comes again, but it doesn't change a thing."

"My words broke his heart and caused him to lose focus."

"You don't know that, Reagan. Snipers do their work unseen. It's what makes them so deadly." Trey brushed the hair from her forehead with the tip of a tear-dampened finger—her tears.

"I've never told anyone what happened. Not even my parents or Bri." She sighed. "You were right. Nothing will change what I did, so what's the point of dwelling on it? It's just that I can't risk hurting anyone else to get my way."

His eyebrows pressed downward. "Is that why you date and

dump guys?"

After hiccupping a humorless chuckle, she wiped her face with both hands. "I'm an excellent candidate for Lane's psychologist friend, huh?"

"Everyone is at some point." He thumbed away the moisture from under her eyes and lifted her chin with a crooked finger. "You can't change Matt's fate, but you can allow God to change you."

"When I'm as guilty as if I'd aimed that rifle?"

"Do you believe Jesus went to the cross to forgive only trivial sins? Do you believe some things are too much for that sacrifice to cover? He's God, honey. He's large enough to carry any burden or wound, even the ones that buckle our knees with the memory."

Reagan stood thunderstruck, yet convicted. For years her knees had buckled on the anniversary of Matt's death, and she was tired of carrying the weight. Tired of the pain each April. Her stomach felt like she'd swallowed a cannonball. "Thank you, Trey."

She shut her eyes and drew in a deep breath. *And thank you, Jesus.*

For so long, she'd fought against the future, living only in the present, afraid she didn't deserve happiness with anyone, especially someone as wonderful as Trey. But she still didn't know how her confession affected their relationship. "Has your opinion of me changed?"

"If you get nothing else out of our time together tonight, I hope you'll understand that you can't scare me off like you do other men, Reagan Hartwell."

For the first time in years, she saw the possibility of a relationship with a man lasting longer than the milk in her refrigerator.

Learning the real reason behind Reagan's yearly meltdowns had almost caused a meltdown in Trey. Hearing the guilt. Seeing those tears. That tremble in her limbs and lips. This woman, who showed weakness only once a year, had done him a favor. She'd given him a better, more realistic view of his competition for her heart. She'd also given him more reason to pursue the type of relationship with her that he'd dreamed of for too long. After all, she didn't want a hero, which described him to a T.

Yet he'd meant what he said. She couldn't scare him off.

A battle brewed inside him. She'd been honest and open, taking a chance that he wouldn't reject her for something that happened years ago. If he wanted a meaningful relationship with her, shouldn't he be as open and honest with her?

"I have my own failings, Reagan. When it comes to my career choice, I sometimes feel I took the easy way out, but I am not my father, my grandfather, or my brother." Those last words came out sharper than he'd intended, but it didn't appear to faze her.

"I know firefighting is a big part of your family's history." She tipped her head. "Are you saying you became a veterinarian because it was a safer choice than fighting fires? Because if you are, you are wrong, Charles Abbott."

"Charles?" His lips twitched. She'd never called him that. No one called him that but bureaucrats who insisted on satisfying paperwork legalities, and his mother when he'd made her mad.

"Don't dodge the question. I've seen you handle a rank horse that threatened to drag you across a pasture. You've calmed more snapping canines than I can count. You don't need to put your life in danger to be a hero. You are a brave man, Trey."

"I appreciate your faith in me, but you don't know my story." He let out a deep, gusty sigh. "For years, everyone—including me—assumed I would become a firefighter like my father and grandfather. It warred with my actual desire to become a veterinarian."

"What changed your mind?"

Trey couldn't get the words to travel from his brain to his tongue.

She laid a hand on his arm. "Never mind. You don't need to satisfy my curiosity." She let go, leaving behind a warm spot on his skin, and rose from her seat.

He stood, too, and his fingers enveloped hers, stopping her from leaving. "Let me tell you who I really am."

She studied him, as though doing so she could search out the real Trey Abbott. "I already know who you are . . . but okay."

This would not be easy, every bit as difficult as her confession. "I was thirteen and at the station house with my dad when they got a call. He told me to wait for my mom to pick me up, but I begged to go. I wanted to prove I could walk in his footsteps, so I hounded him until he had no more time to argue. During the fire, I stayed in the truck like he told me and soaked up every move the firefighters made. Then I heard one of them say they pulled someone from the building. Like any curious kid, I left the truck and pushed through the firefighters gathered around something on the ground." He swallowed the bile raised at the memory of what he'd seen that night and spoke in a raspy whisper. "It's horrifying what fire can do to the human body."

The humiliation roared back at him. Sure, he'd only been thirteen, but some cultures would have considered him a man. He hadn't acted like a man. He'd lost his lunch and embarrassed his father in front of his co-workers.

"My dad took me by the shoulders, leaned forward to get my attention, and said, 'Man up, Trey. Yes, it's an awful thing to see. But we mourn, shake it from our minds, and move past it. If you can't do that, you have no business in the profession.' That's the day I realized I'd never 'move past it.' I'd never make my family proud as a firefighter, and Dad never accepted my inability to 'man up.'"

She pulled her hand free, folded her arms across her body, and shook her head in anger. His heart dropped to his stomach, waiting for her to agree. "How could your father say that to you? You were a kid! I think he gave you an idealistic vision of a job that got real too soon. We all have fears. Not everyone would jump into a lake to save a girl from drowning. I'd like to see his reaction to what you do at the clinic. I bet he couldn't stomach working to save a bloodied and mangled animal hit by a car."

Reagan had been *mad* for him? "The lake incident simply happened. I didn't think about the consequences, because I knew my ability to swim. As for the sight of injured animals,"— he shrugged—"I'm not sure why, but it doesn't bother me."

"Could be because you know you're helping them."

He had to tell her the worst. "There's more. I was a freshman in college, studying for an exam. After several hours in my dorm room, I needed a break, so I took a walk in the woods near the campus to stretch and to clear my mind. Ahead of me, I heard raised voices. A man aimed a gun at another student, intending to rob him. I froze, Reagan. I just . . . froze. My mind. My legs. Every part of me stood as rigid as that cement block wall behind you. While I debated my choices, my risks, the guy looked up and saw me standing half-hidden by a tree."

Reagan's eyes widened. "What happened?"

"Thankfully, he ran off into the woods. The student, one of my classmates, turned around. Seeing me, he thanked me for intervening. He could have died while I stood there unable to move a muscle, and he thanked me! I did nothing, nothing, to help him. Dad was right about me."

After waiting agonizing seconds as she stared at him, Trey checked his watch, not really seeing the time. "Now that you know I'm the Abbott without a heroic bone in his body, let's head back to the gym before our friends send out a search party."

"Not yet." She clamped tight to his arm, preventing him from walking away as he'd done with her. "Only minutes ago, you told me God is big enough to carry all our burdens and forgive all sins. Those were just words to you?"

His eyebrows arched and that body organ that had sunk to his stomach found its way back to his chest, beating like an insane drum the whole way. Were they only words? "No. I believe what I said."

"That's what I thought. So forgive yourself. I need to forgive myself, too." Reagan wrapped her arms around him and squeezed. "I'm proud to work with you. I'm proud to be your friend." She peered up at him, her eyes reflecting a sudden shyness and insecurity he couldn't remember ever seeing from her. She whispered, "If you're willing, I'd be proud and happy to be more than your friend."

Trey had waited three years to hear those words from her. Now that he had, they seemed surreal.

Inch-by-inch, he raised his arms, expecting her to back away as she'd done earlier in the week. When she didn't, he relaxed in her embrace. Nothing that felt this good, this right, could be anything but real. He tightened his hold, pulling her closer. "I've been willing for longer than you'll ever know."

"Then kiss me?"

He'd sold God short by believing the Lord had made him defective—someone less than. A weakling who didn't deserve a strong, beautiful woman like Reagan. But God's power is made perfect in weakness. Why couldn't he remember that?

He grinned and lowered his head, whispering against her mouth. "Yes, ma'am."

Twenty-four

Who knew her mild-mannered vet could turn her inside-out with only the touch of his lips on hers?

It started with a touch, anyway—a light, sweet contact between the two of them that lasted mere moments before turning into a kiss—a oneness—Reagan had waited years to experience with someone after losing Matt. A kiss that meant more than a simple "I think you're okay," but one with a depth of feeling that laid to rest her fears and brought hope to her future.

Trey may have never wanted to become a fireman, but he sure knew how to start a fire to melt Reagan's insides with its heat and heart.

Before getting carried away, she pulled back, her breaths heavy. "Little did I know a dozen years ago I'd make out in my school cafeteria one day."

He chuckled, still holding to her. "I think we should drive to Raleigh and try this in mine."

Her nerves pinged with an expectancy she hadn't felt since the day Matt first asked her to marry him. She'd told Trey her greatest sin—something she'd even kept from her family—and he hadn't recoiled from her. In fact, he'd acted as though she'd been an innocent victim in the matter. She was far from innocent. Her opinion hadn't changed on that score. But she hadn't allowed herself to accept this level of forgiveness in over a decade.

Then God added a bonus.

Not that she hadn't wanted to kiss Trey on Monday. Heaven knew she had. And it hadn't taken a genius to see he'd wanted to kiss her, too. She'd wasted so much time on guilt, on fruitless relationships, on denying her feelings for Trey. No more.

But tonight—

"Where do we go from here, Reagan? I've waited for you for too long to settle for a few minutes of"—he grinned—"absolute amazement. I hope it meant more to you than an emotional response to what we shared earlier."

A pity kiss? Was that what he thought? No pity for his past, just sorrow over what he went through.

First, it was an awful scene for a young teenager to see. What had his father been thinking to take his son to a fire? She imagined Trey as a boy, experiencing such a frightening sight and imagining himself lying on the ground. She understood how it scarred him to the point he believed he could never meet his father's definition of a man of courage.

Second, the incident in college. What did he suppose he should have done? Confront a man with a gun unarmed? She could name plenty of people, herself included, who might have ignored the raised voices or turned around and run in the other direction. He'd investigated. He'd set out to help, and he had helped, solely by his presence.

But he was right in saying they needed to talk. Before they pursued a romance, she had to heed Kaine's warning and be honest with him. She had to tell him of her call to Marshall Burnside.

She still believed selling the kennel land to Briar Park better benefited the town. From now on, though, she would support Trey, even if it meant the other company needed to find their land elsewhere.

"You are one of the bravest people I know. I also think you're one of the most desirable guys on the planet. I wish I had realized it long before now. In fact, I think I did months ago, but I wouldn't allow myself to accept it." Reagan placed a palm against his cheek. "Trey, there's something—"

"There you two are." Brianna marched through the cafeteria doors, a smile on her face. Then, her eyes bulged at seeing the two of them standing so close to one another. "Uh-oh."

Shaina nudged Bri with her elbow and added in a loud, harsh whisper, "I told you we should have left them alone." She flashed Reagan and Trey an apologetic grin, then tugged on Brianna. "They're all right. Now let's go back to the dance and collect."

"Collect what?" Reagan dropped her hand from Trey's cheek. Her narrowed glance slid from one to the other of their intrusive pests.

Trey laughed. "I think some wagering went on in the gym after we left."

Reagan glared at her sister and friend. "Please tell me he's wrong."

Brianna started backing toward the door. "No money was involved, just an ice cream at Locke's."

Someone should tell her college-educated sister that the ice cream would cost someone money. But who? Who else wagered a treat at Locke's Soda Fountain on her relationship with Trey?

"We should probably return to the dance, don't you think?" Trey placed a hand on her back. He leaned closer and whispered, "Time to see who won."

As they walked out the door behind Shaina and Brianna, he caught her hand in his. An hour ago, she wouldn't have imagined his boldness. An hour ago, she would have pulled free, believing she'd only hurt him in the end. Now, she took pleasure in holding his hand, in standing at his side when they faced their unrepentant, gambling friends.

One look at them walking hand-in-hand into the gym brought an array of smiles from the members of their close-knit group . . . and others. Until that moment, Reagan hadn't realized how many people were invested in seeing them happy together.

Sutton—the one person she'd been sure had bet against them—slapped Trey on the back in a show of approval. More and more lately, Sutton had seemed to accept being in the company of the Hartwell sisters, but how would he react if he discovered those same sisters kept secret Paige's potential return to Hidden Veil?

Well, she wouldn't worry about Sutton and Paige's relationship right now. She had her own to focus on and cherish.

Awesome. Incomparable. Romantic. Dozens of adjectives describing the night trotted through Trey's mind.

He dropped his keys on the kitchen counter and nearly danced to the sink for a glass of water. Catching his reflection in the window, his smile grew broader. He hadn't stopped smiling since that kiss and the ones in the parking lot after almost everyone else had left the school.

Until tonight, he hadn't let himself believe in a future with Reagan, but now there was potential. He'd confessed to who he was, his failings, and it hadn't repulsed her.

Other things in his life and business were coming together. He even had an appointment with Oren and Zeke at the attorney's office a week from Monday to sign the leases for the Burnside property.

Thank you, God.

After returning to the gym tonight, he'd asked for Sutton's advice regarding repairs to the kennel. Now may be the time to tell Reagan about Forever Faithful. Surely, she wouldn't object if she knew of the full use of the land.

The door opened and Kaine walked in. He'd already left the dance by the time Trey and Reagan returned to the gym. That was almost two hours ago. Where had he been?

Trey noted his brother's unsteady movements, not staggering but not completely stable. "You okay?"

"Sure." Kaine's foot caught on a kitchen chair leg. He caught himself before he fell, and then kicked the chair.

"You've been drinking."

"I had one beer, Dad."

Trey wrestled with the urge to rush into the garage and assure himself Kaine had wrecked his SUV. "Have a seat. I'll make some coffee."

"I don't need coffee. I don't need a babysitter."

No, he needed an attitude adjustment.

Trey put on a pot of coffee. With the direction of this conversation, *he* could use some. Kaine's moping around and dodging his situation had emotionally exhausted Trey. Tonight, he would discover what happened in Idaho or write off his brother's problem.

Once the coffee was done, he poured two cups and took them to the table, handing his brother one. "Be straight with me, Kaine. Let me help."

"Big brother to the rescue?" Kaine gulped the coffee. He winced and set the cup down. "Hot."

Obvious by the steam swirling from the surface of the drink. "What do you need rescuing from?"

Kaine covered his eyes with his hands and ran them down his face, and Trey waited. Finally, his brother's hands fell away. His bloodshot eyes had turned watery. "The nightmares." Kaine's voice was low and husky and—for once—without anger or defensiveness.

Trey thought back to last night's conversation with him and his emphatic refusal to consider a job teaching skydiving. "Do those nightmares involve planes?"

Kaine drew in a quick breath, and his eyes grew wide. He sat that way for several moments, staring at Trey and saying nothing.

"I won't take no for an answer this time. Tell me what's going on." Evidently, a time of mind-blowing bliss at the high school had pumped him with determination and self-assurance.

"You wouldn't understand."

"How do you know? You haven't told me. Give me a little credit." When Kaine remained quiet, Trey tried instilling a smile into his voice. "Don't make me call Dad."

Kaine huffed a laugh. "You would, too." He wrapped his hands around the hot cup. "I loved my job. It gave me a rush like nothing else—the thrill of a free fall, the hard work on the ground, the sounds, the smells, the challenges. More breath stealing than any extreme sport, you know? Satisfying. Until real life smacked me in the face."

Trey clenched his teeth to keep from speaking, from disturbing his brother's story. He admired Kaine for his courageous choice in careers. Trey's blood ran cold at the image of parachuting into a place that could turn his skin into ash, leaving his body like—

"She died, Trey."

His brother's subdued words burst the image in Trey's mind, the one that sometimes showed up in his dreams and left him drenched in sweat. "Who died?"

"Her name was Allie. Allie Stanton. We worked together. We . . ." Kaine swallowed. "I figured I'd ask her to marry me one day, but I put it off, thinking we had plenty of time."

"Oh, man, I'm sorry." Trey had never seen the brother he'd often considered a ladies' man as a grieving lover. As much as he wanted to prompt Kaine to continue, causing him more pain didn't sit well with him. Still, he wanted to know. How could he help unless he knew the whole of his brother's story?

Kaine inhaled a shaky breath. "The fire was a small one. No worries. Of the eight of us, Allie jumped last. Then the wind shifted."

At Kaine's pause, Trey's stomach twisted with anxiety.

"We fought to keep our chutes from carrying us too far from the landing zone. It was brutal. I twisted my ankle when I hit the ground."

"That's why you limped when you first arrived in Hidden Veil. Why didn't you say something then?"

"Allie was strong, but not strong enough to control her chute that day." Kaine went on as though he hadn't heard Trey. "She went off course, and it tangled in a tree. When the wind shifted, it also shifted the fire. I tried to reach her in time, Trey, but I couldn't get near enough." He covered his ears. "Even over the roar of the fire, I heard the screams."

Trey reached out and laid a hand on his brother's shoulder, unable to say anything but, "I'm sorry."

Kaine breathed deep, no doubt fighting the memory. "I didn't lie when I said my boss wanted me to take vacation time. What I didn't tell you was that I quit my job during our meeting. He expects me to change my mind once I've had some time to clear my head, so he called it a leave of absence. He didn't believe me when I said I could never go back up."

"Kaine, what happened was unfortunate, but you tried to save Allie."

"And I failed! I should have done more."

"What else could you do?"

"I could have shown more guts and rushed into the flames."

"You battle flames with every fire. You show plenty of guts, more than I would. Kaine, you would have died, too."

"Maybe I should have."

"You don't mean that."

"No, I don't. Because I know who was responsible."

Trey drew back at the muttered words. "I don't understand. Who?"

After several moments of silence, Kaine drew in another ragged breath. "Forget it. How did things go with Reagan?"

More secrets. How many did his brother hide?

While he could say more, try harder to ease Kaine's guilt, Trey respected his brother's wish to veer the subject away from himself. He wanted his brother to be happy for him, yet didn't want to rub salt in Kaine's wound, so he kept his answer simple. "We worked things out tonight."

Kaine's shoulders sagged, as though the statement brought him relief. "Good. She told you."

"About Matt? Yes. How did you know?" She said she hadn't told anyone else.

"Matt who? I'm talking about some dude named Marshall."

Marshall? "Burnside?"

"She didn't mention his last name during the call."

"What call?"

"The one I overheard last week." Kaine leaned back in his chair, his jaw hanging. "She didn't tell you, did she?"

Trey's stomach clenched with dread. "What did you overhear?"

Kaine rubbed his forehead. "You know, I had more than one drink tonight. Now, I have a headache." He rose from the chair. "I think I'll head upstairs."

Trey blocked his brother's way and stared into his face. "Honesty, remember?"

"Fine. I walked over to the clinic last week and found her in the parking lot, talking on the phone to someone named Marshall about Briar Park. It was clear she was against your lease."

Every muscle tightened. So Oren didn't tell Marshall about the lease. Reagan did. Why? She didn't get along with him. And she'd been asked to keep the information to herself. Instead, she'd talked to Marshall behind Trey's back. Was that what his brother had meant when he said Trey had no idea what some people hid from him? What else did she hide?

"She asked if he knew about the lease, then told him they had a common interest—a sale of the property. From what I could tell, Trey, he tried to pressure her into making you change your mind."

Trey doubted it took much pressure on Marshall's part. He recalled Thursday night's conversation and her attempt to persuade him from his plan. And here he'd thought she'd been concerned about his business success.

It was one thing for her to attempt to talk him out of leasing the kennel. It was another for her to work with Marshall Burnside against him. For her to double-cross him.

"If it helps, I think Reagan really cares about you, Trey. I don't think she wanted to be disloyal to you."

But that hadn't stopped her, had it? *I heard Marshall Burnside and wanted to be sure everything was all right.* Really? Or had she wanted to be certain her role in his visit remained a secret?

Twenty-five

Reagan turned onto her street and spotted Trey's truck parked in front of her house while he sat in a chair on her front porch. She grinned with relief. Good. He wasn't sick. When he hadn't shown up for church this morning, she sent him a text but received no response. Afraid he was ill she had intended to head to his house after lunch to see if he needed anything.

This was different. Her worrying about a guy and wanting to check on him.

After parking in the driveway, she climbed out of the new Honda. "There you are. I wondered where you were this morning. Did you get my text?"

He met her halfway across the front lawn. She almost stood on her tiptoes to kiss him, but drew back at the scowl that warned her not to take one step closer.

"We need to talk, Reagan."

Shadows haunted the skin under his eyes, like he hadn't slept last night. Maybe he was sick. Or the chill skittering down her back could mean it was something more serious. "Okay. Come on in."

She unlocked the front door, and he followed her inside. Quill whimpered from his crate, his tail beating the wire. She released him. "Do you mind if I take him outside first?" It would give her time to get a handle on Trey's black mood.

When he didn't object, she took Quill out back, returning a few minutes later to find him on the couch, his shoulders slumped, hands clenched together, and his focus on the floor.

Time to get this "talk" over with. "What's wrong, Trey?"

Bouncing around his legs, Quill tried to get Trey's attention but failed, so the pup laid down on the kitchen floor with a soft groan.

"Tell me you haven't been working with Marshall Burnside behind my back."

Her lungs deflated until she couldn't draw a breath to speak. She should have guessed he'd found out. "Trey . . ." What could she say other than the truth?

"You were told Oren wanted the information kept from his son until he'd made his decision." Trey raised his head and met her gaze. Reagan shrank back a step at the hurt she saw in his eyes. "I knew you were against my idea for the kennel, but I never thought you'd take steps to derail my plans."

"What about those who need what Briar Park can provide, a place of healing, comfort, and reassurance for the people of Hidden Veil? People you rely on for your livelihood."

"There are things you know nothing about, Reagan."

"If you're talking about Oren, Marshall—"

"I'm not talking about Oren. I'm talking about people in

need of service dogs—the deaf, the blind, people with PTSD and anxiety issues. People like Alex Newman. People like the blind man who lived in our neighborhood years ago. I've been talking with a friend. Zeke's organization wants to lease the land to use as a facility to train service dogs for the disabled. I want to help support that lease with proceeds from the boarding kennel."

Reagan stood speechless. Why hadn't he told her? She thought of Paige's little girl, Leyla, a child she'd never met. Would she benefit from a service dog trained to alert her to trouble she couldn't hear? How many others would benefit? "You should have told me."

"I didn't intend to tell anyone until we'd signed the paperwork. Why should I have told you, Reagan? It didn't concern you."

"Didn't concern me? You knew my feelings about the future of the property. If you'd said something—"

"I didn't expect you to agree with everything I did or said. You're welcome to your own opinion. But I thought I could trust you to have my back and not stab me in it." He pushed to his feet with the spryness of an eighty-year-old and said under his breath, "Matt dodg—" He pressed his lips shut.

Reagan gasped. Had he really almost said Matt dodged a bullet by not marrying her? Heat whooshed through her, from her scalp to her toes. "Talk about stabbing someone in the back! I didn't tell you what happened so you could make light of it. You know what? You're no better than Matt. You made your plans without even considering anyone else." Well, that wasn't quite true. He had a good cause in mind. That didn't take away the hurt of his throwing her past in her face, or the sting of being left in the dark, as Matt had done to her.

"I shouldn't have said what I did." Trey walked to the front door and stopped. "What happened at the dance last night won't happen again."

He shut the door behind him as Reagan stood rooted to the floor of her living room. She watched as he passed by the front picture window and marched across the lawn to his truck on the street. In moments, he'd driven off, leaving her unsure whether the shaking of her body meant she was angry, sad, worried, or guilt-ridden. All four vied for the top spot in her emotions.

Quill sat at her feet, looking up at her and whining. "You're a male. What plans have *you* made behind my back?"

What a week.

Trey stared at the wall in his office. It started when he learned of Kaine's tragedy, of the potential sister-in-law he had lost before ever meeting her. The next day, Sunday, his brother acted as though nothing bothered him. Now that he knew the truth of what happened, Trey's patience with his brother kicked into higher gear. The only time he'd lost it was when Kaine tried to talk him into ignoring what Reagan had done.

This week would go down in the history of his life as a total disaster.

He'd waited three long years to experience Saturday night. Three years of fearing it would never happen. When it did, it was worth every minute of the wait ... until he learned of Reagan's deception and his misjudgment of her. Now, they tiptoed around one another at the clinic, speaking only when the job demanded it.

Shaina pretended like nothing was wrong, but he'd caught her watching both of them. Clearly, Reagan hadn't confided in her, and Shaina showed the wisdom not to inquire.

He didn't want to lose Reagan's professional skill, but how long could they continue to work this way? When could he trust her and when should he be on guard? What would she do next to prove herself disloyal to him? What else didn't he know about that she had done?

It was like walking down a dark alley at night and having someone jump out of the darkness. Like coming across an armed thief and turning to stone.

Various impulses had flowed through him over the past five days. Follow Kaine's advice and forgive her? Fire her? Let it all wash over him and pretend nothing happened—with Burnside and at the dance? With each question, he thanked God he had come to his senses before becoming one more of her rejected admirers. But he couldn't find any satisfaction in knowing he had done the rejecting.

In addition, since Burnside's visit, multiple people had cancelled their appointments. Not that people didn't cancel or reschedule regularly. But these made a point of telling Shaina they would never use the Abbott Veterinary Clinic's services again and why. Evidently, Marshall had made good on his threat.

After a quick rap on his door, it opened, and Shaina peeked around the thick panel. "The mayor is here to see you."

His dropped chin almost hit his chest. A visit from the mayor. Just what he needed. "Show her in, please."

Less than two minutes later, his door opened again and Mayor Hildenburg strode inside his office as if she were once more a teacher and walking into one of her old classrooms— authoritative and no-nonsense.

Trey stood. "Hello, Mayor."

"Dr. Abbott." The stern woman, somewhere in her late fifties, crossed her arms and spoke his name in a way that prompted him to wait for her instruction to go to the principal's office. "What's this I hear about a plan to lease Oren Burnside's property?"

Conducting their impending conversation while standing only added to the combativeness in their postures. Trey gestured to the chair across from his desk. "Please have a seat."

She accepted, but her gaze never left his face. "Well?"

"You've talked to Marshall?"

"He came to me with his concern."

His concern over being unable to control his father's money, no doubt.

"I've also talked to county officials. Oren Burnside has paid the taxes he owes. Is that your doing?"

"No." It was Reagan's. If she hadn't worked to sell the dogs, Oren could never have paid what he owed. That burned in Trey's gut. Being opposed to his idea didn't stop her from helping Oren and his animals. "What do you know of my purpose for the property?"

"I know you want to bolster your business by using the kennel facilities to board animals. Ordinarily, I would applaud your ambition and welcome the tax revenue for the county. However, this time it comes at the cost of your neighbors' welfare."

Of her constituents. He inhaled a heavy breath. That wasn't fair. Yes, she was a politician, but she cared about the prosperity of the town and its people. "Mayor—"

She raised a hand like she hushed a student. "I also understand Forever Faithful intends to lease most of the acreage at your suggestion."

She knew quite a bit. Trey neither confirmed nor denied, but let her continue with whatever point she had to make.

"I admire your purpose, Trey." She'd softened her voice, probably to put him at ease. It had the opposite effect as he waited for a lead-filled shoe to drop on his toes. "The organization, while worthy, brings little of value to Hidden Veil. How many local people need their services? How much revenue will the county gain? Will the employees and visitors frequent the restaurants and shops downtown?

"Briar Park will provide nursing and rehabilitation services, as well as jobs. They want Oren Burnside's property, but if they can't purchase it, they do have a second location in another county in mind." She leaned closer. "As a fellow citizen of Hidden Veil, I'm appealing to you to consider your neighbors before it's too late."

The words came across as a threat more than an appeal.

Was his plan selfish? She hadn't handled it right, but was Reagan justified in trying to stop him? Whenever he thought about the way she'd gone behind his back—

The mayor stood. "I've had my say, and I can't stop you. I'll leave it to you to do what's right, Dr. Abbott."

Dr. Abbott. She may as well have used his full legal name. "I'm not sure I can disappoint Forever Faithful at this late date."

Or if he wanted to. "But I will give your request more thought."

"Thank you."

Trey followed her to the door and watched as she disappeared down the hallway, heading for the front exit. He stepped back into his office as Reagan left an examination room. They eyed one another. Sympathy mixed with hope on her face. She had heard part or all of the conversation.

The look didn't last long. Her jaw hardened, and she walked away without saying a word.

Twenty-six

Early Saturday morning, Reagan pulled up to the barn at Crooked Creek Ranch and parked alongside one of the other five vehicles. At certain times of the week, like today, the horse ranch changed hats and became Healing Springs Equine Therapy Center. She slipped out of her car and looked around. Two volunteers were in the arena setting up for those coming to heal from mental and emotional traumas.

Lane Becker had accomplished amazing things after allowing his place to be used to help veterans and first responders. Here, they learned to control their anxieties through working with horses. The gentle personalities of the animals brought calm to stressed out men and women whose memories reflected the horrors of their time in service to the country.

"Hey, Reagan." Lane walked out of the barn, a smile on his face as he wiped his hands on a rag. "Are you here to sign up as a volunteer, or to see Macie?"

She hadn't been able to bring herself to volunteer. Not yet.

Not when it required spending time among former military men and women. Too many memories. But she hoped to move beyond that with help. "No, to both. I'm looking for Ron Gregory."

His brows arched. "Oh. He's in the office. Go on in."

"Thanks."

She walked into the building that Lane and Matt's father had built as a workshop years ago. Last year, Lane converted it to an office for the psychologist. It was also a place of rest and fellowship for those using the services of Healing Springs.

Ron sat on a couch, laughing with a man covered in tattoos and whose face hid behind a bushy beard. When he saw her, he stood. "Can I help you?"

She held out her hand. "I'm Reagan Hartwell. We met at the sponsor's picnic last year."

"Oh, sure." He shook her hand. "I thought I recognized you. You were engaged to Lane's brother, right?"

"Yes."

"If you're looking for Lane—"

"I've seen him. You're the one I'd like to talk to if you have time."

He checked his watch. "I'm free for another fifteen minutes. Come on back." He led her to the tiny room at the rear of the building—large enough for a small desk and office chair and one other chair in the corner. "Once Lane and Macie marry, I'll move into what is now the downstairs bedroom of the cabin."

"I'm sure you can't wait."

Last year, Monte Becker had spoiled his nephew's original plan to house Ron's office in the cabin near the barn. While Lane was away, his uncle hired Macie as their cook and housekeeper and promised her the place as a home for her and her son, Alex.

"I'll have more room, but I've grown accustomed to this place." He shut the door. "Have a seat and tell me what's on your mind."

She sat in the corner chair. "I'm not here for free advice, Dr. Gregory. I expect you to bill me."

"It's just Ron." He moved behind the desk and settled in his chair. "We can hash out any potential billing later."

Reagan rubbed away the sudden chill on her arms. "I'm here because of Lane's brother." Using as few words as possible, she told Ron of her reservations about becoming a military wife, the letter she wrote to Matt, the years of guilt played out with Oreos and a day spent in bed, her choice of dating men she knew would never be a lifetime partner, and her habit of sabotaging her relationships. She swallowed. "I'm asking," she tried to laugh, making light of her situation, "do I need your type of help?"

He'd listened with his hands tented at his mouth, his eyes never leaving her face. Now, he folded his hands together on the desktop and leaned forward. "You must think you need my help, or you wouldn't be here."

Did she really need him? Since reciting her list of sins, she felt better. For now. But how long would that last? She rose from the chair. "Never mind. I can handle it. I'm sorry for taking your time."

Ron sat unmoving, studying her in a way that tingled her nerves. "Are you sure you can handle it, or are you running from your problems?"

She'd never thought of her actions as running, more like

saving the lives of others.

"If you don't want to do what's necessary to change, Reagan ..." He'd softened his words, but his brown eyes still pinned her. "You may be correct, and you're not ready for help."

Somehow, hearing those words signaled her to sit down again. Was she ready? How could she move forward with someone else—no longer Trey—when the past still hung over her head?

He's large enough to carry any burden or wound, even the ones that make our knees buckle with the memory.

But God often worked through others, didn't he?

A few minutes later, she drove away with Ron Gregory's card and an appointment for next week.

"I may be dragging you away from your work for nothing."

Sutton settled in the passenger seat of Trey's truck, his head almost hitting the roof, and a tool kit at his feet. He shut the door. "Sounds like you're about to give up."

"I may have no choice." Trey turned onto the road in front of the Vance farm. "People aren't happy with my decision."

"People like Reagan? The grapevine says the two of you broke things off."

The grapevine? Who planted that root? Reagan? Shaina?

Trey had asked Sutton to give him an idea of the cost and time frame to renovate Burnside Kennels to accommodate his boarding facility. The last thing he wanted to discuss was his fiasco with Reagan. "Oren's son threatened me. I've lost patients.

And the mayor paid me a visit." He stopped at the red light in town. "Am I being unreasonable in keeping Briar Park from kicking an old man out of his house and tearing the place down?"

Sutton stared out the side window. "Let's wait until I've seen the place before I give you an answer. Have you signed the lease?"

"When I spoke with Oren about coming today and told him about his son's anger, Oren assured me he hadn't changed his mind about the property. He still plans to sign Monday afternoon."

"You ignored me about Reagan."

"I did."

Trey drove down the highway toward the kennel and his clinic farther south. A dark cloud lifted into the sky in the distance and a faint acrid smell seeped through the truck's vents. "Is that smoke?"

Sutton bent forward to peer out the windshield. "Looks like it."

A surprising sense of urgency hit Trey, and he mashed down on the accelerator until reaching a speed fifteen miles per hour faster than the posted limit. As he reached the turnoff to the road in front of Burnside Kennels, his heart pounded like a hammer on concrete.

He turned and sped up the bumpy road, the source of smoke now clear.

Sutton whistled. "Oh, man."

At the top of the driveway, Trey hit the brakes. The truck skidded on the rocks. Oren stumbled out the door of the kennel building, followed by a half dozen dogs. The older man fell to his knees, coughing. Sutton jumped out of the truck and ran to him, helping Oren to his feet.

A dog barked from beside the truck, dragging Trey's attention to the side window. A black Labrador Retriever stared up at him, his brown eyes showing no fear, only pleading. It jumped on the truck's door and barked again, seeming to plead for him to hurry and do something.

To man up.

Your power, Lord.

Just those three words—that silent plea—gave Trey the strength he needed. He burst into motion, hopped out of the truck, and ran while pulling his phone from his pocket. He reported the fire to 911, then asked Oren, "What happened?"

The old man coughed while staring at the building. "I don't know. Marshall."

"What about him?"

"He yelled at me to leave." Oren coughed and wheezed. "I don't see him."

Trey glanced at the structure. His heart rate skyrocketed, along with his breathing. "Marshall is inside the building?"

"The puppies in a back compartment and my wife's dog ..." He suffered another coughing fit. "Maybe he went after them."

No other dogs came out. Trey stared at the flames.

His brain ordered him to check, to move. His body countermanded that order. He remained mesmerized by a tower of flame shooting through a hole in the roof over the office area of the building. The odor of smoke already choking him. Visions of the burned body of the firefighter from his past flashed before

Trey, followed by a woman trapped in a parachute and hanging from a burning tree. His hands shook, and he stood there for what seemed hours until his gaze slid to Sutton.

Greater love has no one than this, than to lay down one's life for his friends. And an enemy?

"I see that look on your face, Trey. That isn't a smart idea." Sutton gazed at him over Oren's head. "Wait for the fire department."

The flames grew in intensity. It had only been a minute, but no sign of Marshall or the remaining dogs. Minutes meant life and death.

Man up.

He eyed the flames at the front of the building as embers swirled upward in the air. Dogs barked from inside. He set his jaw and forced his feet to move. "Stay with Oren and keep the other dogs out of the way of firefighters." Trey jogged to his truck, grabbed a hand towel from the cab's console, and took off over Sutton's protests.

He found a faucet at the side of the building and wet the towel. With cautious steps, he entered and closed the door behind him, hoping to deprive the fire of some much-needed oxygen. Flames roared and crackled at the front of the building, but the smoke—his deadliest opponent—rolled toward the center, not yet so thick he shouldn't be able to spot Marshall. He glanced around, but saw no sign of the man. Meanwhile, the dogs' barking faded into whines and whimpers.

Trey flattened his body as low as possible. Holding the wet towel against his nose and mouth, he crawled across the concrete floor. His fear screamed to reverse course and wait with Sutton and Oren for the fire department to arrive. But something else he couldn't explain drove him forward, despite the panic knocking inside his chest.

He lowered the towel. "Marshall? Marshall!" No answer from Oren's son.

Renewed howls and desperate barking guided Trey through the smoke and heat, which seemed to seep through his skin and into his lungs. He coughed and wiped away the perspiration running into his eyes. His dad had equipment and turnout gear to back him up. Trey had a towel.

Coughing again, he approached a compartment to his left and saw movement inside. Dogs, but no sign of Marshall.

He used the rag to protect his fingers as he opened the metal gate, then slapped the cloth back over his face. Two large dogs rushed out. He shooed them toward the door, where Sutton's form filled the entrance. The farmer grabbed each dog and flung them out the door.

"Trey?"

"Stay there."

Nearby, the sounds of whimpering drew his attention, and he saw three puppies pressed against the fencing of the rear-most compartment. He opened the door and scooped them up. A fourth pup lay on the concrete, panting. It wouldn't survive much longer.

Sutton crawled a few feet inside the doorway. "Any sign of Burnside?"

"No." Trey's voice croaked, and he coughed.

"Give them to me and get out!"

Trey handed over the three puppies and dragged out the fourth. Sutton disappeared out the door, crawling and coughing. The fire snaked over the ceiling. Trey shoved the fourth puppy across the floor toward the door for Sutton to find, because he knew his friend would return. Time was running out for him and Marshall. He called the man's name as he crawled, but it was getting harder to breathe, much less speak.

He figured he'd been in the building for about three minutes. His lungs ached and his breaths grew shallower in the poisonous smoke. The crackle and whoosh of the fire filled his ears, and the heat threatened to scorch his skin. Over it all, he heard another bark—deep and feeble.

And something else. Coughing? Marshall?

An eerie calm washed over Trey. Turning, he crawled toward the sounds. If his father could see him now, he wasn't sure whether Dad would be proud or call him all kinds of an idiot.

In a matter of seconds, he reached a corner. There, on the floor ahead of him, near the compartment with Mrs. Burnside's "baby," a man lay face down. "Marshall."

The guy stirred and tried to push himself up. Trey tossed the towel aside and helped him to his knees. Both of them stumbled toward the aisle leading to the doorway. Sutton appeared and grabbed hold of Marshall.

Trey stopped. "Take him." Did he have enough time? Even though his chest hurt, he could last another minute if it meant another life saved. He turned around.

"Where are you going?"

He didn't waste time or oxygen answering Sutton's question. In moments, he'd let the senior dog out of the compartment and pushed him toward the door. Before he reached the safety of the outdoors himself, a massive crack caught his attention, and something fell from the ceiling. It hit him on the left shoulder and rolled down his arm. Instinctively, he reached out with his other hand and brushed at it. Rolling on the concrete, he smothered the flames on his shirt sleeve as he gasped for air. Pain burned through the skin on his arm and the tips of his right fingers.

With no more breath to cry out, Trey collapsed onto the concrete.

Twenty-seven

Had it only been one week since she admitted to herself and Trey that she had feelings for him? A week since he had discovered she was the one who told Marshall about the lease? A week since he'd made it clear her feelings for him were no longer welcomed?

Reagan stepped out of the clinic. She'd spent the morning caring for the three dogs and one cat recuperating in cages. She'd enjoyed the time alone, without the stress of working side-by-side with someone who despised her.

Maybe despise was too strong a word for his feelings, but he'd been clear that she'd let him down. Well, he'd let her down, too, by not being forthcoming about his plan for the Burnside acreage.

And if he had told her? Would it have changed her mind? She thought of little Leyla's hearing loss. Surely, the child could use a support animal trained to alert her to voices or danger. Paige had said Leyla received a blow to the head from a baseball one day, because she missed shouted warnings from a group of boys playing in the park.

Reagan approached her car. She sniffed, and her nose crinkled at the odor of smoke hanging in the air. It didn't smell like trash. Maybe dead tree limbs?

She drove out of the clinic's rear parking lot. Turning onto the highway toward her home, she spotted a dark swirl of smoke ahead. Close by. In fact, it looked like it came from— *Oh, no.*

When she reached the road to Burnside Kennel, she turned and pulled up the drive. Flames shot from the kennel building. Had the dogs escaped? What about Oren?

She bolted from her car as a man ran inside the burning building. Sirens shrieked and two fire trucks and an ambulance sped up the drive.

Spotting Oren kneeling on the gravel next to Marshall, Reagan dashed to them. "Are you all right?"

Marshall nodded his head, but it was clear from the coughing and pale skin he'd inhaled too much smoke.

Tears ran down Oren's face. Whether from smoke or fearful sadness, she couldn't say. He pointed to the building. "Trey and his friend pulled Marshall out. They're still inside."

"Trey?" Reagan looked around. How had she missed seeing his truck? "He went in there?" She gestured to the burning kennel. After what he'd told her about his fear of fighting fires, she couldn't believe Trey would enter a burning building.

Yet, she could. Despite what he believed about himself, he was a born rescuer.

Reagan scrambled forward when she saw Sutton backing out of the doorway, dragging something. *Oh, God, please.*

Sutton lowered Trey to the ground, then bent over, hands on his knees, coughing.

Reagan ignored the scrapes on her legs from sliding on the

gravel beside Trey—as though she slid into home base. That's what it felt like. He was her home base. Her destination. Her eyes filled with tears at seeing the red and blistering skin on his arm and the shirt with blackened holes. She touched his cheek. "Trey?"

He moaned and coughed, conscious but lying there with his eyes pressed shut.

Shouts and orders flew through the air from the firefighters behind them.

Sutton gasped. "I thought he would follow me out." His voice and cough were hoarse and congested. "When an old dog came out, and he didn't, I went back inside. I found him on the floor."

Firefighters broached the building, followed by two paramedics. A few feet away, Mrs. Burnside's favorite old boy flopped on the gravel next to a panting puppy.

"Quick! These men need oxygen, and there's a puppy in need of a pet oxygen mask." Reagan knew the fire department had the masks, because Trey had donated three in various sizes a year ago.

Firefighters attacked the fire, but the two paramedics responded to her call, carrying the necessary oxygen. One rushed toward Marshall. The other ran to Trey.

Reagan prayed as she stood back to give everyone room. In moments, an oxygen mask covered Trey's nose and mouth. A male paramedic checked Trey's vitals, while another firefighter held up an oxygen mask for Sutton, who rejected it until the woman insisted. The paramedic's partner helped Marshall to a stretcher and loaded him into the back of the ambulance as another ambulance arrived.

A firefighter had retrieved a small pet oxygen mask and gave much-needed air to the distressed yellow Lab puppy, possibly a sister to Quill. Reagan took over the treatment of the animal to free the man to join his comrades fighting the fire. Behind her, it snapped, roared, and popped ... violent sounds and sights that reminded her of Trey's story.

Sutton drew in a few inhalations of oxygen and handed the mask back to the paramedic. "I'm good."

"You sure?" At Sutton's sour expression, the paramedic gave him the once over, then seemed assured Sutton wouldn't expire on his watch. He shrugged and returned to attending to Trey.

The old dog whined next to Reagan. With the puppy revived, she took a moment to pat his head. "She'll be all right, Bud."

Reagan looked around. Another pair of paramedics arrived with a stretcher and stopped next to Trey. "You're taking him to the hospital?"

"Yes, ma'am."

The fire chief gestured to the Lab in her arms. "You'd better get that girl to a vet. The Abbott Clinic is down the road."

Reagan pointed to Trey. "This is Dr. Abbott."

"Oh. I didn't recognize him with the mask on."

Lying on the stretcher, Trey pulled down his mask. His gaze, filled with pain, locked on her. In a croaky whisper, he said, "Take her," then slid his mask in place. They rolled him, eyes shut and mask on, to the waiting ambulance.

Reagan stood torn. She wanted to follow him to the hospital, but could do nothing more there than sit and wait. Her time was best spent doing her job. "I'm his tech. I'll take her."

On the mile to the clinic, she called Carolyn and gave her a brief report about the fire, Trey, and the dog she was transporting. "I know you haven't started work yet, but I'll need help at the clinic."

"I'll see you in a couple of hours."

"Thanks."

After calling Carolyn, Reagan pulled in behind the clinic building. She took time to send up another prayer for Trey and the other men before she left the car.

Rushing into the hospital that evening, Reagan's Crocs barely made a sound on the tile floor as she searched for her friends.

"Reagan."

She whipped around at the sound of Jo's voice behind her. Kyle walked alongside Jo, both carrying drink trays. "Hey."

Jo handed her a cup of black coffee. "We heard about Trey but couldn't get here until the shop closed. How is he?"

"I just got here myself." Reagan had worked with Carolyn to care for the pup at the clinic. After blood work and x-rays, Carolyn determined they would keep her for the weekend, but that the smoke inhalation had caused no permanent or critical injury.

They reached the waiting area where they found Lane, Macie, Kaine, Shaina, Brianna, and Sutton waiting. Kyle and Jo passed out drinks.

Macie took a cup from the cardboard tray. "You are an angel. The coffee here is awful." She turned to Reagan. "How is the little dog?"

"She'll be fine. The new vet is staying with her for now."

"I thought she didn't start until next month."

"I called her." Reagan was more concerned about Trey. "What is the latest?"

Lane stepped up beside her. "The doctor told Kaine she treated the burns on his arm—first and second degree."

Second degree? Painful, yet it could have been much worse.

"She wants to keep him overnight and maybe a couple of days because of the smoke he inhaled, but she doesn't see any major damage."

Reagan released the breath she'd held during his report. "Good. What about Marshall?"

"They treated him for smoke inhalation, too. He refused to stay overnight, so they released him. Mr. Burnside was fine and said he'd take his son back to his place to monitor him."

Sutton stared at her from his seat along the wall. She walked over to him. "Did they check you out?"

"There's nothing wrong with me." His gruffness sounded even more surly with the hoarse voice. "It's Trey who needs the help."

"If you hadn't dragged him to safety, it would be too late to help him." She swallowed the sob that threatened to escape. "Thank you, Sutton."

A nurse entered the space. Her eyes widened. "Are you all here for Dr. Abbott?" A chorus of yeses filled the room. She zeroed in on Sutton. "You should be home resting."

He eased back in the chair. "Soon."

The nurse looked around. "You can't all see the patient this evening. Whoever you choose has five minutes. Visiting hours will be over soon. Who is closest to him?"

Eight pairs of eyes homed in on Reagan. Hadn't they heard that Trey wanted nothing to do with her? Only Sutton avoided looking at her. It gave her the idea he probably knew everything.

"Kaine should go in. He's family." Something she would never be.

Before Kaine or anyone else could respond, an older couple

appeared in the waiting room doorway, the woman's face frantic. "Excuse me," she said to the nurse. "We're looking for—"

"Mom?" Kaine made his way through the group to greet them. "Glad you came."

The petite woman's eyes watered. "Oh, Kaine." She grabbed her son.

Kaine had to bend forward to accept her hug. When he straightened, he provided his parents with a short update on Trey's condition, then gestured to the others. "Mom, Dad, these are our friends."

Reagan shrank back. Seeing Trey's parents added an extra layer of guilt and sadness. A week ago, she would have been eager to meet them. Now, she sought an escape, a way to slip past them and out the door. Evidently, she *was* that runner Ron described.

Tears tumbled down Trey's mom's face. "Thank you for caring enough to be here for our son."

"Sutton pulled him from the building." Kaine gestured to the only person who remained seated, as though he wished to hide, too.

Mr. Abbott walked over to shake Sutton's hand. "That was brave of you. We're grateful."

Sutton bounced to his feet. "He's the brave one, sir. Not me. He saved another man's life and wouldn't give up until he'd released all the dogs." He shot a glance in Reagan's direction. It hinted that he aimed the comment at her.

"How did the fire start?"

Leave it to a professional firefighter to ask that question.

"I don't know. The kennel was on fire when we got there. Oren and his son tried to remove the dogs but couldn't get them all. When the son didn't come out, Trey went in, found him, and let the rest of the dogs out of their compartments."

Sutton's explanation sounded simple. Too simple.

Mr. Abbott nodded, his Adam's apple bobbing as though he fought against his emotion. At least Trey's father now knew what kind of man he'd raised.

For a long time, even before he'd saved the teen, Reagan had known that heroism was a part of Trey's nature. For even longer, she had fought against falling for a hero type again. She lost the fight. She'd also lost the guy.

How had the fire started? Her stomach twisted at the idea that flashed like neon in her head. She didn't want to believe Marshall was responsible, but he had the opportunity and the motive. And it was oddly convenient that the kennel would go up in flames now.

The nurse approached Mr. and Mrs. Abbott. "You're the parents?"

Trey's dad, a solid-looking man with brown hair like Trey's, graying at the temples and on top, nodded. "How is he?"

"I'll take you to see him. We'll talk on the way."

Once they had disappeared into the hallway and their footfalls faded, Reagan grabbed her chance. "I'd better relieve Carolyn. I'll see y'all later."

She didn't wait for goodbyes but slipped out the door and almost ran to her car, trying to outrun the tears. If she was right and Marshall started that fire to keep Trey from leasing the property, she could lay the blame at her own feet.

She'd almost destroyed another man she loved.

Twenty-eight

Trey jerked awake, bursting through the nightmare that had placed him back inside the burning building. He grimaced, and his arm protested. Movement in the hospital bed reminded him of why he was here. Who was he to complain, though? He'd suffered relatively minor burns—treated with an antibiotic cream and covered by bandages. Painful, but not life threatening. The smoke produced the diciest injuries. Irritated eyes and shortness of breath, a chest that ached like someone pummeled him. Everything combined had earned him a weekend hospital stay.

If Sutton hadn't pulled him out of that building when he did, though . . .

No ifs. Thanks to God—and Sutton—he'd survived his brush with fire. He would be uncomfortable for a while, but he'd faced his fear of fire. He'd also found Marshall and freed the trapped dogs. The way God had used him made the pain bearable. He was alive, but in his weakness, God showed His strength and faithfulness.

The door to his room opened. He expected another nurse.

They had marched in and out over the past hours.

"Hey, son."

"Dad? Mom. Kaine called you?"

His father closed the door behind them, and his mother planted a kiss on his cheek. He hated seeing the tears flooding her eyes. They stood as close to the bed as they could get, considering all the medical equipment.

"Your brother knew we'd want to be here." Mom swiped the moisture away and sniffed. She moved to take his hand, then noticed the bandaged fingers. "How are you, baby?"

"I'll be fine, Mom." He chuckled at the endearment that said he'd always be a child in her eyes. The effort constricted his chest, and the result of the smoke forced him into a coughing fit.

"Of course you will. In the meantime, you'll sound like a frog." Dad grinned as if he'd told a joke at a party not tried to cheer up his son in his hospital room. "From what we hear, you did an amazing job, Trey. We're proud of you."

It took almost dying in a fire to hear those words from his father? Seeing the worry in the man's eyes kept Trey from saying something he'd regret.

"We've always been proud of you." Mom frowned at Dad, then turned to Trey with a smile. "Your friends have filled the waiting room."

"I'm not surprised." He coughed and winced at the pain in his sore throat. Flattered and humbled, but not surprised. "They're good people."

"Besides your brother, there must have been seven or eight others out there."

Trey wanted to ask if Reagan was among them, but he didn't. Part of him wished it were true, that she sat in the waiting room, anticipating a time to visit. Another part of him tried to destroy that wish, as she had destroyed his trust in her. More than likely, with no one to stand in for her, Reagan remained at the clinic, caring for the injured puppy and leaving him with his conflicting emotions.

He still saw her watery stare while he laid on the ground, gasping for air. Worry. Fear. Love? He couldn't be sure. And right now, what did it matter?

A nurse in blue scrubs poked her head around the door. "I'm afraid your time is up for tonight. He needs his rest."

Mom ran a hand over his hair as though he were six, an expression of her love for him. "Is it okay if we stay at the house?"

"No need to ask, Mom. Make yourselves at home." He didn't have the energy to care about the condition of his house when he left it this morning. His mother would probably find something to clean, anyway.

"We'll see you tomorrow." She slipped away from his bedside, followed by his dad.

Trey shut his eyes, but sleep eluded him. He wanted to talk with someone who understood how much it took for him to turn his back on his fear and rush into that burning building. He could talk to Kaine, but his brother wasn't the one he had in mind.

He imagined Reagan sneaking down the hallway and slipping into his room, defying the orders of the nurses regarding visiting hours. A slight lift of his lips caught him off guard. It would be just like her.

Then he recalled why she had no reason to visit him, even during visiting hours.

Intentions worked best when uninterrupted by outside forces.

Reagan decided that would be her new motto.

After picking Quill up at home, she had prepared to go straight to the clinic. But the lingering smell of smoke in the air seeped through the open window of her car and invited her to turn onto the road leading to Burnside Kennel. What remained of the kennel.

She pulled onto the property, seeing Marshall's Lexus still parked near the house. She'd almost convinced herself the visit had more to do with checking that none of the remaining dogs had suffered ill effects from the fire than confronting Marshall Burnside about its origin.

Almost.

Once Reagan left the hospital, her mind on what happened that afternoon, a seething fury built deep inside her. It rose like an angry tide. She aimed most of that anger at Marshall, convinced he started the fire to give Oren and Trey no choice but to abandon a lease. Although Marshall would have discovered his father's arrangement without her interference, she reserved a portion of her wrath for herself. If she hadn't become involved, if she hadn't run to him with the news, she wouldn't feel this overpowering guilt. She wouldn't have lost Trey.

She left Quill in the car and started toward the house, then detoured toward the shell of the burned building. The choking smell of smoke hung over the blackened, roofless walls. It irritated her eyes and throat—a minor irritation compared to what she imagined Trey and Marshall experienced. A few of the dog compartments remained. The rest were shells of concrete block and blackened chain link fencing. Oren's office at the front was a total loss with melted equipment and the charred skeleton of the dusty couch she'd sat on a few weeks ago. Briar Park would have bulldozed the building—a quick, merciful removal compared to this gloomy sight.

Barking came from the fenced area behind the building, answered by the muffled yaps of Quill. She would work harder to re-home the rest of Oren's dogs. With her suspicion about Marshall Burnside, she feared for the safety of those left.

"Can I do something for you?"

Reagan turned. Marshall's hulking presence stood out against the waning light of the day. He didn't intimidate her on a normal day. Now, his slouch, hoarse voice, and reddened eyes gave her the impression of a sick, exhausted man, rather than an arrogant one pleased with having ruined someone else's plan.

She considered asking him about his health and that of the remaining dogs, but she was in no mood for easing into conversation. "What were you thinking to jeopardize the lives of people and animals?" Another question wanted to intrude into her fury. If he started the fire, why go into the burning building to save the dogs? She pushed it away.

"What are you talking about?"

"I know how badly you wanted your father to sell his property and not lease it. So bad you threatened Trey and his business. So bad you decided to burn down the building?"

"Burn—" Marshall's eyes widened. "You think I started the fire, risking not only my life but Dad's? As for threatening Dr. Abbott, I warned him to consider the good of the community." He took two steps toward her. She held her ground. "You wanted to stop the lease, too. I could claim *you* started the fire."

"What?" Was he crazy? "You know I didn't arrive until it was well underway. But you were already here. What better way to ensure the lease fell through than to make the property unusable for Trey's purpose?"

A heavy breath escaped Marshall. The man had perfected the

condescending sigh. "It's been a long day. My father is tired. I'm not recovered. Go home."

He hadn't denied her accusation. "I can't go home yet. I'll spend the night at the clinic, watching over the puppy that suffered from smoke inhalation. She's doing well, in case you're interested. Trey is . . ." Her voice caught. "He's in the hospital, and you and I are to blame."

"I appreciate Dr. Abbott's efforts to save me and the dogs. Dad and I regret his injuries." He stepped away, then turned back. "No, I did not want my father to lease to Dr. Abbott, but I would never risk physically hurting someone, not even the dogs. If you spread your delusion to others, you'll find yourself faced with a defamation suit. Now good night."

As he trudged toward the house, Reagan wrestled with the itch to follow him and continue the argument. But she'd had her say. She'd wait for the Fire Marshal's report before pursuing it.

Trey finally convinced the doctor he was well enough to go home. No smoke in his lungs. No infection. Each day, the discomfort would subside until the worst of the burns healed in two or three weeks.

He entered his house on Monday afternoon, his mom lagging behind, prepared to catch him if he fell. There were two problems with that scenario. First, he was perfectly steady on his legs. Second, if he fell, she wasn't strong enough to catch him.

It was good to be home, but he preferred to be at the attorney's office, signing lease papers. The destruction of the kennel building destroyed that possibility. While trapped in the hospital, he had called Zeke. Without the income from a boarding kennel, he could no longer afford to supplement Forever Faithful's rental of the property, so he'd suggested his friend look for another location. That should please Marshall and the mayor.

And Reagan.

Once they reached the breakfast room, his mother hustled in front of him on the way to the kitchen. "Let me fix you something to eat, Trey."

"No thanks, Mom. I ate lunch at the hospital." When her face fell, he said, "But I could use some water."

She smiled. "Coming up."

Using his left hand, the fingers of his right still bandaged, Trey dug his phone from his back pocket. He winced at the tenderness in his arm. "I need to call the clinic."

"I'm sure Reagan has everything under control. I had hoped we'd meet her at the hospital, but I understand your absence required her time."

Trey brushed off the unspoken question in that last part. "She can handle a lot of the appointments. Others require my attention." He sat at the table and used his left index finger to press the icons that would put him in touch with the clinic.

Yesterday, his friends stopped by the hospital after church. Even Oren had called. Kaine came with their parents but stood in a corner of the room, saying little. Given that fire caused his injuries, Trey understood.

Even Oren and Marshall visited for a short time. Long enough—and only long enough—for the son to express his gratitude for what Trey and Sutton had done. Trey figured, had it not been for Oren, Marshall would have provided his appreciation through a phone call. Maybe even an email.

Everyone visited but Reagan. She sent a message through her sister. He could appreciate the awkwardness of a visit by her, but each time the door to his room opened, he had expected to see her face.

Brianna said Reagan hadn't attended the church service after spending the night at the clinic. However, she mentioned her sister had dropped by the hospital on Saturday evening. That brought him an odd bit of satisfaction.

Shaina picked up his call, and he said, "Hey, Shaina."

"Trey, how are you? Are you home?"

"Just got here. Tell me what's going on." He raised the glass his mother placed on the table in front of him, causing a twinge of pain in his arm. His chest still ached some, and his throat remained irritated. Overall, he was thankful to be alive to feel the discomfort.

"We've rescheduled a few appointments. Otherwise, it's business as usual. Carolyn and Reagan are seeing patients, and—"

"Whoa, back up. Carolyn is there?" She wasn't supposed to start until mid-June.

"Reagan called her Saturday. She's been incredible. They've both been incredible."

Why should he have worried about his practice? Reagan had always kept the place running with precision. She hadn't let him down in this instance. As a vet, he could trust her with anything. Not so on a personal level.

After another couple of minutes of updates, Shaina passed his call to Carolyn. She sounded professional and busy, informing him she had released the puppy to Marshall Burnside this morning. He'd paid the full charge without argument.

Grateful for the smooth continuation of his business through the efforts of three conscientious women, Trey hung up and focused his thoughts on what was next.

"Dad, when do you think the fire investigator's report will be ready?"

His father shrugged. "Probably later this week. Why?"

"Just curious."

With nothing to do in the hospital but think, it occurred to Trey that Marshall benefited most from the fire. He found it hard to imagine the man's greed being great enough to burn down his father's property. Still, Marshall would get what he wanted.

Twenty-nine

"Are you sure you don't need us to stay a little longer, Trey?"

"I think we've stayed long enough, Sue. He's fine and eager to get back to work. Aren't you, son?"

"Dad's right. I'm fine."

Trey had listened from his chair in the sunroom late Tuesday afternoon as his mom and dad discussed their plan to leave in the morning. He had to admit that they were a big help the past couple of days—both of them—but he was ready for them to leave. Mom hovered and Dad watched both his sons in a way that freaked them out. Like he had something to say, but stewed over whether he wanted to say it.

Kaine had made himself scarce since their parents' arrival. Trey wasn't sure if it was due to not wanting to discuss his situation with their father or if Trey's burns reminded him too much of Allie's death. He hated to think his injuries tormented Kaine.

Mom rose from her chair. "I'll say goodbye to Lulu, then start supper." She walked out the back door and crossed the yard.

"Your mom fell in love with that goat after she scared her yesterday. The silly thing fell right over, as stiff as a steel beam. Ever since, she's treated that animal like a member of the family."

Trey chuckled. "I'm afraid Mom and Kaine will have to fight me for Lulu." His brother would roll his eyes, but a slight smile would give him away.

Dad watched as Mom loved on the goat. Lulu ate up the attention. When his mom finished, she came back through the sunroom. His parents exchanged pointed glances before Mom entered the kitchen, closing the French doors behind her. Trey had no time to ponder the silent message his mother sent before Dad leaned forward in his chair, his expression reflecting an edginess Trey had noticed more than once since his parents' arrival. He would put it down to concern over his injury, but it seemed something else was afoot.

Dad cleared his throat, another sign he didn't want to discuss something as innocuous as UNC's football chances next season. "I've been wanting to talk to you and Kaine." Dad offered a tight grin. "I only wanted to do it once, but since Kaine has gone AWOL and we're leaving tomorrow—and while your mother is occupied inside—I may as well say my piece to you now. I'll talk to your brother later."

Trey's shoulders tensed at the gravity in his father's voice.

"I owe you an apology. I've owed you one for a long time."

"An apology?" Not one to admit weakness or wrong, where was Dad going with this?

"As you know, I've always taken pride in our family's devotion to fighting fires." He frowned. "Years ago, your mother reminded me that pride comes before a fall. And she was right. I fell back when you boys were teens, but you and your brother suffered the consequences. I've been unfair to you, Trey. I should never have bullied you over your choice of career."

The subject of his father's apology took its sweet time to sink in, and Trey could only nod his acceptance of it.

"And I shouldn't have gotten angry when Kaine talked about his decision to leave firefighting. That's a discussion I'll have with your brother."

Kaine hadn't mentioned that conversation. How much had he told their parents? Had he explained his reaction in light of Allie's death? Based on their parents' lack of reaction and sympathy, Trey doubted his brother had gone that far. In that case, neither would Trey.

"I knew how the death of that man affected you as a teen, but I pushed you anyway." Dad shook his head. "I convinced myself it was temporary and with time, you would change your mind. You were an Abbott, after all. Being a firefighter was in your blood." His smile didn't lighten the heaviness in his eyes.

"It's true. The incident sickened me." Trey fought against touching the burns on his arm. "But I'd wanted to be a vet long before then, Dad. Maybe if I'd spoken up earlier and not led you to believe I had an interest in firefighting ... Honestly, I never wanted to disappoint you."

"You've never disappointed me, Trey. Not really. I'm the one who disappointed you by acting like a child and treating you as though you owed me something—owed me your future. Even though I knew your passion for animals, I acted like my way was the only way and you couldn't decide your future for yourself.

"It shouldn't have taken almost losing you for me to say how proud I am of the man you are and the life you've built here. It's clear you care about your community and you have friends who care about you."

God had blessed his time in Hidden Veil with great friendships. And the community? Some perceived him as going against the town's—the county's—citizens by not giving up *his* purpose for one that would bring happiness and security to locals.

"I let family tradition affect our relationship, Trey. For that, I'm sorry."

Trey had waited years for those words. Now that he'd heard them, he had a choice. He could hold on to his resentment or do what he knew was right. "God has forgiven me more times than I deserve, Dad. You've done the same. I can't deny you my forgiveness."

"Thank you."

"I'm glad we finally talked this out, Dad."

"Me, too. We should have talked long ago."

Trey swallowed, faced with the irony of his forgiveness. He'd found it easy to absolve his dad of the hurt he'd caused him. What about Reagan? Shouldn't he forgive her?

But that was different, wasn't it? Like Dad, she opposed his intention, but she went beyond opposition to actively working against him. As he'd accused her of doing, she'd stabbed him in the back, and the pain was as raw as the burn on his arm.

Then again, she thought he worked against the people of Hidden Veil. Was he as guilty as Reagan?

"Why do you believe you're responsible for Matt Becker's death, and you also endangered Trey?"

Reagan shifted in the chair across from Ron Gregory's desk at

Healing Springs. Ordinarily, the smell of the hazelnut coffee in his cup would appeal to her, but her nervous stomach had begged her to decline the offer of her own cup. Wouldn't Bri love to know her hard-as-rocks sister not only fought a case of nerves but sat here pouring her faults out to a stranger? "I know I didn't shoot the weapon, and I didn't start the fire at the kennel, but I contributed to the damage both did."

"Matt was a soldier in wartime, Reagan."

"A distracted one."

"Because you sent that letter."

Reagan came within a hair's breadth of rolling her eyes. "Yes." This was her first full appointment with the psychologist, and she counted the minutes until it ended.

"Did Matt contact you and ask you to change your mind about breaking your relationship with him?"

"He called. I didn't answer."

Ron's curious gaze speared her. "Why not?"

"I was hurt and angry. I didn't want him to change my mind and figured he'd contact me again when he calmed down. I guess he had no chance before . . ." She clamped her lips together.

"You've taken a lot of responsibility for that incident on yourself. Have you ever considered that it's misplaced?"

Misplaced? "How? Given Matt's everyday circumstances, I was selfish to hit him with something like that, right? Shouldn't I have waited until he came home on leave?"

Ron leaned back in his chair, fingers wrapped around his coffee cup. Very casual. Very disarming. "What if you'd waited, then he returned to duty and suffered the same fate? Would you still blame yourself?"

A little voice in the back of her mind insisted Matt might never have come home alive, even if she'd waited and talked to him in person. "I'll never know, because it didn't happen that way."

Ron set his coffee cup on the desk and picked up his pen. He twirled it in his hand. "We all do things we regret, especially out of anger. It doesn't make you a selfish, uncaring person."

How long had Ron practiced that comforting smile in the mirror? "Even if trying to get my way hurts someone else?"

"Are we talking about Trey now? You made a mistake by going to the son behind his back, but your purpose was not selfish."

She had spent the first twenty minutes of this session rehashing her sad story, up to and including her betrayal of Trey, who returned to work yesterday. She had tried to apologize to him for not visiting him in the hospital, and for being wrong to trust Marshall Burnside. She got out only a half-dozen words before he brushed her off.

"Is that supposed to excuse me from my guilt?"

"It's supposed to remind you that you are human with human reactions." Ron made a few notes on the pad in front of him. "Are you a believer, Reagan?"

"A Christian? Yes." Why was he asking?

He set down his pen. "Then let's say you're right. You've led a self-centered life, and it's resulted in disturbing consequences. Don't you think it's time to turn your guilt over to God, ask Him to remove it, and work on changing your attitude toward relationships?"

You can't change Matt's fate, but you can allow God to change you. Trey had said those words the night of the dance. "How do you know this guilt isn't part of my ..." Sentence? Punishment?

"Penance for Matt's death?"

Penance? Antiquated, but it would do.

"Do you think God works that way?"

Did she? "I think there are consequences to our actions."

"True. There's also mercy. From what I see, you're the creator of many of your consequences. You're afraid to make a life with someone, so you sabotage your romantic relationships. You can't forgive yourself, so you take one day a year to inflict punishment on yourself."

"I've asked for forgiveness."

"But have you accepted it? Or are you convinced you're too far gone for His grace and mercy?"

Do you believe some things are too much for that sacrifice to cover? He's God, honey. He's large enough to carry any burden or wound, even the ones that make our knees buckle with the memory.

Why did she keep hearing Trey's voice in her head? Their relationship died before it really got started. She'd killed it. She'd sabotaged it.

"I don't know what to do." That sounded frantic.

One side of Ron's mouth slid upward in a sympathetic grin before he turned serious again. "If you've asked for that forgiveness, then God has granted it. To Him, it's forgotten. It's time to move forward. Learn from the past and leave it behind."

Move forward? She thought she'd finally accomplished that with Trey. She'd come to terms with the past enough to love someone again. Now, that man no longer wanted her. "Are you a psychologist or pastor?"

He laughed. "Think about what I said, Reagan, but don't worry. We'll work through this together."

A few minutes later, at the door, she peered over her shoulder at Ron. "What would you have advised if I'd said I wasn't a

Christian?"

"I had a sense you were." He smiled and pointed to a plaque on the wall beside her, one she hadn't noticed earlier. It read, "God makes all things new." He followed her out of the office. "I'll see you in ten days."

Outside the workshop-slash-psychologist's office, she opened her car door, physically and emotionally drained from the visit with Ron. All she wanted to do now was to settle into her recliner at home, watch a lame movie with Quill draped across her lap, and forget her troubles.

"Hey, Reagan. Wait up." Lane jogged toward her, something in his hand, and a sheepish expression on his face.

"What's wrong?"

"Nothing. How are you?"

He was asking about her session with Ron, something she had no desire to share.

When she chose to not answer, Lane raised his empty hand. "I put that wrong. I don't want details. Just remember, Macie and I are here for you."

"I appreciate the offer." One she would never accept.

He held up a stack of envelopes. "I'm embarrassed that I didn't get these to you sooner. They were in a box my parents stored in the attic after the military sent back Matt's belongings. None of us wanted to open it. Over the years, we forgot about it." He shrugged. "We never wanted to deal with what was inside."

Reagan understood. She spotted the handwriting on the top envelope, and her heart jumped into her throat. Her handwriting. Her letters to Matt. With all that had taken place since the dance, she had forgotten his mention of them.

"I thought you might want these back." He held out the

bundle. "Don't worry. No one has read them."

Staring at the bundle tied with twine was like staring into the face of a cobra. Reagan couldn't look away, couldn't move. Somewhere in there lay her last communication—her ultimatum. Should she find it and march back into Gregory's office and let him read it, so he could see the horrible things she'd written? The depths of her selfishness?

Eyes stinging, yearning to shed tears, she wanted to tell Lane to shred the letters. The words remained bottled up inside.

"Reagan?"

With an unsteady hand, she snatched the stack and dropped it on the passenger seat of the car. "Thanks." Her voice was little more than a croak. Before backing away, she rolled the window down. "And thanks for keeping them private, Lane."

He nodded and waved.

While navigating the long driveway, she glanced at the stack of yellowing envelopes. Ron said it was time to move forward. One letter in that group represented her biggest failure. What should she do with it, with all of them? She could toss them in her nightstand, or she could do as she'd almost asked Lane to do—shred them.

For now, she would add Matt's letters to hers, the ones she'd stashed in the drawer beside her bed. She'd decide what to do with all of them later, when she could think straight.

Thirty

Trey rushed into the church twenty minutes later than he'd planned and hoped he hadn't kept everyone waiting to start the wedding rehearsal.

He'd worked late nights with rescheduled appointments and paperwork that had piled up when he'd only spent a few hours a day at the clinic. Without Carolyn helping that first week, he'd be way behind right now. The woman's competence as a vet matched her ability as a team player.

With his approval, Shaina had hired a new tech who started Monday. So far, Morgan had adjusted well. Not quite in Reagan's league, but she was also less experienced.

Reagan . . .

Several times since he'd returned to work, he'd caught her eyeing his injured arm, but couldn't tell whether the inevitable wince was one of pity, regret, or disgust.

He hadn't thanked Reagan for calling Carolyn and providing her with a place to stay. Not because he'd had no opportunity. He couldn't bring himself to speak to her unless the work called for it.

"Trey." Sutton raised a hand as if prepared to slap him on the arm, then lowered it, evidently recalling the injury. "Better?"

Tomorrow would be three weeks since the fire. Although his arm and fingers had mostly healed, some scarring would remain, a reminder of a day that provided a kind of redemption for his previous failure to act. "Better. Almost healed." The burns, not his heart. That would take longer. "No side effects with you?"

"Nah."

"Thanks again for all you did."

"Forget it. You'd have done the same for me."

Trey imagined himself trying to drag the man who bested him by six inches and about forty-five pounds. He might manage it with an adrenaline boost.

Sutton gave him the side-eye. "I'd say you dodged a bullet regarding that lease. I heard old wiring caused the fire."

Dodged a bullet. How had he allowed himself to use that phrase—or almost use it—while arguing with Reagan? "That's what the investigator said."

He couldn't deny his relief at the close call. Had he opened his boarding kennel and lost other people's animals to the fire, it could have ruined him. As for the dogs, Reagan and Oren had already re-homed most of them, which put less at risk that day.

For Oren's sake, Trey was grateful Marshall had nothing to do with the fire. The old man had called Trey often to check on him. He relayed how Reagan had gone off on Marshall, accusing him of starting the fire that burned down the kennel. How he wished he'd been a fly around their heads during that exchange.

One thing Oren told him stuck with Trey. He said Reagan not only blamed Marshall, but she blamed herself.

Her contact with Marshall drove a wedge between them.

Now, his pride in her warred with his failure to forgive her. She hadn't set out to hurt him. He believed that. Until he came to grips with what she'd done, he'd keep her at arm's length. Something impossible to do tonight. He had to walk down the aisle with her during the rehearsal.

And again during tomorrow's wedding.

He stood at the entrance to the sanctuary. Sutton eased alongside him, and they watched the group of people gathered around Lane and Macie at the front of the room—Lane's parents and Uncle Monte, Macie's parents, Alex, Jo and Kyle, Pastor Jim, and Reagan. She turned Trey's way as though she'd heard her name spoken in his head.

He looked away. "Did I miss anything?"

"No. The Beckers were stuck in traffic leaving Wilmington. They pulled in a few minutes ago. They've all been hugging like they hadn't seen one another in years." Sutton voiced that last sentence like announcing a plague.

Trey guessed the Vances weren't a demonstrative family. Given the dynamics, he could understand. When his parents left to return home, Trey had hugged his dad harder than he had in years. It felt good.

"The wedding is tomorrow."

Trey tried to hide his grin. "I know." That's why they had gathered here tonight.

Sutton sighed. "Everyone's getting married." Again with the side-eye. "You're next."

"We don't have time for this conversation."

"Maybe you don't remember, but she was almost hysterical seeing you lying on the ground half-alive."

"Don't be dramatic."

"I don't know what came between you two, but she's here.

You see her every day. Take this opportunity to make things right."

A chance Sutton hadn't had with Reagan's sister. What if Reagan disappeared like Paige? Would Brianna spill her location? Provided, of course, he asked.

"A lack of trust isn't something to ignore, Sutton."

"Yours or hers?"

A woman deserves a man who'll share with her his dreams and plans, not make them without consulting her.

Trey had spoken of Matt, but hadn't he done the same? Reagan accused him of it, and she was right. He hadn't been forthcoming with the secondary purpose for his wanting Burnside's property. Although he'd thought he had a good reason to keep it to himself for a while, by not revealing to her the lease for Forever Faithful, he may have driven her to go to Marshall. Once he explained, she'd been less resistant to the idea. So the trust factor?

"Both. We both broke the trust between us."

Clearly, he had some thinking and praying to do.

Reagan watched as Trey slipped out the door of the small fellowship hall. They had walked down the aisle together during the rehearsal and sat within speaking distance of one another at the dinner table. Yet he said little to her tonight or during the past two weeks at work.

After he arrived at the church, Trey and Sutton carried on a seemingly intense conversation. The whole evening, Trey never cracked a smile. He seemed distracted to the point he'd missed some of the pastor's instructions. She kept him in her sight all evening and, once in a while, she caught him watching her, too. What should she make of it, and how long could she stand his cold shoulder?

If she sought a new job, would Ron tell her she was running?

The Beckers said goodbye to the family members who had attended the rehearsal dinner. Reagan waited in a corner, trying to breathe.

Macie joined her while Lane took a couple of wedding gifts already presented to the couple out to his truck. "Why are you sitting here by yourself?"

"I'll head out shortly." She hated to admit she waited to leave until sure Trey had pulled out of the parking lot.

Macie glanced over her shoulder at the nearly empty room. "Were things too awkward tonight?"

It looked like she wouldn't avoid the topic. "A little, but we'll learn how to handle being together without 'being together.'" She emphasized the last two words with air quotes.

"I wish I could do something for you."

She nudged Macie with her shoulder. "You can focus on your marriage and living happily ever after."

"I almost forgot." She dug into a back pocket of her jeans. "Lane gave you the letters."

Reagan nodded. She'd thrown the batch in her nightstand with the others that day and hadn't opened the drawer since.

"Did he tell you we dropped them in the attic?"

"No."

"We thought we'd gathered them all before tying them together with the twine." Macie held out an envelope. "I found this on the floor beside another box yesterday. One we'd overlooked."

Reagan stared at the envelope. More specifically, she stared at the postal date. This was the one, the last letter she had written

Matt. The one that led to a tragedy Ron Gregory insisted was not her fault.

She'd never believed in out-of-body experiences, but watching her arm straighten and her fingers clasp the letter delivered what must be a similar sensation. It didn't burn her skin like she'd expected. It didn't cause her heart to stop. It was simply paper and ink. Deadly ink.

Something odd struck her about the feel of the envelope. She turned it over and—

"Macie, did you reseal this envelope?"

"No. We took it out of the box like that. Why?"

Reagan studied it a little longer. "I don't understand."

"You are white as a polar bear, Reagan. What is wrong?"

Her gaze locked on Macie, and she whispered, "I didn't kill him."

"Kill who?"

She held up the envelope, flipping it front to back. "It's sealed. Matt never opened it. He never knew."

"Knew what? You're scaring me." Macie's eyes widened. She glanced at the others in the room, then lowered her voice to match Reagan's. "Are you saying you thought something in that letter led to Matt's death?"

Reagan shoved the envelope back into her friend's hand. "Read it."

"Are you sure?"

She couldn't say why she wanted Macie to read the letter. Maybe it was a first step in no longer running from the consequences of the past. "Go ahead."

Almost as if the object were sacred, Macie slid her index finger under the flap with care, separating it from years of attachment to the rest of the envelope. She unfolded the single sheet of unlined paper inside, the message short and anything but sweet.

After reading, Macie sat a moment, then folded the paper again, slid it inside the envelope, and handed it back to Reagan. "Did you mean what you wrote?"

Reagan nodded. "Yes. After he died, I received his last letter. In it, he said he wanted us to get married. I thought it was a reaction to my letter."

"Would you have changed your mind?"

"I don't know."

"You hide away each anniversary."

"Because I've blamed myself for his death. I thought my rejection preoccupied him, and he let his guard down." Reagan breathed a pathetic half sob and half laugh. "Could that sound any more conceited?"

"You're talking to the woman who thought, had she been on that raft with her husband and son, her husband wouldn't have died." Macie wrapped an arm around Reagan's shoulder. "It's called guilt, and it's misplaced. The seal proves he never saw your letter."

"Ron Gregory used the word misplaced with me."

Macie smiled. "Where do you think I heard it?"

Reagan glanced at the Beckers as they said goodbye to Pastor Jim. Fay Becker looked her way. She must think Reagan and Macie appeared too serious. Even across the room, Reagan felt the woman's curiosity. "They're nice people."

Macie followed her gaze. "They are."

She had grown tired of secrets. Matt's. Trey's. Her own. "Should I tell them the truth?" What if they hated her afterward?

Macie said nothing for several moments, focusing on the floor. "Given the situation, why would you?"

Because she had repaid Matt's parents' kindness by letting

them think she would have waited for and married their son. "It's something I probably shouldn't keep from them anymore."

Pointing to the envelope, Macie asked, "Will Fay and Cliff be better off knowing? Or will you be the one better off because it eases your conscience?"

Was that the real reason Reagan wanted to share? Was she thinking only of herself once more?

"If you believe what you wrote still matters, then talk to them. Otherwise, why stir up sad memories?" Macie squeezed Reagan's hand. "On a brighter note, after talking to Lane, we met with Oren Burnside. When we return from our honeymoon, we'll pick up the puppy you saved from the fire. Alex is beyond excited."

"That's terrific. She's sweet." The news reminded Reagan there were still a handful of dogs left at the kennel. She hadn't summoned the desire to work on finding them new homes.

Fay and Cliff Becker crossed the room toward them. When Macie saw her soon-to-be in-laws approaching, she hugged them, told everyone goodnight, and went to find Lane.

Reagan slipped the letter into her pocket. "Mr. and Mrs. Becker—"

"Why so formal, honey? You used to call us Fay and Cliff."

"I know. I just ..." Didn't feel she deserved to show such familiarity? That had changed, hadn't it? Even though she saw them at the sponsor event at Healing Springs last year, she said, "It's been a while, Fay."

"It has." The woman's eyes darkened with a sorrow Reagan suspected would never go away when something or someone reminded her of Matt.

Macie was right. Why torture them with memories that affect only her?

Cliff grinned. "We're glad to see you and Macie hit it off."

"She's a good friend, and she'll make Lane an excellent wife."

Fay nearly bounced on her toes. "And we love Alex, too."

Reagan hugged this couple who, at one time, expected her to join their family. "Time for me to leave and let you rest back at the ranch. See you tomorrow."

Reagan walked out of the church building, her mood lighter than it had been all night. Sitting in her car, she closed her eyes. *Thank you, God, for the knowledge that I didn't cost Matt his life. And thank you for providing Macie to keep me from making another mistake, one that would bring nothing but sorrow to Cliff and Fay.*

A few minutes later, she pulled onto her street to find Trey's truck in front of her house. Again.

Thirty-one

Trey should have waited until after the wedding to do this. He risked things going further south.

But no, he had to settle things between them. It had been hard enough walking down the aisle with her tonight. To do it again tomorrow, during a ceremony he'd often prayed they would experience for themselves? Nope. It had to be done tonight.

Reagan pulled into her driveway. With her attention on him, she wasn't watching where she was going. He held his breath, half-expecting she'd roll through the fence in the backyard. His breathing eased when she stopped in her usual spot under the carport.

He left his truck and met her halfway across the yard. "Hi."

"Is something wrong? An emergency?"

"No. Nothing like that. I was hoping we could ride out to the lake . . . to talk."

She studied him a moment, then her head bobbed. "I'd like to take Quill. He hasn't had his exercise today."

"I'll wait here while you get him."

After the way he'd acted lately, Trey had prepared to be grilled on the reason for the trip before she said no.

Neither of them spoke during the drive to the lake. Reagan sat in the shotgun seat of his truck with Quill tethered in the back seat, poking his head between them.

Trey parked in the lot used to launch the kayaks last month and dropped his glasses into the console's cupholder. While Reagan attached Quill's leash to his collar, Trey walked around and opened her door.

They ambled through the calf-high grass toward the dock near the boat launch. From the opposite shore, the laughter of children skimmed across the surface of the lake.

"What is this about, Trey? You've ignored me for weeks. Suddenly you want to stroll by the lake?"

That was the Reagan Hartwell he knew . . . and loved.

Their footsteps echoed on the dry wood of the dock as the sun dropped lower in the sky and added a golden glow to the water's surface. Trey stopped at the edge and stuffed his hands in the front pockets of his jeans. He stared at the water. Its calm and peaceful flow contrasted with the waves of apprehension sloshing in his stomach.

"I don't blame you for being upset with me, Reagan. I've acted like a jerk."

"Oh, really?"

He glanced at her, standing at his seven o'clock. The slight smile and humor in her eyes took the sting from the question. "Really."

She joined him at the edge and gave Quill a hand signal to sit.

She said nothing for a few moments, then exhaled. "I don't blame you for your reaction to what I did, either. I was untrustworthy, not acting like a friend or a faithful employee. I'm sorry for going to Marshall behind your back. I'm sorry for thinking your reasoning for the kennel was self-seeking."

She didn't realize how right she was about him. He took a chance and reached for her hand, pleased when she didn't snatch it back. "Marshall would have found out soon enough."

"But he—"

"He did nothing I wouldn't have done. Well, I probably wouldn't have thrown threats around or talked people out of using his business."

"No, you wouldn't."

The passion in her voice lessened some of the turmoil inside him. "I could have told you about Forever Faithful the day you found me meeting with Oren." The day he'd supposed she lingered in bed, feeling sorry for herself.

"I understand why you didn't mention it. You wanted to be certain the deal would work. You wanted all your ducks in a row as my dad would say. It still hurt not to be included."

"I know."

Quill barked at a blackbird that landed on the dock a few feet away. Reagan kept a tight hold on the leash when he lunged for it.

"It's true that I wanted the lease to work out before word spread about the service animal training center. But it wasn't my main reason for keeping it secret." Moistness from nerves clung to his hand, and he let go of Reagan. "You were right. It was self-seeking. Part of me expected a pat on the back. After all, the mayor pushes for good publicity and building the town's image. What a great way to show the town had heart." He huffed his disgust. "Truthfully, I did it to build my ego. I saw myself as doing something noble, something heroic. Something to help me gain your respect and everyone else's. I think I recognized that and didn't like it."

"Oh, Trey." She reached over and squeezed his hand, thankfully the uninjured one. "You've never needed to prove anything to me or anyone else around here. People see you as a good, caring man. It's how I see you."

But was what she saw enough to love him for the rest of their years? "I also pushed Forever Faithful for a personal reason."

"What?"

"I told you about the robbery in the woods. The guy who thought I saved him?"

"I remember."

"That guy was Zeke. He's with Forever Faithful."

Her head bobbed with her understanding. "You used Oren's property as a way to pay him back for letting him think you ran the off the thief."

"If I were to delve deep into it, yeah. That's what I was doing."

"You did run him off. If you hadn't investigated the loud voices, there's no telling what would have happened." She wrapped her arm through his, avoiding the still tender scar along his upper arm. "My sister has a little girl with partial hearing loss. When you told me about the organization, I pictured Leyla being helped by a service dog for the deaf."

"Paige has a daughter?" How would Sutton react if he knew?

"Two daughters and a son. All adopted."

Three children. While Trey didn't know the details of Sutton's break with Paige, he knew the farmer nixed the idea of kids of his own long ago. "You and Brianna rarely speak about your sister."

"When Paige left Hidden Veil, she wanted a clean break, which meant keeping a certain someone from contacting her. None of us agreed with how she handled it—well, Brianna was too young—but we went along with her request. People stopped asking about her years ago. We don't discuss Paige with others and won't until she's ready."

"Sure." He wouldn't breathe a word to that certain someone.

"What will Forever Faithful do now that Oren signed a contract to sell to Briar Park?"

"They'll continue to look for a place. I hope it's around here." Trey grinned. "Once word got around about the organization, Hidden Veil's mystery philanthropist donated ten thousand dollars to them."

She gasped. "Really? First it was ten thousand to help with Ryan McCormack's kidney transplant, then ten thousand to Healing Springs, now the same to Forever Faithful. All anonymous. I'm seeing a pattern and am dying to know who is behind all the charity."

"Whoever it is, it's clear they want to keep their donations private."

"What about the boarding kennel?"

"We'll put that on hold for now, but I'm believing something will come up down the road."

She reached down and ran a hand over Quill's head. "I saw your parents at the hospital. They worried about you."

"Whatever the age, no one outgrows a parent's concern. Dad apologized for his attitude toward me."

"That's great, Trey."

He focused on the approaching sunset. "Dad also apologized to Kaine."

"Why?"

"I only found out a few weeks ago, but Kaine lost someone special recently. Because of it, he left the fire service. Not knowing the reason, Dad expressed his unhappiness."

"A repeat of history?"

Trey nodded. "Similar. Kaine finally told Mom and Dad the story. It seems the Abbotts are good at keeping our business close to the vest until we're forced to bring it out in the open."

"What will Kaine do now?"

"He isn't sure. Kaine and my dad used to work on cars in their spare time, so Harley hired him." Car repair. Something else his father enjoyed doing that Trey had shown no interest in. "He found an apartment downtown and is moving out Sunday afternoon."

"I didn't know the circumstances of Kaine's loss, but I wondered, based on what he said to me the night he came to my house."

He turned to Reagan. The comment raised jealousy like yeast in bread dough. "He visited you at your house?"

"Kaine overheard my call to Marshall and chose to warn me. He said I shouldn't play with fire, because I could lose what I wanted most. I played with fire years ago when I thought I could change Matt's mind about re-enlisting."

"Reagan." Trey cupped her cheek, her explanation throwing

cold water on his misguided jealousy. "Please stop blaming yourself for Matt's death." Those green eyes peered into his. Strangely, he no longer saw the darkness of guilt and sadness. He saw a healthy glow of calm and acceptance. "What happened?"

She laughed. "You know me well."

Not as well as if they had a lifetime together.

"Like Paige, I didn't handle the situation right, but I don't blame myself for his death. Not anymore. Macie found the letter I wrote to Matt in Lane's attic . . . unopened. Matt never read it. I guess it arrived too late." Her shoulders rose and fell with a deep breath. "The point is, Kaine was right. I played with fire concerning the Burnside property, and I lost you."

"You haven't lost me, Reagan. That's what this is about." He swept his arms out to indicate their surroundings. "I brought you here to apologize for letting my lack of self-respect put us at odds. Then I compounded it by refusing to talk to you."

"We're talking now."

"And I have more to say." First, he'd ask what he'd wondered about for weeks. "Why didn't you visit me in the hospital or afterward?"

She scuffed the toe of her shoe on a crack in the board. "I didn't think you'd want to see me."

I did.

Trey planted a palm on each side of her face and wove his fingers into her hair. He tilted her chin until their gazes met. "I've been miserable this past month, and not from the fire. I've missed talking to you about subjects that had nothing to do with business, hearing you laugh, eating takeout with you. Being around you without having the Lord knock on my heart, urging me to make things right. I love you, Reagan, and I'm sorry. Do you think you could love me?"

"There's a better question to ask. Is there any way you can keep me from loving you?"

Trey's heart stuttered. "Is there?"

"I don't think so."

Holding her other hand in his, he went down on one knee. "In that case, Reagan Hartwell, if you'll have me, I'd like nothing more in life than to marry you."

"I don't do emotion well, but you're determined to see me melt into a puddle, aren't you?" She swiped at the wetness under each eye. "I haven't let myself get close to a man in so long for fear I'd ruin his life. For that reason, I was terrified to get close to you. Ron Gregory reminded me that asking forgiveness from God means He's forgotten the things I've done wrong. It's a new day, a new time. And I'm ready for a new relationship. But only if it's with you."

He stood. "So your answer is yes?"

She wrapped her arms around his neck. "There is one more thing."

"What?"

"Does Lulu come with the deal?"

Trey released an exaggerated sigh. "Love me, love Lulu."

"Then that's a yes, written in capital letters and with three exclamation points at the end."

He arched an eyebrow. "Only three?"

"It's a start. If you kiss me right now, I'll add more."

Trey gathered her in his arms and captured her lips with his. It was an amazing start.

Reagan stood at the doorway to the church's sanctuary as Shaina played "You are My All in All" on the violin. Macie's mother walked down the aisle, then Lane's mother. It was all Reagan could do to keep from shimmying and swishing the full skirt of the emerald dress back and forth as she waited for her turn.

Trey leaned closer from his place beside her and whispered, "You look amazing."

"Thanks." She smiled as her gaze scanned him from head to foot, appreciating the way his tux fit him. "You'd give James Bond a run for his money."

In front of Trey, Sutton cleared his throat. "Enough of the love fest. I thought you two weren't speaking."

Reagan sucked in her lips to keep from laughing while Trey ignored him. The music changed to "Can't Help Falling in Love" and Sutton, Lane's best man, stepped forward. A moment later, Trey followed. The men took their places at the altar beside Lane.

Then it was Reagan's turn to walk down the aisle. She concentrated on each step to be certain she proceeded at the right pace. Faster than a sloth but slower than Quill. Got it. She also kept her focus forward and not on Trey.

She took her place at the front, getting a glimpse of why Paige used to nearly swoon over Sutton. He was extra handsome in his tuxedo. But Reagan reserved her swoon for the guy next to him.

She touched the bare spot on the ring finger of her left hand. They wouldn't announce their engagement until after Lane and Macie returned from their honeymoon. It was their friends' day, after all.

But once the couple returned and Reagan and Trey had picked out their rings, she would shout their engagement to the world.

God, you've made all things new, including me.

Jo stopped beside Reagan, the material of her matching dress bulging with the tiniest of baby bumps. How long before Macie and Lane expected a new arrival? An unforeseen excitement pricked Reagan over the idea of starting her own family in the future . . . with Trey.

The music changed once more. Everyone in the rows of chairs stood as Macie walked down the aisle on her father's arm. Wearing a tea length white dress of lace and tulle, her long blonde hair caught in an elaborate chignon at the back of her head, she nearly floated past the friends and family gathered to witness her vows. She carried a bouquet of deep green magnolia leaves surrounding one large white magnolia flower. The whole ceremony came across as intended—simple, yet beautiful.

Reagan sneaked a peek at Lane. Gone was the practical horseman in boots, jeans, and a western shirt, replaced by the dashing image of a well-dressed man ready to grace the pages of GQ.

Before she wrapped her head around the idea of standing in Macie's place in the near future, the ceremony ended. The couple walked arm-in-arm down the aisle to the cheers of those in attendance. Sutton linked arms with Jo. A moment later, Trey held out his arm for her.

While walking with her fiancé—a man of grace, compassion, and courage—Reagan stood taller and smiled with a joy she thought she'd never deserve. All because of this man.

Her hero.

Sandra Ardoin

Coming up in the town of Hidden Veil

A Father's Promise

The November wind sent invisible tentacles through the shrunken slats of the dried-up barn wall. The temperatures this time of year fluctuated. One day they climbed into the sixties or seventies. The next they dipped into the forties. It would only get colder in another month.

Sutton Vance decided long ago that living in Hidden Veil was better than living where he'd struggle through two feet of snow simply to feed the cattle. And this was his hometown. He had no desire to tear up his roots and move somewhere else.

Besides, responsibilities tied him to the area. Responsibilities thrust on him.

His thoughts slipped to the vacant house down the road. He'd kept an eye on it while saving for a down payment. Now, he needed Fitz Johnson to put up a For Sale sign.

If he didn't get away from the crowded farmhouse, the bickering, the drunken stupors, and the chronic sickness, he'd go crazy. Even if he only went a short three-quarters-of-a-mile closer to town, it would save his sanity. But he couldn't go too far and still fulfill the responsibilities laid on him as the oldest Vance child, responsibilities he'd never asked for.

Sutton tugged on the corduroy collar of his denim jacket until it stood up, then he went back to work. Parts of the building had gotten so bad he refused to stall Rocket inside for fear the whole thing would collapse on his roping horse—the personal indulgence he allowed himself. The one living being he could talk to and not worry about him mouthing back.

Last month, he'd ordered the lumber that would give new life to the barn, and with the winter wheat planted, this time of year was ideal to make a few more of the repairs his father's farm desperately needed.

His father's farm.

Sutton's snort competed with the wind whipping through the large structure. If there was a God and He had any sense of justice, the deed to the farm would contain Sutton's name, not his father's. After all, who kept it up? Who provided the most support for the man, his often-ill wife, and their five kids? Who worked his behind off, both on the farm and through construction jobs, to ensure his half brothers and sisters had what they needed to survive? Who got no thanks for any of it?

The place wasn't always so rundown. When his mama was alive and Daddy hadn't soaked his brain in alcohol, the farm was neat—a showplace—and provided a good income. Leastwise, that was how he remembered it.

After slipping the claw of a crowbar under a board, Sutton pried it loose as the rusty nails creaked along the wood. Halfway free, it broke into two odd-shaped pieces that fell to the dirt floor. He added them to a pile he'd eventually either chop up to heat the wood stove this winter or repurpose for someone else's home. People liked that kind of thing.

As he moved on to the next board, he noticed something he hadn't seen in years. Or maybe he'd just ignored it. He crouched and removed a work glove to examine the grooves carved into the gray wood. He ran his index finger down a vertical line, then around a half-loop. Sliding his finger over a space, he found two more vertical grooves connected by a horizontal one.

His heart raced, and he swallowed. No need to risk a splinter to know what came next.

Sutton recalled the day he carved his and Paige's initials into the board. Paige had lived off the road that ran behind and parallel to the farm. One or the other of them would cut through the woods and across the fields. They'd spent hours roaming the countryside together, both as kids and teens.

He recalled a day of cold weather—like today. They ran to the barn to warm up. As they sat next to the wall, talking and laughing, he took his pocketknife from his jeans and carved her initials in the wood. He added a plus sign beneath, then looked at her. When she grinned and nodded, he carved his own initials. Then he leaned over and kissed her in that awkward way of a thirteen-year-old. Their first kiss.

"PH plus SV." The whisper was as close to reverence as Sutton had ever managed.

He and Paige were in love then, and those feelings only grew stronger over the years. Or so he'd thought.

Then she left Hidden Veil. She left him without a goodbye or a way to ask for one.

Sutton stood and grabbed the crowbar. With two powerful yanks, he pulled the board free. He should have figured this one would remain intact. He tried to toss it on the pile of discarded wood, but his hand wouldn't let go.

Just as he'd never really let go of Paige Hartwell.

Reader Friend,

If you have multiple children, you know there can be that *one* who battles against everything.

Well, authors have their book children. Some make life easy, and the story bounces off the fingertips. Others wander off the path and try the patience. After a while, they straighten up and cooperate. Then there are books like *A Hero's Nature*. Five months after my hoped-for release date, the version I envisioned from the beginning was ready for people to read.

This book proved how necessary it is to get someone else's eyes on the project, and Heidi Chiavaroli had perfect vision. Her priceless suggestions strengthened the weakest spots in the story (and there were several). Thank you, Heidi! What a blessing to still be working with you after all these years.

I also want to thank my Brainstormers, especially Marie Wells Coutu, for assistance with a plot point that stumped me. Many thanks to Marie, Jerusha Agen, and Angie Arndt for being there when I need you.

There are so many other authors I could thank for their support and encouragement. Just know it does take a village to raise these book children, and I'm glad to live in a village with so many talented and faith-filled people.

As for you, cherished reader, I couldn't do this without you, either. Well, I could, but it wouldn't be as much fun. I'm so grateful for those who have read all or most of my books, those who have read a few, and those who are new to my stories. I pray to always provide entertainment, a little romance, and a word or two of spiritual wisdom that will make your life easier.

I hope you took away from Trey's story the amazing comfort found in knowing God waits to show off His strength through our weaknesses.

If you enjoyed Trey and Reagan's story, please do other readers, and this author, a favor. Show *A Hero's Nature* that all-important review love. It only takes a couple of lines to give others your insight into what they can expect (without giving away the story). Review the book on your favorite retailer, BookBub, and/or Goodreads.

Happy reading!

Sandra

As an author of heartwarming and award-winning historical and contemporary romance, Sandra Ardoin engages readers with page-turning stories of love and faith. Rarely out of reach of a book, she's also an armchair sports enthusiast, country music listener, and seldom says no to eating out. Visit her at www.sandraardoin.com.

Connect with her on BookBub, Facebook, Twitter, and Goodreads.

Grab the historical romance novella, *Unwrapping Hope*, when you sign up to receive the Love and Faith in Fiction newsletter. Stay informed at www.sandraardoin/newsletter.

Don't miss the first two books in the
HIDDEN VEIL HOMETOWN SERIES

A
MUSICIAN'S
HEART

*She's the woman
of his dreams.
He's her worst nightmare.*

A
HORSEMAN'S
MISSION

*She seeks healing for her son.
He's looking for atonement for
his brother's death.*

www.ingramcontent.com/pod-product-compliance
Lightning Source LLC
Chambersburg PA
CBHW030647260626
47157CB00007B/2525